A CANDLELIGHT ROMANCE

CANDLELIGHT ROMANCES

The
Flowers
of
Darkness

Elisabeth Barr

A CANDLELIGHT ROMANCE

Published by
Dell Publishing Co., Inc.
1 Dag Hammarskjold Plaza
New York, New York 10017

Dell ® TM 681510, Dell Publishing Co., Inc.

ISBN: 0-440-12624-X

Printed in the United States of America

First printing—June 1980

PROLOGUE

It was 1797, four years since the death of the king and queen of France and the beginning of the Reign of Terror. During that reign, all France had become a great river of blood, bearing away tortured, butchered men, women, and children whose one crime was their position in a society no longer tolerated by those who had usurped its power.

The terror left its dark and bloody stain indelibly imprinted on France; those who could, fled the country—or remained in hiding, like Eleanor La Vanne, who, for nearly four interminable years, had hidden in the home of her two most faithful and loyal servants.

Eleanor had seen Marie Antoinette ride to the guillotine in order to satisfy the insatiable thirst for blood of those who had risen up against her; she had seen her sitting proud, dignified, and silent in the tumbrel passing jeering crowds of people who had once strewn flowers in her path; the queen's appearance shocked Eleanor—she was prematurely aged by her long and humiliating imprisonment—as now Eleanor was aged.

Twice, attempts to smuggle Eleanor to England had failed, ending in near disaster and narrow escapes from death; the price on her head was high when it was known that she was carrying a very precious treasure with her; with the death of the two old servants who had sheltered her, Eleanor had believed that she would never reach England, to fulfill the promise she had made to the queen.

When her position had seemed most desperate, there had come a third offer of help—from the Englishman who now shared the miserable accommodation that was their temporary hiding place.

They had traveled far through France, with frustrating slowness, and fear always hard at the heels of Eleanor; her companion, who called himself simply "Jackson," had urged the utmost caution if this final attempt was not to fail. She lay now, against a heap of damp straw in a crumbling, almost roofless barn, part of a derelict farmhouse, on the outskirts of a small French town. The farmhouse had been gutted by fire, its occupants long since dragged out, and their throats cut in front of an approving crowd, when it was discovered that they were sheltering two of the hated aristocrats. The rotting bodies of two defaulting neighbors, who had taken bribes for trying to help the unfortunate farmer and his wife, hung from roughly made gibbets in the yard. Eleanor could see them from a gaping hole in the wall of the barn, and the sight made her physically sick; she longed to be on her way, but Jackson had pointed out that the Channel ports were well watched and they could not afford to take unnecessary risks but must wait for a signal from one of his compatriots before proceeding on the final stage of their journey.

Both Eleanor and her companion wore rough, peasant clothes; her once-thick, lustrous hair had been cut short and was prematurely gray, her face looked tired, her brilliant eyes sunk deep in their sockets; but her voice betrayed her English nationality and her gentle birth; her hands, small, slender, pale, were those of a woman who had never done manual work.

She kept her hands hidden, and never spoke. When they were halted and questioned, Jackson spoke in the patois he had mastered so perfectly, declaring that his companion was his elder sister who had been deaf and dumb since birth.

Eleanor was very tired and hungry. They were only miles from the nearest Channel port, and she dared to let hope sustain her, just a little. Already she could smell salt on the breeze, hear the familiar tongues she had not heard for so many years, speaking English.

Jackson rose to his feet, staring down at her.

"I shall go into the village and get some food," he announced.

6

She, who had shown no fear, shivered suddenly.

"I would rather that you did not leave me," she faltered.

"You will be safe enough; no one comes this way. The tale is told that this place is accursed and haunted."

He smiled, a thin-lipped smile that did not reach his light-colored, narrow eyes.

"I am not hungry," she lied.

"We are *both* hungry," he said suavely. "I shall not be long. There is some kind of celebration going on in the village; they are all feasting and drinking. It will make my task easier and ensure your safety. Sleep while you can."

She shook her head, though her eyelids were heavy. The moon gave thin, unsubstantial light, coming through the hole in the wall and illuminating the dark shadows of the swinging bodies.

She did not want Jackson to leave her, but before she could protest further, he was gone, lithe and quick as a fox, out through the broken door that hung drunkenly from its hinges.

Silence lay heavily about her. She groped in the straw for the small leather satchel for which she was risking her life and discovered that it was not where she had hidden it earlier that day.

Eleanor frowned, her heart beating fast; frightened, she groped through the straw in every direction.

Her fingers shook, her pulses were racing as she fought down rising panic. Jackson must have taken the satchel, hiding it in his clothing, as he had done once or twice before, but why had he taken it *now*? Did he, after all, fear that some home-going revelers might pass that way and find her with incriminating proof that she was no peasant woman?

Shaking, her breathing rapid, she struggled wearily to her feet and leaned against the wall. Her tired brain refused to form conclusions that would satisfy the sixth sense lurking in every human being, and sometimes alerted when the need for an extra sense is greatest. Until now, such sense had lain dormant within Eleanor; suddenly it was unhappily coupled with the reflection that she had never quite trusted "Jackson" in spite of the expert way with which he had managed to smuggle her so far upon her mission.

What if he planned to steal the jewels she carried and abandon her here, without any hope of help from anyone, she reflected fearfully?

He *would* not do that, she told herself, with sudden anguish. He is an Englishman and a gentleman!

Sometimes she believed that the jewels were as accursed as this decaying farmhouse was reputed to be. She saw them again in her mind's eye, proudly adorning the woman who had been queen of all France: necklace, earrings, a magnificent ring and twin bracelets, all made of diamonds set in fine gold, and flashing frosty fire; fashioned in the form of flowers, diamond-petaled, with rubies at the center of each flower, and with leaves of emeralds to set off their perfection—priceless, magnificent jewels that she, Eleanor La Vanne, had promised to take to England and hand over for safekeeping, far from the reach of those who ruled France with an iron rod.

She could see them clearly, worn by the queen, the stones flashing and winking in the light, so dazzling that they hurt the eyes; yet the queen herself had spoken with sad prophecy, declaring that the rubies looked like drops of blood, and she would sooner have seen sapphires in their place. . . .

It was the queen who, accepting the gift from an admirer, had christened the jewels the Flowers of Darkness.

Eleanor, remembering, felt beads of sweat break out along her forehead. Greed, she reflected uneasily, made murderers out of men and women.

Jackson Parnall's work in the village was quickly done. It was a matter of the utmost simplicity to ingratiate himself into the nearest group of drunken revelers and whisper the news that he had seen a woman hiding in the barn at the burned-down farmhouse, a woman who looked to him very much like an aristocrat.

At first they laughed and shrugged, but the wine and his repeated suggestions that they should all investigate inflamed them and roused their hunting instincts. They took lanterns and torches, singing their songs as they marched from the village. Jackson, stumbling along with them, feigned a drunkenness that caused ribald comments when he staggered into a ditch along the road to the farmhouse; he lay there, shouting and cursing his own stupidity until the torchlight procession had passed him. Then, when quietness flowed back over the countryside, he scrambled to his feet, dusted himself down, and felt for the satchel that he had strapped against his body. The jewels were heavy and his burden was uncomfortable; to the onlooker they merely added to his girth. For his part, he would be glad when he reached the far side of the Channel.

He could have left Eleanor La Vanne to make a bid for freedom instead of delivering her into the hands of the mob and certain death, he reflected dispassionately, but it was folly to leave witnesses who might live to testify against him and bring disaster upon him.

When Eleanor heard the songs and the sound of marching feet, she knew at once that her instincts had not lied to her; she knew also that it was too late for escape. It was ironic to reflect that the Flowers of Darkness would undoubtedly be taken to England, as the queen had wished, but would never be handed over to those who would look upon them as a trust, to be safely housed against the day when a sane and peaceful France would rise from the ashes of the Revolution.

Her last words were a curse.

"Everlasting ill luck to you," she whispered bitterly to the man who had pretended to be her friend. "May the Flowers of Darkness bloom terribly for you, and may your blood be spilt in agony, every last drop, to avenge what you have done. The Flowers are responsible for the death that awaits me this night; they will be responsible for *your* death and eternal damnation, before they are given into the keeping of those who have a right to them!"

Her words went winging out into the darkness. Jackson Parnall, hurrying away to the safety of a waiting ship that would take him home under cover of darkness, heard nothing, but he fancied that the wind blew more coldly in from

9

the sea, and he shivered, huddling himself deeper into his rough clothes.

It was an icy wind that seemed to cut into his flesh, gone in a moment. He remembered an old saying he had once heard.

"May the winds of fate ever blow coldly about you; may their breath chill you and shrivel every small green shoot of hope in your heart, until they bear you away in death, to the place that no man knows."

He shrugged—pretty, fanciful words, for the superstitious. He was not superstitious, and the winds of fate had blown all his ships into harbor, so far as he was concerned. Now he was going home with the last and the richest prize of them all.

In the safety of his attic room, at the top of an inn overlooking the tiny French harbor, he closed the shutters, lit a candle, and bolted his door. His movements were stealthy as he opened the leather case and spread out its treasures on the shabby coverlet of his bed.

When they were all laid there, he caught his breath with sheer ecstasy, his eyes bright with a greed that surpassed any emotion he had ever known.

No stars would ever match the Flowers of Darkness for beauty, sparkling with an unearthly light, the candleflame striking small fires from every facet of the diamonds, until they glittered like frozen rainbows; the rubies flashed like drops of blood at the center of each flower. Had he been a fanciful man he would have said that the blood-red rubies seemed to grow until they were larger than the diamond petals and the emerald leaves surrounding them, dominating the whole room, until it seemed filled with their fire. The walls seemed to reflect the deep red of the stones, and suddenly it was not fire but blood that stained them. . . .

Angry with himself, he swept the jewels back into the case. He was tired after a long and hazardous journey, he told himself; he was not yet out of danger and still in a hostile, foreign country. With luck, he would soon land safely in Dorset, and the possession of such treasure as he carried would make him one of the richest men in England.

He smiled with immense satisfaction and gave no thought at all to the woman he had betrayed.

When they surged through the door, in an obscene and evil-smelling tide, Eleanor was waiting, calmly, for them. Now that she was near to death, she prayed only that that end would come swiftly and cleanly.

They thrust her violently against the wall and rained blows on her, increasing their furious assault with terrible savagery when she would not answer their questions. Someone set a flare to the straw around her feet, but it was too damp to fire, and smoldered sulkily, making them all cough and retch, so they dragged her outside into the muddied yard and stripped her clothing from her. There, beneath the gibbets with their sad burdens, they threw her to the ground and stamped upon her body again and again until only a huddle of bloodied, mangled flesh remained as mute testimony of one man's greed and treachery.

CHAPTER 1

Luella March was sixteen and a half years old when she ran away from Henrietta Spencer's house in a busy Devon market town.

The flight marked, for her, the end of six months of misery and physical torment; it was also a journey into adventure and danger such as nothing in her life had ever prepared her for—although she did not know that at the time.

Luella possessed an unquenchable spirit, optimism, resourcefulness, a quick tongue, and a pert charm that infuriated Henrietta, who tried to beat it out of her.

Henrietta's sole pleasure in life was the infliction of physical pain and mental torment—it satisfied all the abrasive qualities in her, easing the frustrations of a plain, childless widow. She had picked Luella from a dozen other girls at the charity school—all of them waiting to be "placed" in homes. Luella promised to be a very satisfactory candidate for the task of creating a broken and contrite spirit, Henrietta thought; she was wrong, which enraged her. Luella's spirit did not break under the merciless finger of a cane thrashing her back, her shoulders, her arms and legs, nor under the strain of working eighteen hours a day, sparsely fed, and housed without comfort in a cheerless room at night.

Luella was small, slim, boyish looking; in the year 1797 it was more fashionable to be rounded and feminine. Her small, pointed face made her green eyes look enormous. One of the girls at the school had hinted that her mother must have been a witch to have bequeathed her such emerald eyes, which, with their thick, dark gold lashes, were her chief claim to attraction. Her hair was thick, the same dark

13

gold in color, and it refused to curl; it spent most of its days bundled under a cotton cap.

She had never embraced the charity school precepts of meekness, piety, humility, obedience, and thrift; she was too rebellious a spirit, and that fact had often got her into trouble with authority.

She had been found on the doorstep of the school one cold March evening—hence her surname—a baby about three months old, well clad and well nourished. The school matron, in a fanciful mood, had added the "Luella," derived from her own name, "Louise Ellen."

Life at the charity school, in Somerset, was dull and circumspect, but not harsh. Luella had been taught to read and write, and she was proficient in all the domestic arts when she left the school to take up a position as maid to Henrietta.

One day Luella dropped a dish and broke it. It was a kitchen plate of no value, but Henrietta vowed that Luella had deliberately smashed it in a spirit of defiance and beat her mercilessly. Luella went to bed in the dark that night, for it was one of Henrietta's favorite punishments to leave her without a candle. The punishment had afforded her great pleasure ever since she discovered that Luella disliked being alone in the darkness.

Lying under the rough blanket, Luella wept bitterly for the fiery pain in her body and wished passionately that Henrietta would die.

Four days later, Henrietta had a seizure, fell downstairs, and broke her neck. Luella thought it might well be an asset in life to have had a mother who was a witch. She felt no remorse for having wished Henrietta dead; her body bore too many bruises and scars, her mind too many unhappy memories, for that.

Her relief at Henrietta's death lasted until the day of the funeral, when she discovered that she was to be sent to live with, and work for, Henrietta's cousin, a woman of even more sour disposition and temper.

It was then that Luella made her decision. That night she packed her few personal possessions in the straw basket she had brought from the school. Very early next morning

14

she rose, dressed, and crept downstairs, past the door of the room where Agnes Dewey, Henrietta's cousin, snored in happy ignorance of the impending loss of a cheap maid of all work.

It was quite dark, and Luella had to gauge her movements carefully. She made her way to the drawing room and lifted down the Wedgwood vase from the mantelpiece, cupping her hand under the rim as she tipped it.

There were five gold guineas in the vase. None of Henrietta's family knew of their existence.

She had never been paid one penny of her promised wage, and the money was her due, Luella thought, as she put it into her reticule.

She went out by the kitchen door, through the garden, and unlatched the gate to the narrow lane that ran along the backs of the houses. Luella moved swiftly, keeping close to the wall, though no one was about. She did not feel safe until she reached the crossroads beyond the town.

It was a cold morning, almost four years to the day since Marie Antoinette had mounted the steps to the guillotine. There was a sharp note in the air, but the woolen cloak Luella wore had been given her when she left the school, and it was both warm and all-enveloping. Under it she wore a thin cotton gown. Her stockings were of cotton, and the damp struck through the worn soles of her scuffed kid slippers.

However, she was happy as she waited at the crossroads for a farm cart to go by; her spirits rose with her awareness of freedom. She tossed her hair over her shoulder. I will *never* wear a cap again, she told herself; I shall go to London, make myself useful, become rich and respected.

Exactly how this was to be accomplished she had no idea. In spite of her justification that Henrietta owed her wages, she knew she had stolen the five sovereigns, and she had been taught that stealing was a crime—a person could be hanged or transported for the theft of even a rabbit.

She could not consider the theft a stain on her conscience, though she tried to feel remorse and told herself that when she was rich she would return the money; the idea of flinging five gold coins at the feet of Henrietta's cousin gave her sufficient pleasure to warm her against the cold.

Luella touched her neck to reassure herself that she was still wearing the locket she normally kept concealed in the lining of her basket, fearful that Henrietta would find and keep it. The locket had been handed over to her when she left the school, because it had been around her neck when she arrived: an oval of gold, set with pearls and corals, on a fine gold chain. There were no portraits inside the locket, but the initials E.F. were inscribed on the back. So far as Luella was concerned, the locket was a clear statement to the world that she had a rightful name, a family, and roots somewhere.

Dawn was no more than a sliver of light in the east when the first farm cart creaked into view, drawn by a plodding and reluctant horse. Luella hid behind a tree until it had almost passed, then swung up on to the back, amongst the piled vegetables, unnoticed by the hunched, sleepy figure who sat with the reins slack between his hands, a lantern hanging beside him.

Luella relaxed, feeling enormous triumph and relief as the rhythm of the hooves put distance between her and the possibility of being discovered and returned to Henrietta's house.

As they journeyed, morning light sliced the darkness wide open with a thin blade and let the sun pour through. Though it was a sun without warmth, it made diamond lace of every spider's web that was traced with dewdrops. A breeze came as attendant to the sun, shaking down hhe leaves, making them dance a ballet along the road, all of them red and gold, brown and amber; the dry sound of their movement was like ghost laughter.

On the outskirts of Axminster, Luella jumped down, dusted herself, and walked the last half-mile into the town. When she reached the inn yard, by the market square, it was obvious from the bustle and confusion that a coach had just departed.

There was an ostler outside the inn, a lanky boy with straw-colored hair and pink eyelids.

"When is the London coach due to leave, please?" she asked briskly.

"Gone," he said, with malicious pleasure. "Not five minutes since. Won't be no more, not till tomorrow. You'll 'ave to get the afternoon coach to Dorchester and go from there."

Luella was bitterly disappointed; she was also ravenously hungry. She stepped inside the inn. A wave of warmth flowed out to meet her, laced with the smell of food.

The innkeeper looked at her with covert interest; he saw a shabby young woman, traveling alone, and having the effrontery to demand breakfast with a haughty air. He stopped picking his teeth and shouted for his wife.

Luella sat by the fire, spreading chilled fingers to the warmth. The innkeeper's wife slopped in on her noisy pattens, bringing hot chocolate, fresh bread and butter, cold bacon, and gooseberry pie left over from the previous evening. She took the golden guinea Luella proffered and gave her very little change.

"That's a lot of money for breakfast!" Luella said.

"Take it or leave it," the woman said tauntingly, ready to whisk away the food at the slightest sign of mutiny.

Luella surrendered, because the food was good and she had never eaten so well in her life, not even on Christmas Day, when the school governors came with gifts of cold goose and plum puddings. Luella sighed contentedly, daintily licked her fingers, and promised herself she would eat like this every day when she had made her fortune.

She dozed by the fire until the woman roused her sharply and told her to get along unless she wanted to pay for a room. Luella gathered up her possessions, head high, and marched out into the street.

It was market day. Crowds thronged the square, and she moved with them, still exhilarated by a sense of freedom she had never known before. She bought a few sweetmeats, carefully hoarding the rest of the guineas, for she had no idea of the fare to London. She looked with interest and delight at the people around her: tinkers, beggars, prosperous-looking farmers and their wives, farm laborers, and giggling girls, tossing their heads and flouncing their petticoats. Her attention was suddenly caught and held by a figure on the edge of the crowd—the figure of a heavily veiled woman who seemed to be trying to remain concealed while she looked for someone.

The thick black veil completely hid the face and descended from a black velvet bonnet trimmed with feathers; the rest of the figure was entirely hidden by a full, black velvet cloak. The effect was funereal, and the wearer was obviously in mourning. Luella stared curiously; as though aware of the scrutiny, the wearer of the veil slowly turned toward the girl. It was impossible to make out the face behind the concealing veil; Luella had only a vague impression of blurred features.

Luella shivered, with a strange feeling of dread, and turned away, but she paused on the edge of the crowd and looked back. The figure in black still stood there, as motionless as a statue.

Luella ate the sweetmeats but did not buy lunch, afraid of depleting her small store of money. The fare for the coach to Dorchester seemed very high; as it was, she had bought an outside seat, because it was cheaper than riding inside. She sat high up at the back of the coach, wedged between a large man who smelled of stale sweat and drink and a thin young man with a mournful face and a bead of moisture permanently attached to the end of his long nose.

It was an uncomfortable journey, bouncing over rough roads, the wind stinging her face, but the scenery delighted her; it was some of the wildest and most savage on the Devon and Dorset borders. The bleak heathlands with their low-growing scrub and furze bushes faced the continual challenge of the fierce gales that rode up the English Channel.

The Channel was a narrow enough strip of water between England and France, where one of the bloodiest wars in history was being fought. Louis XVI and his queen had already been put to death, and a Corsican soldier with the curious name of Napoleon Bonaparte had emerged from obscurity to command the French army and begin a triumphant conquest of Europe. Britain stood alone, but unconquered, against France and her allies, two great sea victories behind her, and the boats that slid stealthily into

18

the rocky inlets along the Dorset coast often brought refugees as well as silks and brandy and tobacco.

Luella knew little of all this. The wind blew coldly, but it smelled of the sea. Ahead of her was the promise of London, behind her all the degradations and humiliations of life with Henrietta.

A seagull swooped above her, its raucous cry reminding her of Henrietta's voice when she was in a temper, and Luella laughed to herself; at that moment, the coach gave a sickening lurch, which almost catapulted her from her seat, and then stopped, tilting at an alarming angle.

The coach was jammed in one of the ruts that had been softened by recent rains; it was the beginning of a chapter of minor mishaps. When the coach was righted and the passengers again on board, it was discovered that one of the horses had gone lame. An exchange had to be made at the nearest inn, which fretted Luella. If the London coach should leave before they reached Dorchester, she would have to pay for a night's lodging.

They had scarcely started out on their journey again when a band of redcoats rode up, armed with muskets, led by a sergeant, who commanded that the passengers be apprehended and the coach searched.

The coach driver argued angrily.

"We're late, as 'tis! The Lunnon coach won't wait."

"Can't help that," said the sergeant inexorably. "Got my duty to do. Prisoner escaped from Dorchester jail. Orders to search every conveyance along this road and apprehend every man, woman, and child."

"He *must* be a person of importance!" said one of the inside passengers scornfully, as she gathered her skirts together and stepped down.

"Aye, ma'am. Wanted for treason. It's a French spy—and he's wanted for murder, too; killed an old woman in a cottage, nigh Dorchester. Come on, then, we haven't got all day!"

The soldiers began their systematic search and inspection. Luella stood apart from the rest of the passengers, fearful that she might be asked where she had come from and why she was traveling to Dorchester. One of the soldiers came up to her, young, bright-eyed, swaggering. He whipped through the meager contents of her basket and stared at her curiously.

"You're not carrying much luggage, ma'am," he said suspiciously.

"No. I'm paying a short visit to my aunt in Dorchester," she said quickly.

She held her breath as he moved closer to her. She was not prepared for his action: He pushed his hand inside her cloak and squeezed one of her firm young breasts in his hand, winking at her as he did so.

No man had ever touched her before. With a furious exclamation she backed away, one hand raised, but his eyes narrowed, and he caught her wrist in an iron grip.

"Well, you're a hot-tempered little piece, and no mistake!" he murmured, with a grin. "Reckon some man 'ud enjoy giving *you* a tumble in bed! Not me, though. You're too skinny for comfort. I like 'em plump!"

He laughed, pushed her aside, and went on with his job. Luella almost fell, and she clutched at the wheel of the coach to save herself. She was trembling and angry as she climbed back on to her seat.

The soldiers galloped away inland, the coach creaked on its way, and Luella settled herself as comfortably as she could between her fellow passengers, the basket on her lap. They had not gone half a mile before she discovered that the reticule was no longer attached to her wrist by its drawstring.

She searched frantically, as best she could, to loud complaints from the men on either side of her. Finally, she managed to stand up and shout loud enough to attract the driver's attention. He reined the horses to a standstill, swearing angrily. The coach stopped, and irate heads poked out from inside.

"I have lost my money!" Luella cried. "I must have dropped it when the soldiers searched the coach. I *must* go back and look for it!"

She jumped down from the coach with difficulty, landing

on her knees, bruised and shaken. From the cushioned warmth of the inside, passengers stared at her with hostility, their eyes blank.

"I've no time to wait about!" the driver shouted angrily. "We've wasted too much time already."

"My wife and I *must* catch the London coach," a white-haired man told her importantly.

"It is *my* money—*all* my money!" she retorted. "If I do not find it, I shall have no money to continue my journey to London."

"My dear young lady, that is no concern of mine," the man replied smoothly.

His smile was bland. His disbelief was not entirely heartless: The lost-purse trick was an old one, often used on such journeys by innocent-looking young women.

"Either you gets back on my coach this minute," the driver said heavily, "or I goes without you, and that's that. I got my other passengers to think o'."

"Please, please, *please*!" she cried. "You *must* wait while I find my purse!"

A fierce argument broke out; angry passengers demanded the instant departure of the coach. Luella, desperate, stood her ground, begging for just five minutes—she would run all the way there and back again.

The men who had ridden on either side of her said nothing. Suspicion grew in her mind; it *could* have been the soldier, she thought hopelessly, or the reticule *could* have fallen to the ground in the scuffle.

The driver surrendered to the angry threats bombarding him from the inside of the coach; he raised his whip and cracked it across the backs of the horses, who plunged forward, leaving an incredulous and horrified Luella standing alone, in the middle of nowhere in the fading light of an autumn afternoon.

For seconds, she raged against the inhumanity, the cruelty, the total indifference of her fellow travelers. Something was tossed from the coach; she saw that it was her basket. Then the horses rounded a bend, and the sound of their hooves died away in the distance.

Sheer disbelief froze her into immobility for a moment; then, with the realization of her position, she—who never shed tears easily—began to cry bitterly.

She ran forward and picked up her basket; then she turned back along the road she had just traveled in the coach. It was a long walk; soon her stockings were splashed with mud, and stones cut the flimsy soles of her shoes. Dusk was riding in on the wind from the sea when she reached the spot where the soldiers had halted the coach; with desperate hope she prayed that the reticule might be lying there—in the grass, in one of the ruts, by a stone, *anywhere*. But there was no sign of it.

The suspicion that had first taken shape grew stronger. The reticule had been attached to her right wrist, and the fat man had sat on her right-hand side. He had not spoken throughout their journey, but she remembered the sly brightness of his eyes as he had watched her climb on to the coach and dismount from it again. He had offered no hand to help her.

Luella bit back the tears. This was a setback that she had not anticipated, and for a moment the bright candle-flame of her spirit was almost quenched.

She took stock of her surroundings. Inland, she could see a cluster of cottages and some farms, but they seemed to be very far away. To her left, the heathland fell away to the sea. In the distance, near the sea, she saw a church tower and, a little to the left of it, the outlines of a big house, like a castle, with castellated turrets.

Ahead was the road back to Axminster. To walk on to Dorchester was her only alternative, but it would soon be dark, and to make matters worse, the wind had rain on its breath, damp and cold against her hair and face.

She turned up the hood of her cloak, deciding to make for the church; might she not find some help there? she wondered.

So she left the road for a rough path, but her progress was slow; her feet were sore, she was miserable, and the going was rough. Then the rain came sweeping toward her in great, gray swathes, cutting down the horizon; she saw the vague outline of a derelict cottage, its door half-open and creaking eerily in the rising wind, its windows like black, gaping holes.

She was resigned to the fact that it would probably be her only shelter for the night; she stumbled thankfully toward it, pushing the door inward very cautiously.

Inside there was a quantity of mouldy-smelling hay; she collapsed on it. Then she realized that someone occupied one of the shadowy corners of the hut; she could just make out a pair of bright eyes.

Terrified, she scrambled to her feet, backing away toward the door. A man's voice, educated and precise, spoke from the shadows.

"You have nothing to fear. I am in no mood to ravish a woman, even if my condition permitted me to do so."

Slowly, warily, she went toward him. He sat on the floor, his back against the wall. His thin face was white and tired beneath a crest of dark hair, and he had a graze on one cheek. There was a large, fresh bloodstain on the thigh of his breeches.

He lifted the flask by his side and held it out to her.

"Here—you look to me as though you are in need of this. I pray you, do not drink it all, for I shall have need of its contents myself before this night is out."

Thankfully Luella took the flask and put it to her lips.

She had never before tasted brandy; it scalded her throat and burned a fiery path all the way to her stomach. Choking and spluttering, she wondered if he had deliberately poisoned her. The warmth of the spirit crept through her veins, even though it had an odd effect on her sense of balance, making her sit down heavily.

Fortified, she looked at her companion with more curiosity than fear.

"Are you the man the soldiers are looking for?" she asked.

"How do you know that soldiers are out searching for someone?" he demanded.

She told him of her misfortunes on the coach journey; he listened attentively.

"Will you run all the way to Dorchester jail and say that you have found me?" he demanded bitterly.

23

She sat back on her heels, looking at him thoughtfully.

"No. Even though they say you have murdered an old woman."

"They lie. If an old woman has been murdered, it was not by my hand. I stole food from a cottage along the Dorchester Road. Food—nothing more. There was no man nor woman nor child in the house when I entered it, nor when I left."

"The soldiers may come back here and search," she pointed out.

"Not tonight. They searched this hut whilst I lay screened by furze bushes in a nearby hollow. They are stupid, and anxious to get back to the warmth and comfort of their quarters."

"*Are* you wanted for treason? *Are* you a French spy?" she asked, wide-eyed.

He shook his head slowly. "A trap was baited for me, with deceit and treachery."

"I don't understand," Luella said, frowning.

He smiled wanly, but offered no explanation. When he tried to move, he winced with pain.

"How did you hurt your leg?" she demanded.

"I fell heavily and gashed it on a stone."

She rummaged in her basket, pulled out a cheap cotton shift, and tore it into strips.

"I see you are a resourceful young woman," he said dryly. "The blood has caked on the wound and you will need to bathe it. There is a pool of rainwater outside, none too clean, I am sure—but we have no choice."

Luella went outside, her head still on fire, and dipped a piece of the torn shift into a pool near the door. She had to make two trips before the wound was successfully cleaned; then she bandaged his thigh, while he cursed and swore at her, grimacing with pain.

"What is a child of your years doing alone on the moors?" he demanded.

"I am not a child. I am turned sixteen," she retorted, affronted.

"That is still too young to be out alone in some of the wildest country in Dorset," he pointed out.

24

"I am running away," she answered simply.

"You, too?" His laughter was harsh. "From what?"

She told him her story, and he eyed her cynically, his mouth and eyes bitter.

"The world is not a kindly place when you stand alone, with your face to the sea and the open countryside at your back, like a hunted stag," he told her.

She thought it a curious remark; it was one she would long remember.

She finished the bandaging; he lay back again, against the wall, closing his eyes, swamped in utter weariness of mind and body. On the screen of his closed lids the picture formed and re-formed: diamonds, rubies, and emeralds exquisitely fashioned into glittering flowers and leaves. Jewels once worn by a queen now dead. They had been truly named the Flowers of Darkness, he reflected bitterly.

He opened his eyes. He was almost too tired to go on, he reflected. Escape had been difficult enough; to remain free might well be impossible.

He was aware of Luella watching him and asked abruptly, "Are you hungry?"

She nodded eagerly. He reached into a deep pocket inside his coat and took out a hunk of bread and a piece of cold bacon. The bread was stale and the bacon greasy, but Luella was too hungry to be fastidious.

"Is this all your food?" she asked.

"No matter," he said, with a cheerfulness he did not feel. "I shall get some more. What will *you* do? Without money you cannot travel anywhere to find work."

"Oh, I shall find something," she said, trying to sound confident.

"Listen," he said. "There is a house near here. It looks like a castle and stands on a headland, facing out to sea."

"Yes. I saw it," she told him.

"It is called Westhaven Park. The owner is a man named Quinn Mallory. I do not know him well, and he is at present away from England. It *is* possible that you may find work there. Ask for Mrs. Graddle. She is the cook, and a more kindly soul than Mrs. Farley, the housekeeper."

She nodded, memorizing what he had told her. Suddenly

he leaned forward and caught her wrist, so roughly that she cried out with pain.

"Do not tell *anyone* that you have seen me. Tell no one that you met a stranger on the moors. *Do you understand*?"

She nodded, and he let her go with a muttered apology. He would go secretly to Mary this night, he thought, and with luck no one else would know he was back. He would have to tell her the truth, he realized. If *she* did not believe his tale, he was truly lost.

He scrambled to his feet, the stiffness of his injured leg making him move awkwardly. He did not like the ominous throbbing of the wound nor the way it burned so fiercely.

"Hunted men must move under cover of darkness," he told Luella wryly. "I have been fortunate. Today the soldiers missed me by a hairsbreadth. They will return to the search tomorrow."

His face was gray with pain, and small pearls of sweat lay along his forehead. As he limped toward the door, Luella protested, "You are ill! You *cannot* go tonight! If you do I shall be left here alone!"

"You will be safe enough." He stared down somberly at her.

"What is your name?" he asked.

"Luella March," she whispered.

"You will have to stay here for the night; it is not safe for a young woman to travel on foot in the dark. Besides, you do not know the countryside as I do. In the morning, go to the house and ask for work. Remember not to mention that you met me."

He smiled with difficulty and limped away into the night; she knew it would be useless to try to detain him.

Luella clenched her fists and sat, rigid, listening for every sound; she heard only the fret of the sea, the voice of the wind walking over the moors, strange scrabblings inside the hut, and the whisper of the rain.

The evening had scarcely begun; there were hours of solitude ahead of her before daylight. Perhaps it would be better to ignore the advice she had been given and go to Westhaven Park as soon as she could.

She debated the possibility for a while, but when she put her head outside, the darkness was almost complete—and frightening in its vastness. She could see only clusters of faint, far-off lights, like distant stars; they were cottages. She could never reach them, she reflected despairingly. Besides, it was still raining, she was desperately tired, her feet ached, and she craved sleep. She pulled her cloak tightly around her, eased her body into the hay, and closed her eyes, worn out by the events of the strangest day she had ever known. Her last waking thoughts were for the man who had gone stumbling into the dark, without clear idea of where he was going. She hoped he would be far away by first light.

Several times she awoke, startled; the mice and the rats scurried nearby. Outside, the rain fell steadily, and Luella slept again, her sleep full of nightmares.

In spite of the nightmares she awoke refreshed early next morning. She looked a sorry mess, she thought ruefully, shaking pieces of straw from her cloak and trying to wipe the mud from her stockings.

However, her spirits had risen with the sun; if there was work for her at Westhaven Park, that would mean food to eat, a decent bed to sleep in, no one to beat her. She would be paid wages; she would work hard and save, and one day ride into Dorchester to take the coach to London. . . .

The sun sparkled coldly on a placid sea. There was a small stream along the path; Luella knelt and washed her face, using the last piece of her shift as a towel. She drank some of the water and found it fresh. Revived, she went more jauntily on her way, thinking about the strange man who had given her his food, hoping he had escaped his pursuers.

The road dipped toward the great headlands. Luella came to a small village, held snugly in a green hollow: thatched cottages with thick white walls, a duckpond, a sprawling farmstead—and the rectory, snug beside a tiny stone church with a solid-looking tower and a tiny cemetery.

The gate of the cemetery was half-open, and a path went through it, between the headstones, to a gate and another path on the far side that wound toward the house by the sea. She could see the house clearly, for it stood on a green rise, splendid and remote, its windows shuttered.

Luella went into the cemetery. The church clock struck seven, and she thought: It is much too early to knock on a door and ask for work. I must wait until they take the shutters from the windows.

She had a vision of herself tugging at the bellpull of the gates, rousing startled servants, and laughed aloud.

It was peaceful in the cemetery; she amused herself by reading the names on the headstones. Some of them were very old, sunk into the grass, crooked as Henrietta's teeth, she thought, and ribboned with ivy. "Master Charles Barton, ten years old" . . . "Annie Benham, Grace Richards, Patrick Curling" . . . "Tobias and Mildred Biddlecombe, in death not divided" . . .

Near the far gate there was a new headstone, gleaming white in the pale sun. She read the inscription curiously: "Marianne Walton, aged twenty, whom the sea took from us, August 1797."

Marianne. She spoke the name aloud, fascinated by the sound of it. Marianne Walton made music; Luella March sounded harsh, she thought.

Twenty was not very old; it was a sad little phrase, "whom the sea took from us." From whom? A family of brothers and sisters, a mother and a father? *How* had the sea taken her? She must have been drowned, Luella decided.

"Marianne," she said again, and the grasses seemed to murmur it softly. A seaward-winging bird cried harshly as though it mourned the girl who had died when she was still so young.

The silence flowed back; even the grasses were still, and Luella could not hear the sound of the sea. She did not want to be here alone, with that name singing through her mind.

She walked to the far end of the cemetery and leaned on the gate, wondering about the man named Quinn Mallory, who was master of such a splendid house as Westhaven.

It would not do to arrive at the house looking untidy,

she decided, so she bent and opened her basket; inside was a ragged petticoat, a chemise, a discarded ribbon she had found lying in a road one day, a handkerchief, a Bible, and a plain wooden hairbrush. The two latter items had been given to her when she left the school, with instructions that both were to be used regularly.

She began to brush her hair with long, slow strokes. There had never been time for the luxury of grooming her hair at Henrietta's; she had been too tired at night, too sleepy in the morning. It was the same with reading the Bible, even though she knew long passages of it by heart: Henrietta never allowed her enough light by which to read it.

So she brushed her hair and sang to keep her spirits up, wondering who had stolen her money and what it would be like to live in Westhaven Park. When she heard hooves clatter along the road outside, she expected the rider to gallop on toward the rectory and the village; instead he slowed the great coal-black horse on which he was mounted and turned it expertly through the gate Luella had left open.

Man and horse had traveled hard: The horse glistened with sweat; the man looked tired. He was over six feet tall and splendidly built, with powerful shoulders; his hair as black as his horse, thick, strong, and curly, growing low on his neck. He had strong, well-marked features, a high-bridged nose, a look of arrogance—and, for contrast, a long firm mouth slightly uptilted at the corners, suggesting a readiness to amuse and be amused. His eyes were a clear, vivid blue beneath heavy black brows. He rode his horse with superb grace, in spite of his weariness after his long sea journey; he sat upright, lifting his head and drawing a deep breath as he viewed the house ahead of him.

He smiled to himself at his audience of tombstones, doubting that the sleepers would be affronted at his presence, though the rector had hinted more than once that to take a short cut on horseback through the cemetery was a mark of incivility to the dead. Such hints always vastly amused Quinn Mallory.

Luella, hearing his approach, looked over her shoulder

in surprise, and that was how he first saw her: a small, bedraggled figure, performing her morning's toilet, her thick, honey-coloured hair shining in the morning sun.

He reined a few yards from her as she turned to face him; his smile was amused.

"So? A mermaid is stranded on dry land and takes refuge amongst the departed," he said lightly.

"Mermaid?" she repeated, puzzled.

"Come, you have surely heard of the sirens who sit on rocks and comb out their golden hair while they sing sweetly to lure poor sailors to their doom? Do *you* sing sweetly, mermaid?"

He was laughing at her, and she was angry; she tossed her head and made no reply.

She had a pert little face, he thought, and those huge green eyes surely belonged either to a mermaid or a witch.

"Are you perhaps a witch then?" he demanded, keeping a straight face with difficulty.

He *was* laughing at her. She glared at him.

"'Yes, I *am*!" she cried, with a child's defiance. "I wished ill on a woman who had mistreated me, and four days later she was dead, with a broken neck!"

Quinn laughed delightedly, throwing back his head. She saw the white gleam of his teeth, the contractions of the strong, muscular shoulders, and felt despair as well as fury.

"Tell me your name," Quinn ordered, when he had stopped laughing.

She folded her mouth into an angry line, glaring at him stubbornly. He leaned forward and poked her gently with his riding crop. She pushed the crop away and replaced her hairbrush, closing the basket without looking at him.

"Tell me your name!" he repeated sharply. He was not used to being defied. Who *was* this child to stare at him with such silent insolence? he wondered.

"Well?" he cried impatiently. "Are you going to tell me, or would you prefer the taste of my riding crop?"

Luella smiled mischievously at him, hiding her uneasiness.

"My name is Marianne," she told him.

"Indeed?" He sat motionless, his eyes very bright. "What is your other name?"

"Walton," she retorted brazenly. "I am Marianne Walton."

It sounded rather splendid, she thought. She was unprepared for Quinn's reaction.

"*You*?" His glance swept contemptuously over the muddy stockings and shabby slippers, the crumpled and dusty cloak. "You? Needing a good wash and with no flesh on your bones? Marianne Walton is asleep in her bed behind those drawn shutters," he cried, pointing toward Westhaven. "She likes to lie abed until late, though she will rise soon enough this morning when she knows I have come to set our wedding date. So now, how dare you say *you* are Marianne Walton!"

Her eyes grew enormous. he saw the uneasiness in her look and cried impatiently, "Who the Devil are you?"

"Marianne!" she cried wildly, suddenly frightened.

She wondered how long he had been away from home; involuntarily, she glanced back the way she had come toward the bright new tombstone shining in the sunlight.

His eyes followed her glance; puzzled, he dismounted and walked back along the path to read the inscription.

"Marianne Walton, aged twenty, whom the sea took from us, August 1797."

He stared at the words in utter disbelief; then he looked at Luella, who was trying to still the trembling of her hands as she held the top bar of the gate.

"*Open the gate*!" he thundered, his face savage with fury. "By God, someone shall pay for this prank!"

She held the gate open, still trembling; he mounted his horse, then bent down, scooping her up as though she was a bundle of old rags, setting her with scant ceremony in front of him.

She felt the physical power of him as he held her against the hardness of his body; his face was like granite, his eyes like ice.

"We shall see what this is all about!" he cried. "You shall come to Westhaven with me and answer for this! Who has such an evil sense of humor as to pretend that Marianne is dead?"

He spurred his horse into a gallop. It was the first time Luella had ever been on the back of a horse; they seemed to be flying through the air, the horses' hooves scarcely touching the ground, this fearsome stranger at her back, and it was exhilarating. She did not want the ride to end, but the great animal took them at tremendous speed over the track to Westhaven and up to the great, closed gates.

CHAPTER 2

Luella had a clear impression of the great house as Quinn
rode up to the gates and shouted at the top of his voice for
someone to open them at once; she saw a long gray façade,
with deep-set mullioned windows, with castellated towers at
each end; a flight of broad, shallow steps led up to a terrace, in the center of which was a massive oaken door,
flanked by stone carvings. The shutters remained drawn,
giving the place a secretive air. In front of it, formal gardens were laid out with a precision that spoke of constant
care and attention.

Near the gates was a small stone lodge, with a gray
plume of smoke curling from the chimney into the crisp
morning air. Luella's cheeks were pink, her eyes bright, her
heartbeats fast and uneven; as for Quinn Mallory, he was
beside himself with rage as he struck the gates with his
crop and cried that the lodgekeeper would earn a sound
thrashing unless he appeared at once.

The front door was flung open and a man ran out, hastily pulling on his clothes. Luella saw the corner of a curtain
twitched aside, and the startled face of lodgekeeper's wife
appeared cautiously in the opening.

The little gray-haired man was muttering what sounded
like an apology and gave Quinn a look of mingled horror
and surprise as he unfastened the great gates and swung
them back, but so far as Quinn was concerned, he did not
seem to exist; as soon as the gates were open, he urged the
horse through them and raced up the long drive to the foot
of the steps.

There he dismounted and jerked Luella down after him;
he set her on her feet and caught at her wrist as though she

33

were an erring child being dragged home from some esca-
pade. She shouted furiously at him as he hauled her with
scant consideration up the flight of steps, across the flag-
stones on the terrace, to the front door.

Again and again he pulled at the bell chain, and she
could hear the sound clanging brazenly, with metal tongue,
throughout the house. He beat on the door with his riding
crop, just as he had hammered at the gates. Luella stood
beside him, fascinated, horrified, and bewildered, her basket gripped tightly beneath her free arm. She tried to wrig-
gle away from the great, dark giant who held her prisoner,
but he shouted at her angrily to be still and went on with
his violent tattoo until the door creaked open and a white-
faced woman stood in the opening, looking at Quinn with
the same mixture of fear and dismay that the lodgekeeper
had shown.

She was plump and middle-aged, dressed in a neat prim
dress with a white apron; from beneath her cap strands of
gray hair escaped into small curls. She began to stutter an
apology that Quinn brushed aside with a wild torrent of
words.

"Betty Graddle! Where is the housekeeper? Where is the
footman? Since when has it been the task of my cook to
answer my knock? Why is everyone abed at this hour?"

He did not wait for answers to his questions; he strode
past Betty Graddle into a hall that seemed to Luella to be
bigger than the whole of Henrietta's house.

There were rich-looking carpets on the stone flags, china
urns splendidly painted with Oriental scenes and with gilt
lids to them, standing in niches. There were gilt-encrusted
mirrors supported by smiling cherubs, lacquered cabinets, a
huge, velvet-covered chair with a footstool, a scarlet sedan
chair—and behind it all, a broad sweep of shallow steps
leading up to a landing that had a stained-glass window of
enormous proportions, running from floor to ceiling. The
window had been painted in rich colors, depicting Adam
and Eve being banished from Eden by a wrathful God.
Luella looked at it with awe.

The house dwarfed her; she was aware of servants coming from all directions, several of them still half-asleep,

gathering around the figure of Mrs. Graddle, who stood trembling before her master. Someone closed the front door; there was a terrible silence everywhere. All eyes were on Quinn and his odd companion.

"Go and awaken Miss Marianne," said Quinn, and his grip on Luella's wrist did not relax.

Not a sound broke the stillness; no one moved.

"Do you *all* dare to disobey me?" Quinn demanded, his rage icy now.

Sefton, the young footman, stepped forward, the Adam's apple in his throat working nervously. Luella only just caught his words, for he spoke very quietly.

"It is not possible to awaken Miss Marianne, sir," he said.

"Why not?" Quinn demanded, quietly. "Is something amiss with her?"

The silence was like that of a tomb. It was Betty Graddle who gathered her wits together and spoke up, looking her master straight in the eye. Her own eyes were full of tears.

"Miss Marianne is dead, sir; she met with an accident some weeks ago, and we had no way of sending word to you, for we did not know where you might be found."

No one moved. They all appeared to have been spelled to sleep, like the courtiers in "The Sleeping Beauty."

Quinn's face seemed to be cut from marble; only his eyes glowed, a brilliant, burning blue in his still face.

At that moment there was a commotion at the top of the stairs. Every head turned toward the stained-glass window; in front of it stood an imperious old woman, with a slightly younger woman holding her arm and speaking protestingly.

"Madam, I do beg you, come back to your bed."

"Quiet, Emmie." The old voice held authority. "My grandson has come home."

The grandmother wore a great many wraps, and jewels flashed fierily on her fingers; fine silver hair lay about her shoulders, and she had eyes as clear as a child's. They rested briefly and with curiosity on Luella before their owner began to walk slowly and majestically downstairs.

"So you are back from your travels," she said softly.

Quinn walked toward the bottom step; his grandmother

stood on the last stair and bent to kiss his cheek. From this distance Luella could see the wrinkles. She looks as though her face has been stitched together and has puckered where the needle pulled the thread too hard, Luella thought, fascinated.

"Grandmother," said Quinn, with terrible calmness, "they tell me that Marianne is dead. Is this true?"

She bent her head.

"Yes. It gives me great pain to tell you this: Marianne was walking along the cliff path, when she fell and was drowned."

"Drowned?" he thundered, remembering the inscription on the stone. "Was no one with her?"

"No. You know she liked to walk there alone at times. Only her bonnet and cloak and her betrothal ring were found; weeks later, there was a great storm, and her body was cast up on the beach, near Lyme Regis. I traveled to identify it and arranged all the burial details; there was no one else who could do so in your absence. Mary kept to her room, as always, and showed no emotion for what had happened."

Quinn still seemed to be carved from stone as he stared over his grandmother's head at the picture of the banishment of Adam and Eve from paradise.

Jessica Mallory looked with renewed interest at the small, lonely figure behind Quinn.

"Who is your companion?" she asked him.

He did not turn his head, but his voice held scorn and bitterness.

"I found her in the churchyard. She told me that her name was Marianne Walton."

A murmur of surprise passed, like a wind over a cornfield, through the assembled servants: they looked, with varying degrees of hostility, at Luella.

"The world is not a kindly place when you stand alone . . . like a hunted stag."

She remembered the words clearly.

Jessica Mallory stepped down, and leaning heavily on her stick, she came toward Luella, the assembled servants

36

standing back to let her pass. She looked down at the girl; her eyes were as blue as her grandson's.

"No, my dear, you are not Marianne come back to us," she said regretfully. "Your hair is the wrong color, you see; and you are altogether too small and thin. Her eyes were not green, like yours, nor brown, but a color midway between the two. Her hair was like copper, and her skin like cream. She was a great beauty, and she would never have worn such clothes as yours."

Stung, Luella retorted, "She might have been glad to, had she nothing better!"

Jessica looked at her with deepening interest. "What have you in your basket?" she asked, with a curious eagerness, like a child's.

Luella's hands closed tightly and defensively around it, but her fingers trembled, and the bag fell to the floor and split open, showering its pitiful contents over the floor in full view of everybody.

A maidservant giggled and was hastily silenced. Whispers of amusement and scorn rippled through the small crowd.

Angrily, Luella bent to gather her possessions together, her cheeks red-hot. Jessica stopped her, twitching a garment out of her reach with the tip of her stick.

"Is this all you own, child?" she asked.

"Yes!" cried Luella defiantly.

"Parsons," she instructed one of the servants, "remove these garments and burn them. Emmie, take the Bible and hairbrush to my room."

Emmie, long and thin, with a crooked nose and a sandy wig, picked up both items disdainfully in her fingertips and walked up the stairs, her back like a ramrod.

"Now," said Jessica, "Mrs. Graddle, see that this child has a bath and some food and then bring her upstairs to me."

She smiled at Luella.

"What is your *real* name, child?"

Before Luella could answer, the immobile figure at the foot of the stairs came suddenly to life; he had been staring unseeingly at the window beneath which he had asked Marianne to marry him—and had received her breathless, laughing "Yes" in answer.

"She dared to say her name was Marianne!" he cried furiously to his grandmother. *"Marianne,* do you hear? I do not care *what* you do with this child, so long as *I* do not hear her call herself by *that* name ever again!"

With that, he was gone. He strode past them all, with the fierce energy of a whirlwind, brushing against Luella with such force that she was almost overbalanced.

He wrenched open the door and strode out, slamming it violently behind him. Seconds later, the sound of hooves was heard as Quinn Mallory galloped down the drive and away across the heathland.

"Back to your work, this instant," Jessica said briskly. "It is high time the shutters were opened. Get along, all of you!"

She turned and walked upstairs, slowly. Mrs. Graddle gave Luella a small push toward the baize-covered door at the back of the hall.

Beyond the door was a bustle of activity, a maze of rooms, a warren of passages. Luella looked bewildered at store rooms piled with pots and pans and knives and saws and all the instruments needed for the kitchen of a vast house; she looked at sacks of flour, salted hams hanging from ceiling hooks, piles of vegetables; she saw the ranges and the bread ovens, the great scrubbed tables, and everywhere the hustle and bustle of life in the servants' quarters, the men and the women talking in subdued whispers to one another as they went about their business, all of them turning to look at Luella and make some comment in a loud voice, so that she could hear.

She held her head high, but she was as close to tears as she had been when she found her money had been stolen. Betty Graddle looked uncomfortable, telling them sharply to go about their business and leave the child alone.

The cook took her to a small room, comfortably furnished, where a fire was beginning to crackle into life. She shouted orders in her broad Dorsetshire voice to a sulky-looking young maid, who brought a large tin bath and a kettle of hot water, flouncing out to bring another kettle of water with a disgusted glance at Luella and a wrinkling of her nose.

Luella cast about in her mind for the most crushing remark she could think of, and came up with one she had heard Henrietta use to a tradesman.

"You are vulgar and offensive," she said coldly. "You should not stare at me so!"

The girl's mouth dropped open. There was a smothered sound from Betty Graddle, and then a pin-drop silence, before Betty said testily, "Are you going to stand there all day, Alice? Isn't my time to be wasted enough as it is, looking after this child, without you looking stupid? Bring some more water, and soap and towels."

Betty stripped off Luella's clothing with no regard for modesty and ordered her to get into the bath, where she proceeded to clean her with a piece of coarse yellow soap. The water was too hot, the soap stung her eyes, the towel in which Betty commanded her to wrap herself was rough and scratched her skin, but she made no complaint; she just stared at the older woman with those great green eyes, and Betty shook her head, looking troubled.

"Who are you?" she asked.

"That is a secret," Luella said, with dignity, "which I shall tell to no one."

"You'll answer questions right enough when old Mrs. Mallory asks them," Betty retorted grimly. "Where'd you get those bruises, and those marks on your back and legs?"

"Henrietta did that," Luella said simply.

"Henrietta?"

"Mrs. Henrietta Spencer. I was her maid. She beat me most days. The worst I ever had was for breaking a plate. I didn't break it on purpose, but *she* said I did. It was just an old plate that I had for my food. I wished she was dead, and she fell downstairs and died. I suppose I'm a witch."

"Oh, indeed, miss?" said Betty, torn between compassion, amusement, and curiosity. "Well, you're skinny enough for one, I must say. Dry yourself properly, mind. What on earth possessed you to say you was Miss Marianne, eh?"

"I read the name on the tombstone and liked it better than mine. Was she *very* beautiful, Mrs. Graddle?"

"That she was. The master was going to marry her; he was head over heels in love with her. Terrible shock for him, poor man, coming home like this, and finding her had died."

"If he loved her so much, why did he go off and leave her?"

"Because he had to; he was on secret business, and that's all I know. You ask too many questions, that you do!" Betty scolded.

She was, to use her own words, "fair flummoxed." This child, with the pointed face and the cats' eyes that made her uneasy, was certainly not gently born and reared; neither was she a vagabond or a street urchin—she spoke well, held herself properly, and had a fair command of words, pert though they were in Betty's eyes. She had been educated and taught her manners.

"Who was your mother?" she asked.

"I don't know," Luella said flatly.

"What's this, then?" Betty held out, accusingly, the locket that Luella had taken from her neck and tried to conceal in the folds of the towel. "Did you steal it?"

"No!" Sobbing, Luella tried to snatch the locket from her. "It's mine, I swear it is!"

"Don't take on so, then." Awkwardly, Betty handed it back and got to her feet. "What I'm supposed to dress you in, heaven knows. You can't put them stockings on again, that's for sure, they're in ribbons; and your gown is torn into great holes. I suppose I'll have to find you something."

In the doorway she paused, eyeing Luella with a worried frown. "You don't want to take too much notice of what Mrs. Mallory says. She'll no doubt make a great fuss of you, and pet you, and then get tired of you. Old people are full of such whims and fancies. Besides"—Betty hesitated, trying to choose her words with care—"her isn't—well— what you might call—like other people. She's odd—strange in the head. Most times she's sharp enough, but now and again she'll be a bit . . . *queer*. She talks about Miss Marianne as if she was still here."

40

Luella shook her head uncomprehendingly. Betty sighed and went away; she came back with a faded print dress that had belonged to one of the maids, a chemise, and some clean stockings. Alice followed her in with a tray of food; her lips were pressed tight together, and she ignored Luella.

The child must be ravenous, Betty thought, as Luella tucked into eggs and toast and tea and ham without waiting to get into clean clothes. The towel fell away from one bare, pink arm, and her damp, golden hair lay spread about her shoulders. For all her hunger, she ate daintily enough, Betty thought, surprised. She did not approve of what Mrs. Mallory had done, but Luella won from her a reluctant approval.

"How'd you get your clothes in such a state, all torn and muddy?" she wanted to know, watching Luella eat.

"I walked a distance. I've run away, and I'm going to London," Luella said.

"Lunnon? Whatever for?"

"To find work."

"That's foolishness. 'Tis no place for a young woman on her own, that's a fact," Betty said positively.

"Why not?" Luella asked naively.

Betty stared at her in astonishment and shook her head.

" 'Tis a wicked city, don't you know that? Full of thieves and cutthroats and men that'll take a young woman and use her badly and then throw her in the gutter. Don't you understand what I mean?" Betty asked.

"Oh yes!" Luella spoke airily, delicately licking her fingertips. "I know all about men!"

"Ah, well!" said Betty, rising to her feet, with a bewildered headshake, "if you've finished your food, then I'll take you upstairs to Mrs. Mallory as I'm told to do. Mind you speak respectful and behave yourself and see to your manners."

With which admonition Betty led her from the room, back the way they had come through the servants' quarters, into the hall, and up the stairs.

Luella looked curiously at the great window with its rich jewel colors and its picture, which seemed to dominate the whole house. There was an inscription, in old English lettering, above the head of the vengeful, fierce-eyed God, who stood with his hand upraised.

"In the beginning, God made Heaven and Earth."

Beyond the window was another, shorter flight of stairs, leading into a very wide gallery that had long windows, with deep window seats, looking out over the front of the house.

Around the walls of the gallery were several large coffers of carved oak. In the center of the gallery, at the back, another flight of stairs curved upward, and there were doors, also, at each end of the gallery.

This gallery was a place in which, long ago, Mallory children had played on wet days, and young men and women had sat out between dances in the great ballroom, or had done their courting. Old people and young, men and women, had looked from the windows, feeling safe or imprisoned, according to their circumstancs.

The windows gave a splendid view of the sea, which tumbled ceaselessly inshore to the wild, scrub-covered heathland, where twisted bushes crouched low to escape the wrath of the wind. The small, rocky inlets that lay beneath the headlands were completely concealed from the house, though several rough paths crisscrossed the half-mile from house to sea.

At each end of the house the towers jutted out like wings, hiding the view of the church on the right and the view along the coast on the left, and were connected to the gallery and the main part of the house by important-looking carved doors.

Betty commanded Luella to follow her to one of these doors, in the meantime pointing out a small flight of stairs tucked away at the back of the gallery.

"That's the way the servants come," she told Luella. "Leastways, the rest of the servants have to use it; 'tis only me, and Mrs. Farley, who's the housekeeper, and Emmie, who looks after Mrs. Mallory, that's allowed the use of the front stairs. 'Tis a privilege."

Betty spoke proudly and Luella asked, "Have you been here a long time?"

"Nigh on thirty years—since Mr. Mallory was a babe in arms."

"Does Mr. Mallory have brothers and sisters?"

"He has one sister, but you'll not be seeing much of Miss Mary Mallory," Betty said shortly. "Here we are: this is the sea tower, where Mrs. Mallory has her private apartments."

Betty rapped on the doors, and they were opened by a small, dark maid for all the world like a gnome, who scuttled away and left Betty and her charge standing in a large, richly furnished drawing room, with thick carpets, a great deal of gilt furniture upholstered in crimson velvet, and console tables holding a variety of small objects in silver and ivory, as well as some splendidly lacquered cabinets. The walls were hung with damask, and the ceiling was painted with a design of flying birds and clouds against a pale blue background. On one wall there was an ornate carved golden eagle surmounting a huge mirror in which Luella saw herself reflected as very small and insignificant.

She had never been in such a room in all her life; this, she thought, must be the paradise from which God had banished Adam and Eve.

There was a window at the far end of the room, its velvet curtains looped back with heavy gold tassels to show a view of sunny skies above a whitecapped sea that came running swiftly into shore. Far out, a small boat plowed its way valiantly through the waves.

The view entranced Luella as much as the room, but she had no time to enjoy either, for Emmie came in, stared down her long nose at Luella, and said, "Come with me."

Luella followed Emmie into a room as big and richly furnished as the one she had just left: the same damask-hung walls, a great many needlework stools and small tables, and many mirrors. Amidst all this luxury Mrs. Mallory sat in state in the most splendid bed that Luella had ever seen.

The mahogany bedposts were delicately carved and tapered to a dome at the top, which was surmounted by a carved sphinx; beautifully wrought lamps decorated each corner; around the base of the bed was a silk valance over-draped with tasseled swags. The many pillows against which Mrs. Mallory was propped were covered in silk; the coverlet was of thick, pale-green damask decorated with birds and flowers and sprays of cherry blossom.

Luella was overawed; Jessica, seeing this, was delighted. She had a child's pleasure in showing off splendid possessions to impressed audiences.

"Emmie, bring a stool to the bedside. Sit down, child. Walking downstairs tired me so that I have come back to bed. It is a splendid place to be. Do you not agree?"

"I never spent much time there, ma'am," Luella said wryly.

"You shall tell me about yourself. Sit down. Emmie, leave us." The old hand waved the disgruntled companion away.

The door closed behind Emmie. On the far side of it, she tossed her head so that her wig came askew, and went in search of Miss Mary to tell her the astonishing news.

"So you are Luella March," said Jessica, indicating the flyleap of the Bible, on which Luella had written her name in fine script. "That is a very pretty name indeed."

"I have never thought so," Luella said doubtfully.

"That is because you have grown accustomed to it; one becomes accustomed to something and it seems neither strange nor sad nor beautiful, but part of everyday life."

Jessica settled herself against the pillows, adding, "I have been lonely since Marianne left us. She would come and sit with me, and say things that made me laugh, and play backgammon with me. She was very gay and full of spirit and beautiful. There is a portrait of her in the gallery. It is very lifelike."

She sighed, looking sad and tired for a moment.

"Did she live in this house?" Luella asked.

"Yes. She was my goddaughter and an orphan. There was an accident, fifteen years ago, when Marianne was a little girl and Quinn almost a young man. Marianne's parents were staying with me and had gone to a ball with my son, who was Quinn's father, and *his* wife. On the way home a sudden thunderstorm frightened the horses and the coach crashed into the river; a flood of water swept them away, even the coachman. They were all drowned."

"Marianne, too, was drowned," Luella said, "the sea took *her*; how strange!"

"Yes." Jessica's eyes were full of tears. "She was full of life and laughter, and Quinn was going to marry her; that was my dearest wish."

She was silent for several moments; she lay so still that Luella thought she had fallen asleep.

"I have done as you would have wished, Marianne," Jessica said suddenly.

Luella was startled; the blue eyes that had been bright and clear were suddenly clouded. Jessica smiled vaguely at the girl by her bedside.

"She will be pleased with me," Jessica said. "So very pleased. I have told no one. It is *her* secret and *mine*. We liked to share secrets."

Luella was silent; Jessica plucked at the bedclothes with aimless fingers.

"The sea is cruel," Mrs. Mallory whispered. "Cruel and greedy; it swallows up ships and men to satisfy its appetite. It took my poor Marianne; but this time the sea gave her back, though all her beauty was gone, rotted away, her soft flesh being eaten. . . . I did not want to go to Lyme Regis that day, but I went. It was my duty."

The voice went on; Luella listened, puzzled and fascinated. She had no idea what a body looked like after it had been in the sea for a little while, but she understood that Quinn's beautiful bride-to-be had been sadly disfigured; she, who had never known any emotion save hatred in her short life, felt sudden compassion for him. The feeling was one of strange tenderness that made her want to weep.

"Tell me how *you* came to be in the cemetery," Jessica commanded.

Luella looked at the woman in the bed. Her eyes were clear and properly focused again; she had returned to the present.

Luella told her tale; Jessica listened, expressed indignation at Henrietta's behavior, and asked Luella what she proposed to do with herself.

"I shall go to London to find work," Luella told her.

"London? It is not such a wonderful place, my child; the streets are dirty and full of rogues, who live by cheating and swindling and stealing. The young men have no manners, the old men are great bores. You will stay here; you can keep me company and help poor Emmie, whose rheumatism troubles her."

"I *must* go to London," Luella insisted, feeling suddenly trapped.

Jessica waved her hand imperiously. "Utter nonsense; have I not just told you that you will do far better to stay here?" She looked with sly speculation at the girl by her bed. "Why, this is a better life than you'd have, trying to fend for yourself. We shall find a handsome young man for you to marry one day. How would you like that, eh?"

She patted Luella's hand as though she had tidied the world around her to her satisfaction. Luella said nothing, but was thinking furiously. She needed money, and if she could earn it here, then her prospects would be the better when she set out for London, she reasoned. After all, this was sheer paradise compared to the misery of her life in Devon.

"Show me the locket of which you spoke," Jessica ordered.

Silently, Luella handed it over, and Jessica Mallory examined it with interest.

"Hm. Yes, finely wrought, I must say. These initials now—'E.F.' The locket was especially made for someone. Who knows, you may be the daughter of someone who is wellborn; on the other hand, you may be a rich man's bastard." She smiled impishly, handing the locket back and adding, "It matters more *what* you are than *who* you are. Few would agree with me, of course. You appear to have had a good education at the charity school. Not that I approve of education for the children of the laboring classes; it is a scandalous waste of time."

"I believe I did not come from such a background," Luella retorted. "Even if I did, is it not the right of every child to have such learning as will help it through life?"

The old eyes danced.

"A rebel, I see. You remind me of my grandson. I do not agree with you, but I own that I like your mind; it is sharp and clear as a frosty morning. Go away now and leave me in peace. I am tired."

She drifted into sleep as easily as a child. Luella leaned her forehead against the window pane and looked at the tumbling seas. Jessica slept with her mouth open, snoring gently, and Luella wondered how old she really was. She did not turn from her contemplation of the sea until Emmie came in, bearing two delicately fluted cups and saucers and a silver pot of chocolate on a beautifully chased silver tray.

The sound of Emmie's arrival, quiet though it was, awakened Jessica; her eyelids flickered back from her tired eyes.

"When will Marianne come?" she asked fretfully.

"Later," Emmie soothed. "She has gone for her walk; you know how she hated to be indoors all day."

"She is a very long time coming," Jessica pointed out, her voice still querulous.

"I daresay she has walked farther than usual, madam."

Emmie tucked the clothes around her mistress and poured the hot chocolate. Luella's eyes met Emmie's for a moment, and there was gentleness and understanding in the rather prim face of Jessica's companion.

Luella drank her chocolate in silence; Jessica continued to talk about Marianne.

"I hope she will bring me some shells from the beach, Emmie, or a pretty stone for my collection, that I can put in my room with the others. Marianne *always* brings me something from the beach. The sea has given her back, Emmie—I knew it would—and she will bring me treasure from the sea as a token."

Jessica seemed suddenly aware of Luella's presence; her eyes lost their restless look and her voice became brisk.

"Show Luella the old nursery suite, Emmie. She can sleep there. The maids are to put clean linen on the bed and put in a warming pan. There are some of Marianne's

47

clothes there; they will surely fit this skinny child. Let her have what she pleases. Now, go, both of you. I am too tired to talk; I shall sleep until Marianne comes."

"Come with me, miss," Emmie said repressively to Luella.

Outside, in the long gallery, Luella said, "I should like to see the portrait of Marianne."

Emmie smiled thinly and led Luella toward a big portrait hanging on the far wall. Gravely, Luella looked up.

The girl in the portrait wore a gown of gauzy material with a knot of silk rosebuds tucked into the low-cut bosom. She was the most exquisite person Luella had ever seen: Her limbs were softly rounded, her hazel eyes large, brilliant, and full of life; she wore her thick, reddish-gold hair looped into the chignon that had been fashionable since 1790, a few stray curls escaping on her smooth, delicate cheeks. There was a pink ribbon around her forehead, exactly matching the rosebuds at her breast, bracelets of gold and turquoise on her wrists, and an elaborately wrought pendant of gold and turquoise around her neck. She had a full, laughing mouth, a rounded chin, a delicately modeled nose; it all added up to a beauty that aroused tremendous envy and longing in Luella.

Yet Marianne was now only a name on a tombstone; as Jessica had said, the sea had destroyed her beauty and ravished her before returning her again to her family.

"Come," said Emmie impatiently. "*I* have no time to idle."

She led the way toward the curving flight of stairs that rose to the floor above. Luella followed slowly, savoring everything she saw because it was all new, strange, and wonderful. She had not known such richness and opulent splendor could exist, and she marveled at the people who lived amongst it, taking it all for granted.

Down in the kitchens the servants had plenty to talk about.

"Where'd she come from, *I'd* like to know? Not some fancy woman of the master's, that you may be sure of; she ain't no more'n a child."

"Did you *see* 'er? Her stockings and her gown all torn and muddied, dirt on 'er hands and legs. Reckon the gypsies turned 'er out."

"Gypsies? More like, some lad give 'er a tumble in the hay!"

There was laughter. Alice said, "Speaking to *me* like that! Cheeky little madam! And Mrs. Graddle trying not to laugh, you could see that!"

"A fair shame, Alice! What a day, to be sure! Poor Mr. Quinn coming home for his wedding and finding his bride dead and buried. And what did 'e mean, saying that skinny little creature called herself Marianne Walton? She's not right in the 'ead, if you ask me."

"No one asked you, Lily Parsons," said Mrs. Farley, the housekeeper, grimly. "Get on with your work without so much talking. What with all that's going on here today, and the military out looking for an escaped prisoner from Dorchester jail, there's been enough distraction to last us all for a while."

The man with the wound in his thigh had limped on through the rain and the dark, his progress slow and uncertain, but he blessed the firmness with which Luella had fastened the bandage, for it gave him some support. Nevertheless, darkness cheated him. He had decided to make his way toward the sea, where Westhaven lay; confused by the darkness, he turned inland, away from the sea, trying in vain to find the paths he thought he knew so well.

He had no idea how far he walked. The pain began to throb in his leg again, fiery and agonizing. He was hungry and exhausted, craving sleep and food, knowing he would find neither. When he saw the red glow in the distance, he stumbled toward it, like a drunken man, praying for strength to reach it. He was so weary and in such pain that he did not care if the soldiers found him; he only knew that the red glow was a campfire, warm, friendly . . .

He crawled, sobbing like a child, for the last few yards before he dragged himself into the light of the fire and lay there, gasping for breath, his face buried in the cold, wet grass.

The fire burned fitfully because of the rain; it had been lit, not by gypsies, but by a small band of tinkers, their makeshift wagons covered with canvas hoods. The soldiers had already been that way, searching the wagons with anger born of frustration, showing brutal disregard for the occupants. They had hurled out the women and children, overturned all their meager possessions, questioned the men, jabbing them with the butts of their muskets if they did not answer fast enough, unconcerned at the hatred smoldering in the eyes that stared back at them.

In the end they had gone away, leaving the children crying, the men and their womenfolk in a state of sullen fury. They shouted back through the dusk that if the lot of them weren't on their way first thing in the morning, then they'd be in for trouble, all right, nothing but vagabonds, and see if the *next* parish would have them . . .

A woman who came from one of the wagons and found the stranger lying there touched him with surprisingly gentle hands. If *this* poor devil was the man the soldiers were seeking, it would be a great pleasure to cheat them, she reflected.

The tinkers were gone at dawn; the stranger lay in the back of the woman's wagon, covered by a blanket, a fresh dressing on the infected wound. He was in a fever, his cheeks like hot coals, and the woman squatting beside him moistened his lips from time to time with water from a tin cup.

The wagons moved away inland up toward Somerset. They were well on their journey when Quinn left his horse grazing peacefully and walked toward the edge of the cliff, many miles along the coast toward Lyme Bay. The agony in his heart was worse than any physical pain. Marianne was dead, and he was bereft; the sea had clawed her down into its cold, dark depths and then spewed her out again, to lie, a heap of rotting flesh, waiting to be identified and taken away for burial.

That soft flesh rotting, those warm limbs cold? Laughter gone from her lips, mischief from her eyes? The thought

50

was torture such as he had never known, anguish that wrenched his soul apart. He remembered Marianne's trick of tossing her head at him, smiling over her shoulder . . . the way her curls bounced when she moved quickly . . . her provocative, teasing, amusing ways . . . the girl he had wanted to marry.

He knew he would have to return to the house sooner or later; there were questions he needed to ask. He had seen Marianne's name carved on a tombstone; he had heard a green-eyed urchin call herself by that name—and hated her bitterly because she was not Marianne.

Perhaps there had been some ridiculous mistake; his grandmother was old, she could have looked on a stranger battered by the seas and thought it was Marianne . . .

Quinn sighed, knowing the folly of such reasoning. He left his horse to graze and walked a long way over the scrubland; the storm raging within him was one of overwhelming violence that left him exhausted.

He stared out over the Channel; beyond the horizon lay France, in her death throes, weakened by the terrible uprising of the Revolution. He had seen dreadful things done there in the name of freedom and justice; the mission he had just completed was to have been his last—a dangerous and difficult one, taking more than a year, traveling through France to Italy to find a safe passage for the man the British government wanted safe in its care.

He, Quinn Mallory, had done as Sir Julius Margrave had asked, and the Count Jean-Baptiste Riennes was in England. If I had *not* gone to France, Marianne might be alive today, Quinn thought bitterly.

CHAPTER 3

The nursery suite was at the top of the house, separated from the servants' bedrooms by a stout door. Emmie left Luella alone in the suite, with instructions to behave herself.

Luella explored her surroundings; there was a night nursery, day nursery, schoolroom, and a small sitting room. From every window there were views that excited; she had never lived with such freedom and space all around her.

With its bleakness and bareness and its look of being continually fretted by the sea and harried by the winds, Dorset was a wild, sinister place. Even the stone-walled cottages huddled together as though for protection from the fury of the winds, and they had deep-set windows, like secretive, watching eyes. There were a few farms and a road of sorts leading away to the main Dorchester-Axminster road; a number of rough paths crisscrossed the paths that ran between the low, twisted bushes of furze and scrub.

There was a view of the cemetery from one of the back windows; away to the left she could just make out the bulk of a house standing, like Westhaven, with its face toward the sea, but very much smaller than Quinn Mallory's house. She could also see the path that ran along the top of the cliffs; in places, it was within a few feet of the edge, and the cliffs had crumbled, as though the sea wind had nibbled away at them.

This was the path from which Marianne had fallen. Luella thought of the laughing girl of the picture and the lonely grave in the cemetery; the wind and sea seemed to roar in her ears, yet at the center of the tumult there was a core of silence, cold and terrifying, full of evil.

She closed her eyes, willing herself to weld the fragments of a strange picture into a coherent whole; she could not do so, but she had impressions that puzzled her, for she was not aware of possessing any kind of sixth sense. She thought she heard the sound of wheels rolling over stones, of jeering crowds; she seemed to feel a terrible bitterness and despair, worse than anything that life with Henrietta had produced; all around her the darkness seemed to blossom with a burning, white light . . .

She felt the sweat bead her forehead, but the vision had gone, though it left her feeling sad and lost. She shook away feelings she could not understand and turned her attention toward the cupboards on the wall of the bedroom.

It was full of clothes that Marianne had discarded when she left the schoolroom, but the size and variety of Marianne's wardrobe took Luella's breath away. There were muslin gowns, sprigged, spotted, and plain, most of them white; summer gowns of cambric; winter ones of fine wool and sarcenet; a great variety of cloaks and pelisses in kerseymere and velvet.

The luxury of deliberation was something entirely new to Luella. She finally chose a green dress with tiny silk tassels at the waist; with it went a cloak of green kerseymere, fastened at the neck with silver tassels. Having found what she wanted, Luella turned her attention to drawers filled with petticoats and shifts and chemises, all in delicate silk or chiffon or cotton, and with silk stockings. She had never possessed a pair of silk stockings. She stripped off the cotton ones she was wearing, as well as the rest of the clothes Betty Graddle had brought to her, and sat on a chair, without a stitch of clothing on her body, delighting in the sensuous feel of the silk against her bare legs, as she carefully eased on a pair of Marianne's stockings.

She found gloves and scarves, bonnets with ribbons, reticules of velvet, shoes of soft leather and satin; plus a lacquer box containing items of jewelry: a coral necklace, another of seed pearls with a matching bracelet, a bracelet of silver bells, and a gold and turquoise set of jewelry.

Luella put the jewelry back in the box and hastily shut the lid, feeling she had no right to touch it. Then she dressed herself leisurely in the rest of the clothes she had chosen and stared at herself in the mirror.

Excitement had put color into her cheeks. Startled, she realized she no longer seemed a skinny waif. At the school she had worn hand-me-downs, and she had never owned a brand new gown in her life; even these clothes had belonged to someone else, but they transformed her. She was already older, more womanly, her small bust more clearly defined, her thinness concealed by clever cut; she lifted her head high and put her shoulders back.

The astonished servants coming to put sheets on the bed in which Marianne had slept until her fifteenth birthday saw a well-dressed young woman, sitting in Nanny Varley's chair, reading from a book of John Donne's poems that she had found in the schoolroom bookcase.

Luella smiled at them and politely gave them good-day; they went about their work in silence until they were outside in the corridor once more.

"Did you ever?" whispered the first maid, round-eyed. "Acting like she was a lady to the manner born. Don't seem like only this morning she was wearing them raggedy bits of clothes . . ."

"Well, you know what they says," the second maid replied scornfully, "fine feathers makes fine birds."

Reading palled; the hours passed slowly. Luella's restless, rebellious spirit was unsatisfied. They had forgotten about her, she decided; it was well into the afternoon and certainly time for dinner.

She went down to Mrs. Mallory's rooms, but when she walked into the sitting room, she found Mrs. Mallory alone, propped against the pillows, looking frail and old in sleep.

There was no sign of Emmie nor the little dark maid, so Luella left the sea tower and began to explore the house. She met no servants, though there seemed to be plenty of activity downstairs.

She opened a great many doors and looked inside—at suites of rooms for guests; bedrooms for members of the household with enormous, elaborate beds; sitting rooms; vast cupboards filled with linen, bigger than the bedroom in which she had slept at Henrietta's. She saw the huge ballroom, a music room, a study; she saw a replica of Jessica's apartments in the rooms of the other tower, but so austerely furnished that she guessed that they were occupied by Quinn Mallory.

He is like a great eagle, perched high on a rock, Luella thought; there was a picture of an eagle in the assembly hall at school: a huge, proud bird with bright, hooded eyes, a cruel beak, an air of majesty, of ruthless strength. Quinn Mallory would swoop down from his great height to crush anyone who angered him, she reflected.

From each end of the gallery corridors led away to other corridors, each with rows of doors, so that Luella became thoroughly bewildered and lost.

She tapped endlessly at doors, but the rooms behind them were empty. She gave up tapping and simply turned the handles, to look quickly in, and then go on her way.

At the end of one of the larger passages she opened a door and had a sudden shock.

She looked at a well-furnished sitting room, with a bright fire blazing in the hearth to soften the chill of autumn; by the fire, on a brocaded chair, sat a woman, her hands folded idly in her lap. She seemed to be staring into the heart of the fire.

She was wearing a high-waisted dress of some supple, dark material, with full sleeves and a brooch pinned between ruffles of net at her breast; it was impossible to tell her age or her looks, or even the color of her eyes and hair, for her face and head were entirely covered by a black lace veil.

Luella was instantly reminded of the woman she had seen in the marketplace at Axminster. This woman turned her head sharply and drew a deep breath; Luella had an impression of being closely scrutinized from head to toe, but she stood her ground, head held high, though her heart beat fast as she remembered how sinister the woman in the marketplace had seemed.

"Who are you?" the woman demanded, and Luella had an impression of dark eyes flashing behind the concealing lace. "What are you doing here, and why are you dressed in the clothes that Marianne wore when she was in the schoolroom?"

"My name is Luella March, and I was told I might wear these clothes," she said clearly.

"Were you indeed? Emmie told me some garbled tale of Quinn coming home with a little ragamuffin, some urchin he had picked up . . ."

"I am neither a ragamuffin nor an urchin!" Luella retorted angrily. "Emmie had no right to say such a thing."

"How dare you answer so impertinently!" the woman snapped.

"You sound exactly like Henrietta Spencer!" Luella cried.

"Who is Henrietta Spencer?" the woman asked coldly.

"I was her maid. I ran away; she paid me no wages, and I was going to London to look for work, when my money was stolen . . ."

"How could you have money if you were paid no wages?" said the woman, sharp as a needle.

"I—borrowed five guineas."

"*Borrowed*! It is more likely that you stole it. Are you a thief?"

"No, I am not! I shall return the money one day—not to Henrietta, for she is dead . . ."

The woman sat back in her chair, staring thoughtfully at Luella, her lips pursed.

"Come in and close the door; I feel the cold. Stand over there, where I can see you properly, and answer my questions. The truth, mind, I want no lies," she said sharply.

Luella obeyed, though not submissively; she shut the door and walked across to stand opposite the pointing finger of the woman in the chair.

"Do you know who I am?" the woman asked.

"No," replied Luella, staring back at her, unblinkingly.

"I am Mary Mallory. Quinn is my brother. Do you know where he is now?"

"No," said Luella again.

57

"He is out on the moors somewhere. Trying to forget that he was going to wed Marianne and she is dead. She was beautiful, but all beauty dies. Time touches it, and it melts like snow in summer; the sea takes it and gives it back broken and ugly. I have seen ugliness—I saw a woman who had been burned in a fire; a woman with a harelip; and another with a great stain like spilled wine on her face. They never knew what it was to be beautiful; perhaps they yearned to look as Marianne looked. Do you understand what I am trying to say, Luella March?"

"I think so."

"Oh, how *can* a child like you understand such things? Of what use is Marianne's beauty now?"

The voice was almost triumphant. Mary Mallory settled herself comfortably and refolded her hands, nodding to Luella.

"I wish to know everything about you," she said.

So Luella told her tale, for the second time that day, and Mary Mallory's reaction was not sympathetic as Jessica's had been. She merely nodded and said, "It is for Quinn to decide what is to be done with you. If you are honest and clean and mind your manners, you may be allowed to stay here and work."

"I am not sure that I want to stay!" Luella cried suddenly.

"Why not?" Mary demanded, affronted.

"I should feel like a prisoner here," Luella said simply. "This house is so big, the people in it are so strange. I shall stay only long enough to earn my fare to London."

"London!" The voice held blistering contempt. "What will you do there, you skinny little brat? Do you fancy some rich old man will make you his mistress? No man wants such a bag of bones to hold in his bed!"

Luella was furious.

"You have no right to say such things!" she cried.

The woman laughed shortly.

"I have every right! You are a servant in this house!"

"I am *not* a servant!" Luella cried, her eyes flashing fire. "Mrs. Mallory wishes me to stay, but I am not bound to do so. I am free as the gulls that fly in the air. I can find work where I please!"

"Fine words!" Mary mocked. "It is not so easy to find employment. You must hold your tongue and not answer back; you will get your ears boxed and be sent packing if you behave as you do now."

Luella glared at her; there was nothing this woman could tell her about the pain of punishment. She said angrily, "Why do you cover your face with a veil? Is it because you are so ugly?"

There was a moment's terrible silence. Mary stood up, towering over her, and Luella thought she was going to strike her, but she scorned to show fear, and stared back at the veiled woman, her green eyes brilliant and unblinking.

Mary gripped her by the shoulder and propelled her toward the door.

"Go!" she choked. "Go! I never want to see you again, you impudent, sniveling little chit!"

When Luella was on the other side of the door, Mary put her hands to her scarred face, beneath the veil, and wept bitterly.

"Oh, Philip!" she whispered forlornly. "If only you were here! Why did you go, without a word to me, without a farewell? Where are you now?"

He lay in the back of the tinker's wagon, burning with fever, shivering and muttering strange things. The husband of the woman who watched over him grumbled uneasily.

"What if the military finds out we've got him?"

"They'll not, rest on that," she retorted. "They're far behind, and as stupid a bunch as ever we'll set eyes on."

"What if he dies, then? Thought on that, 'ave 'ee?"

"I've thought on it." Her voice remained calm. "He'll not die. I have my remedies. There's things you'll need to gather for me."

He said nothing; he would go willingly enough, she knew. The tinkers were not thought much of; it was the proud Romanies who were the royalty of the roads, the chosen people of the highways and byways. *They* had a vast store of knowledge concerning herbs and medicines, charms and potions, that they seldom revealed; but sometimes, during the long years that Romanies and tinkers had traveled the same road, a few Romany secrets had filtered through to the people they looked down upon, and women like Kyra were quick to learn.

So Kyra watched her patient, tended him, used her remedies upon him with skill and conviction. The wound on his leg grew more angry and full of pus; when she lanced it, he screamed out at her in agony, while the wagons wound their way towards the fair at Horcastle, and the rest of the tinkers shrugged, saying among themselves that Seth's woman was a fool thinking she could patch a dying man like he was an old pot or pan.

They were a loyal bunch, though; not one would have revealed the fact that a fugitive from Dorchester jail lay fighting for his life in the back of Seth's wagon.

Kyra listened to the fragments of talk that he muttered in his delirium, and made little of it; sometimes he spoke rapidly in a foreign tongue that she did not recognize, for she had no book learning and could neither read nor write.

Once he stared at her vacantly, his lips moving, his words so quiet, she had to put her ear close to his mouth.

"The Flowers of Darkness . . . do you know where they bloom?"

She considered the words, thinking they made a pretty phrase; when she thought she had found the right answer, she smiled and nodded.

"The Flowers of Darkness, eh? That'd be the stars in the sky. Little silver daisies, they be. Yes, I likes that, mister."

"No stars," he muttered, his face contorted, as though with terrible pain. "France is torn and mangled and the vultures eat her flesh . . ."

She shook her head. She was lost; there was a war going on across the sea, she knew *that*, but what was it to *her* and her kind? Little information filtered through to the tight-knit tinker community, who went about their own business and let the rest of the world do what it would.

Often he sighed as he tossed and sweated, and he spoke a

woman's name; Kyra could not quite catch what it was, as he mumbled it incoherently.

Mary's furious dismissal left Luella feeling resentful and startled; she went back to the gallery and sat in the window seat. The day dragged its feet as heavily as though they were iron-shod. Emmie sent her to the kitchen, and they gave her a meal in Betty Graddle's room. Afterward, Luella went back to the long gallery, wondering at the number of servants needed to look after so few people.

She was feeling like a bird in a cage when Emmie came from the sea tower and told her that Mrs. Mallory wished to see her.

Jessica had awakened refreshed from her sleep and eaten an excellent lunch; she eyed Luella approvingly.

"That dress was made for Marianne's fifteenth birthday party. It becomes you. She will not mind you wearing it. I suppose she has gone to see the Cazelet woman again."

Luella was learning quickly how effortlessly Jessica made her flights from fact to fancy.

"Who is the Cazelet woman?"

"She lives at Dunbury House."

"Where is that?"

"Along the cliffs. It is an ugly, dark old place. Mrs. Cazelet will not see anyone—except Marianne. She is a recluse and scarcely ever goes out. Marianne says that she is in mourning for her husband; the Frenchies are supposed to have killed him. I have had enough of the wretched war with France; I am tired of all the alarms and frights, and the rumors that the French are about to land and attack us. Such nonsense! We are safe enough here; this house is a fortress. Quinn went to France, secretly. Oh, he did not tell me that, but I *knew*. He went to help those who are victims of the uprising. You spend too much time with Mrs. Cazelet, Marianne. *I* need you beside me; you look so pretty in that dress, and you make me laugh. Perhaps Simon will come this afternoon."

"Who is Simon?"

"You know very well who he is; he lives at Bellminster,

though he hates it there now that his father is dead and he must manage his estates himself."

"Tell me more about Marianne," Luella persuaded softly, for the very name fascinated her.

Jessica was only too willing to talk about her goddaughter.

"She was so full of mischief, so eager for life. She was as restless as a butterfly, never still, and no one knew what she would do next. Do you not remember the day she made Paynter the coachman hand over the reins and drove the coach into Dorchester, right through the main street at a gallop? She was barely fourteen years old and Quinn was angry, fearing she might have been hurt; but she had such *spirit*, even as a child. *Nothing* daunted her!"

Luella sat with her hands in her lap, listening. Marianne was like the sea. Wild, untamed, changeable of mood. I wish I had known her, she thought.

Jessica grew tired; she fell silent. Luella bent forward and said softly, "I have met your granddaughter, Miss Mary Mallory."

"Mary keeps to her rooms," Jessica said, with a sigh.

"Why does she wear a veil over her face?"

"Because she has had the pox, child; do you not know what scars it leaves?"

Luella did know; one of the teachers at the school had borne the scars of the dreadful disease: small pits in the flesh of her cheeks and on her forehead.

"Is it—so bad?" Luella asked.

"She thinks she is so ugly that no man will ever look upon her. Bring my cologne, and ring the bell for Emmie. Draw the curtains; the light is too bright for my eyes."

Luella did as she was told; the old woman watched her, shrewdly.

"You shall stay here," she pronounced. "You shall sit with me, and amuse me, and talk to me. I do not like many people; I am old, and they weary me. Now that Quinn is back, it will be easier for us all. Marianne is a long time coming home. Perhaps she has stopped at Bellminster to see Simon; they are such good friends."

"She will not be long," Luella said softly. Hesitantly she put a hand on Jessica's forehead. It was the first time in her life that she had touched another person. No one had ever put their arms around her or kissed her, and she could not imagine what it would be like to be loved as Marianne had been loved.

The rest of the day passed as slowly for Luella as the first half had done. Mary Mallory took her meals in her own suite; Betty sent one of the servants up to the nursery suite with a well-laden tray, and another maid brought candles, for it grew dark early. It was cold, for no one had thought to light a fire, and Luella tried to read by candlelight for some time; finally, she tossed the book across the room and wept, tears of frustration and loneliness.

Quinn came home exhausted and hungry; his man-servant, Cowles, was too old and too well trained to make any comment on his masters's disheveled appearance. He merely brought hot water and clean linen and attended to the master's immediate needs. Downstairs the servants scuttled around the kitchen preparing a meal.

Quinn left the meal untouched; he drank half a bottle of brandy, sitting alone at the table beneath the magnificent gilt chandelier, remembering how, the night before he had set sail for France, Marianne had sat opposite him, wearing a magnificent gown of shot silk, with the diamond brooch that had been her mother's sparkling at her breast. He remembered how the light had caught the sheen of her hair, with its ribbon bandeau; how it had sparkled in her eyes; how she had teased and laughed and lifted her glass to wish him safe return for their wedding day.

In sudden fury he hurled his glass to the floor, where it shivered into fragments. The footman, Sefton, never moved, not even when Quinn rose unsteadily to his feet; he held the door open for his master and heard him mount the stairs with a slow and heavy tread.

The moonlight came through the long gallery and lay in silver stripes across the polished floor; with his fingers on the handle of the door to the sea tower, he paused.

His grandmother would be sleeping, he thought heavily; in the morning, he would talk to her and discover that she had made a mistake. He would *prove* that Marianne was not dead, even if he had to claw the earth from her grave and lift out the coffin of a stranger.

His mind stumbled in the dark, but all his senses were inflamed by thoughts of Marianne, who should have been waiting to greet him on his return; as he turned from the door that led to the sea tower, the moon came from behind a cloud, and by the pale light he saw Marianne standing at the foot of the stairs leading to the old nursery wing.

She wasn't as he last remembered her, but as she had been on her fifteenth birthday, wearing the green dress that was his favorite. She looked pale and still; Marianne was never either of those things, and he wondered, fleetingly, if she was ill.

He saw her put a hand to her breast; triumphant joy flared in him.

"*Marianne!*" he cried thickly. "So you tease me? Hide and pretend to be gone for ever from me? You'll pay for such a prank!"

He reached the small figure standing by the stairs and pulled her into his arms.

"You shall pay, Marianne!" he whispered softly. "You owe me a forfeit. Do you not remember the game we used to play? The forfeit was one kiss from your pretty lips; tonight I demand much, much more, though it is not our wedding night. You owe me *that* for the miserable day you have given me!"

Horrified, Luella ducked free of the encircling arms and ran upstairs to the nursery suite. She had come down in search of someone to talk to, never expecting to see this man who frightened her as no one else had ever done.

She heard Quinn pounding up the stairs in pursuit; wildly, she looked around for a way of escape. She ran into the night nursery, where she had left two candles burning; the flames dipped, bowing their heads at the tumult of her entrance. She could hear Quinn moving in the other room, and very cautiously, she moved forward to close the door.

But there was no key in the lock, and even as she tried to push the door shut, Quinn was there and had flung it wide open again.

He came slowly toward her. She looked beautiful, he

thought, with her disheveled hair and enormous eyes. He had never before realized that Marianne's eyes were more green than brown . . .

"Take off your gown!" he said softly.

"No!" she cried.

"Then I shall do it for you!" he retorted, smiling.

Sobbing, her hands shaking, Luella fumbled with the fastenings on the bodice and let the gown fall around her feet; she stood there, shivering, in her white cambric petticoat; then, with a sudden, furious movement, she scooped up the dress and flung it in his face.

"Take it!" she choked bitterly. "I shall never wear it again! I wish I had never set eyes upon you! I wish I had died of cold and hunger out there on the moors; *I* did not want to come to this house! *You* dragged me here. You are as dark and fearful as a wild animal, and I would rather live with one than stay here!"

He stopped in amazement, suddenly realizing that this was not his beloved Marianne; this skinny little child, who was like a small, spitting stray cat, was the girl who had taunted him with Marianne's name in the cemetery.

The brandy burned like fire in him; his head throbbed, his body ached with the fever of his loss, and desolation swept like a burning wind through him. How dared she pour out her scorn and fury on him, he thought savagely, when she had pretended to be Marianne, fooling him, cheating!

He put his two hands around her waist and swung her up into the air, dropping her with scant ceremony onto the bed. He flung himself on top of her; his breathing was hard and heavy; his mouth sought hers relentlessly.

She could not move; she was trapped by his weight, but she fought back wildly. His mouth found hers and held it prisoner, wide open, bruising her lips; his hands tore away the petticoat from her shoulders, ripping it down to the waist.

Luella's knowledge of her body, its emotions and functions, was sketchy indeed, for the physical facts of the relationship between men and women had never been properly explained to her. She had gathered hints, whispered from behind upraised hands, at the school; she had been given lurid accounts of how a man's body differed from a woman's, horrifying tales of how children were begotten; she had been informed that mistresses were handsomely paid to please men, but were expected to perform strange acts for their fees.

Before she left the school, Luella had received a short homily on the virtue of modesty, which, so far as she could see, meant keeping her body covered, not behaving riotously (whatever that meant), and not allowing men to take liberties with her person.

No one had told her about the delight that would pour through her veins, nor of the mingled fury and torment that was part of physical contact with a man; no one had prepared her for such quickening of soul and spirit, as well as of body. When Quinn's seeking, demanding hands raked over her, part of her longed for him to find every crevice, every corner of her and make it his own; part of her burned with outrage at his treatment of her.

So, tossed giddily on a wave of emotions that threatened to engulf her, Luella felt herself stifled of breath by the savage joy of his kisses, and his lips moved downwards, over her neck, her shoulders, her breasts.

She remembered that she had recoiled from the soldier's touch, but he had been a pasty-faced, strutting little gamecock, not a man who could crush her beneath his weight; she felt Quinn's hands move purposefully onward, between her thighs, and some deep-rooted instinct of preservation surfaced suddenly, sending her crashing from the pinnacles of ecstasy; in sudden panic, she pushed against the hardness of him with all her strength; his head jerked up, and by candlelight she saw the surprise in his face.

She knew she must be free of him and the domination he represented; she lifted her head from the pillow and sank her teeth deep into his chin as he stared down at her.

With an oath he let her go abruptly, rolling away from her and getting to his feet.

She looked up at him as he stood by the bed, tall and splendid, in his breeches, his shirt open to the waist, his dark hair curling in wild disorder around his haughty face with the high-bridged nose and piercing eyes.

There were tears on Luella's lashes, though she did not know why she was crying; he saw a disheveled little creature, the candlelight shining on her golden hair, petticoat torn and rumpled around her waist, leaving the whole of the lower part of her body exposed to his gaze; but there was anger in the green eyes, too; her open mouth showed small, sharp white teeth, and she was breathing quickly, as though she had been running.

It was her helplessness that shattered him; he knew he could have taken her easily; it would have been only a question of minutes before her body became one with his. She was only a child, and one very ignorant in the ways of men with women, he suspected.

"Don't cry," he said curtly. "I have not harmed you."

He bent and picked up the green dress; she glared at him.

"Tomorrow, when I leave here, I shall go in the clothes that Betty Graddle lent me!" she cried.

"How foolishly you talk! Where will you go?"

"To London, to find work!"

"Without money?" He was angry; he flung the dress on top of her, so that it covered her exposed limbs.

"How did you come to be in the cemetery?" he demanded. "Who are you? Where are you from?"

Wearily, she told him; he stared down at her, seeing properly for the first time the fading bruises and marks that Henrietta's beatings had left. Gently, he turned her over and looked at her back; the weals had not faded, though the woman who had made them had been dead for a week.

He felt for Luella some of the pity and horror he had felt for the dead and dying men, women, and children of France. He walked over to the window and angrily jerked back the curtains, staring at the sky with its sprinkling of stars and the moon making ghost country of Dorset.

"My grandmother appears to have taken a liking to you," he said shortly. "There is no reason why you should not stay here. You will be paid. When you have saved enough from your wages, you can go to London, and I will give you the address of people who will employ you there."

She did not seem to hear him; she whispered forlornly, "You have broken my locket!"

He looked over his shoulder; she was holding something that glittered in the candlelight. He walked over to the bed.

"Give it to me!" he ordered peremptorily.

She handed it over, with an angry look; he held the locket in his hands, letting the broken chain dangle and examining the stones and inscription as best he could.

"How did you come by this?" he demanded.

"It was around my neck when I was left at the charity school," she replied.

"I will have the chain mended. When next I go to London, I may be able to trace where it was made. It probably bears the mark of the goldsmith who fashioned it."

He pulled the curtains into place again and walked toward the door.

"Go to sleep," he said as though she was a child. "You should not have looked like Marianne; what happened was your own fault."

With that quixotic remark he left her; she lay awake, going over and over in her mind all that had happened, trying to recapture the strange feelings he had aroused in her. Finally, she fell asleep, and the candles burned down to a stubble of wax.

She was awakened next morning by movement in her room; she sat up, realizing that only the green dress still covered her, and she saw Lily putting a loaded breakfast tray on a table near her bed.

The maid glanced significantly at the rumpled bed and the torn petticoat that Luella was trying to pull over her shoulders. Her eyes were knowledgeable, her mouth buttoned up into sour disapproval.

"The master said your breakfast was to be brought to you," she said, outraged. "You're to have a fire in the sitting room if you wish. *Do* you—*miss*?"

"Oh, yes, please!" said Luella happily. "I *should* like a fire."

She watched the stiff, retreating back of the maid; when the door had closed behind Lily, Luella's lips curved into a smile of childlike pleasure. She had no idea why Quinn Mallory had ordered her to be so pampered, but it gave her a delicious feeling of luxury.

She was like a stray cat that had sneaked in from a cold, unfriendly world and knows it is going to be allowed to sit by the fire.

She thought soberly of the happenings of last night; they had left an indelible mark on her; she was unchanged, yet not the same prson as the girl that Quinn had dragged into the great hall at Westhaven. She felt pleasure, of a purely sensuous kind, though she could not have named it as that; she felt feminine in a way she had not felt before. It was all very pleasant . . .

Luella poured coffee from the pot and listened to Lily, who had brought up fire irons and fuel and was working at the empty grate in the day nursery, making a lot of noise, as though giving expression to her resentment.

The task Lily performed was a very familiar one to Luella; one *she* had once performed, every day, under Henrietta's critical and merciless eye.

CHAPTER 4

Quinn slept soundly after all; he awoke early, took a long walk alone, and then spent half an hour with his grandmother, who reiterated her sorrow at his unhappy homecoming.

He listened and said little; she was vague about the events leading up to Marianne's death. Betty Graddle would tell him what he wanted to know. Mrs. Farley would sulk when he summoned Betty, considering that, as housekeeper, she alone had the right to be summoned to the master's study.

He did not care a jot about that; Betty had been with the Mallorys ever since she was a girl of sixteen.

Before he sent for Betty he sharpened a new quill and wrote to Sir Julius Margrave, telling him that his mission was successfully completed and the Count Jean-Baptiste Riennes delivered safely into the hands of those who were to care for him in his exile. He was aware that the letter was a mere formality; Sir Julius would know, by this time, that the count was safe.

Quinn added a postscript to the effect that he considered the exile of the count and those like him would be a long one, in view of all he had heard and witnessed while in France.

Finally, he told him, in a single line, that Marianne was dead. He stared at the words he had written, and for the first time he recognized and accepted the reality of her death. Somehow its very finality lessened the agony he had felt for the last twenty-four hours.

* * *

71

Betty sat awkwardly on the edge of the big leather chair, hands folded in her lap.

"Well, sir, it was a dreadful shock to us all. I spoke to her in the hall; she was wearing her bonnet and cloak and said she was going for a walk. I told her the light was going, but she said she'd been indoors all day and needed fresh air. She wouldn't have one of the grooms with her; you know how she liked to walk on her own."

Yes, he knew very well; he stared down at the blotter on his desk.

"How did she seem? Happy, as usual?" he asked.

"Well, no, sir. As if she had something on her mind. It wasn't like her, but it wasn't my place to ask questions."

He had written to Marianne—several times—sending the notes to England by couriers who were engaged on the same work as he was. It was a tricky, dangerous business, he knew; to be found with such a letter meant almost certain betrayal and death. He wondered how many of his brief notes had got through to Marianne; he should not have left her alone so long, so soon after their betrothal, he thought bitterly.

"You had no idea what was wrong with her?" he pressed.

"I *did* ask, sir. She said she had a headache. She'd been on her own, most of the day, in her room. That wasn't like her, either. She loved company, sir, and she was never quiet, if you know what I mean; but she was quiet all that day."

"Did she have any visitors?"

"No—not even Mr. Janson, sir; she sent word to him that she didn't wish to take a lesson that day."

He looked up sharply.

"Who the devil is Mr. Janson?" he demanded.

"The tutor, sir. He rented a cottage from Mr. Simon on Bellminster land. He taught painting and sketching to the rector's little girls, and the doctor's niece, and to Miss Mary and Miss Marianne."

He had known nothing of Marianne's life for the last year; there had been no way in which she could communicate with him.

72

He felt a fierce, angry pain within him.

"I see. So Marianne went for a walk along the cliff path?"

"It would seem so, sir. Sometimes she went to Dunbury and saw Mrs. Cazelet, but not usually so late; and she wouldn't have gone *that* night in any case . . ."

The quill he had been holding between his fingers snapped suddenly as he bent it.

"There seem to have been changes during my year's absence," he said. "Dunbury House was unoccupied when I left England."

"That is so, sir. Last spring a lady came to live at Dunbury. She was a widow, whose husband had been killed in France, so I heard, and the lady didn't welcome visitors. Wore a black veil, like poor Miss Mary does, when she went out—which was a rare occasion, sir. She seemed to have taken a fancy to Miss Marianne, though; I understand Miss Marianne walked over there one day, out of curiosity, she said, and they became good friends."

"Where is Mrs. Cazelet now?"

"She left Dunbury just before Miss Marianne died. I understand from Miss Marianne that the sea didn't agree with her and she was going to relatives in the country. That's why Miss Marianne couldn't have gone to see her that night."

"Tell me exactly what happened after Marianne left the house," Quinn commanded.

"Well, she'd been away an hour, the light was all but gone, and I couldn't see no sign of her. So I told Mrs. Mallory and she sent a couple of the grooms and Sefton with them to look for her. They came back in a terrible state. Sefton had Miss Marianne's cloak over his arm and said he'd found it on the path, near a little hollow that was a favorite place of hers for sitting in and looking at the sea."

Had she looked at the French coast? Thinking of him, wondering when he would return?

"Go on," he said remotely.

"We all went out, then, except Mrs. Mallory and Emmie. We took lanterns, but we couldn't find anything, not in the dark. Next morning we was all back early, looking.

73

We saw her bonnet caught fast in a little bush, halfway down the cliffs, and her kerchief just below it. We found one other thing, sir: the ring you gave Miss Marianne before you left, the one with the blue stones in it. Wedged in some rocks it was, near the top of the cliff, like it had been tore off her finger."

She had not fallen, she had been attacked, he thought, horrified. There were bands of cutthroats, many of them army deserters, who robbed country houses, farmsteads, and travelers; there were outbreaks of fierce fighting among rival bands of smugglers, there were tales of innocent people being killed by the French spies who were landed all along the coast, to pave the way for an invasion.

Marianne had been attacked or robbed and had fallen from the path or been hurled into the sea; Betty saw the agony in his face as he bowed his head briefly.

"There must have been a struggle for the ring to have been torn from her finger," he said. "I understand that my grandmother later—identified her."

"Yes, sir. A few weeks later, after the storm. Worst I can ever remember. Word was sent that the body of a young woman had been washed up near Lyme Regis. Mrs. Mallory insisted on making the journey, though she wasn't fit for it. She took Emmie, and they identified Miss Marianne. Upset Mrs. Mallory dreadful, sir, but she had poor Miss Marianne brought home; after the funeral she took to her bed for a week and wouldn't see no one."

He looked up and stared unseeingly at Betty.

"Thank you," he said.

Luella ate her breakfast, poured water into a bowl, and washed herself. Then she hung the green dress at the back of the cupboard and chose a plain, dark one with long sleeves and a chemise-tucker of white cambric. Her Bible and hairbrush had been placed on the dressing table. She fingered her Bible, sighed, and left it unopened. Then she brushed her hair and tied it up with the red ribbon that she had brought to Westhaven in her basket.

She met Quinn on her way to the sea tower; they came face to face in the long gallery and her heart beat painfully

fast beneath the demure bodice of her dress. She was remembering how he had lain with her the previous evening,
how most of her body had been exposed to his gaze.

Color flared in her cheeks. She stammered "Good morning" and discovered she could not meet his eyes.

It did not matter, after all; his eyes were blue ice, and
they looked through her, toward the portrait on the wall. If
he heard her greeting, he gave no outward sign.

Jessica Mallory was out of bed, seated in a chair by the
window, and in a lively mood. In Luella she had a brand
new audience for the tales she loved to tell of a world more
than seventy years in the past . . .

Luella listened, fascinated; hearing about the wealthy
and handsome Captain James Mallory, who had inherited
Westhaven on the day he married Jessica; of his sudden
death from typhoid when their only son, Quinn's father,
was twelve years old; of the girl Quinn's father had married,
and Amy, Marianne's pretty, willful mother . . .

Jessica talked about Mary.

"She rarely leaves her room. Poor child, she will die of
melancholy unless something is done, but she insists that
she is ugly to look upon and hides herself away. She and
Marianne were never good friends, alas. Only Mr. Janson
found favor in Mary's eyes; he was a charming young man
who came to teach painting and sketching. *I* liked to talk to
him, but he was reserved and would not speak much of
himself. He was greatly attracted to Marianne." The old
eyes danced with faint malice. "He knew she was to marry
my grandson; oh, there was never a word out of place, but
I could tell by the way his eyes followed her. I'm an old
woman, and tired. Quinn must marry; I want to hold my
great-grandchild in my arms before I die."

Luella listened and marveled at the lives of people who
lived in great houses, rode in carriages, went richly gowned
and jeweled to balls, slept in soft beds, and were fed on fine
food, with servants to wait upon their every whim.

Emmie brought the morning pot of chocolate and looked
covertly at Luella. The girl would be useful and save her
aching legs, she decided. She would keep Jessica amused, a
task that Emmie was finding increasingly difficult.

75

The old woman who had looked after Jessica for so many years felt again the weight of the lie that lay on her conscience; but what purpose could be served by telling the truth *now*, she asked herself?

Simon Corbie rode over to see Quinn as soon as he received news that the master of Westhaven was back from his travels; Sefton admitted him, and he was standing in the hall handing his caped coat to the footman when Luella came hurrying down the stairs on an errand for Mrs. Mallory, who wished to see the housekeeper.

She stopped short halfway down the stairs, and the visitor regarded her with curiosity and interest; he saw a golden-haired girl in a dark dress, not pretty with Marianne's warm, full-blown rose beauty, but with an air of distinction. Not a young woman who would put all her goods in the shop window, he thought shrewdly.

She saw a tall, slimly built young man, with restless brown eyes, his thick brown hair curling almost to his shoulders; his smile was slow and impudent, though his eyes remained unsmiling, and his manner was guarded.

"So Quinn has brought back a souvenir of his travels?" he drawled. "He has chosen an uncommonly attractive one!"

Slowly, Luella came to the bottom step, so that her eyes were on a level with his. Simon had never seen such brilliant green eyes; she was a skinny little thing, but her eyes and the way she held her head gave her an intangible charm, he reflected.

"I am companion to Mrs. Mallory," she told him coolly.

Before he could reply, Quinn came into the hall to greet his visitor; he looked briefly at Luella, who swept past him with a rustle of skirts and went on her way in search of Mrs. Farley.

Simon looked at Quinn with raised eyebrows.

"Where did you find *her*?" he asked.

Briefly, Quinn recounted the story; having explained the reason for Luella's presence at Westhaven and observed the deepening interest in Simon's face, he led his visitor to the study, where a cheerful fire burned; he poured wine into two goblets and said shortly, "If you have come to offer condolences on the death of Marianne, then I have no desire to discuss what has happened."

"Naturally, my dear fellow," Simon replied soothingly.

"How are things at Bellminster?" Quinn demanded, after a brief silence.

"I am there as little as possible and can afford only a couple of servants. I detest the role of country squire, as you know."

"In which case, you should sell your estates and retire to Bath or Exeter or some such lively city, where life offers the diversions you seek."

"Perhaps I shall take your advice in due course." Simon looked at him with narrowed eyes. "I am aware of your opinion of me, Quinn; I am a young man who has dissipated a fortune at gaming tables and in whorehouses."

"That is your affair," Quinn retorted.

"I find life tedious here, Quinn. The estate will never pay its way."

"The land needs good men!"

Simon laughed shortly.

"Tell that to the wretches who fire my hayricks and steal my livestock! A curse on this bloody Enclosures Act that robs a man of land on which to graze cattle, grow vegetables, and gather fuel. With his strip of land taken from him, he can no longer support himself and must needs claim parish relief. A fine state of affairs."

"The purpose of the act is to merge small pieces of land into a greater whole on which to grow better crops and raise fine stock," Quinn pointed out. "The drift from the land is an unhappy result of the act. Already, there is talk of machines replacing men, and the cottage industries will dry up like streams in summer because the small master cannot compete with the Great God Machine."

Simon shrugged, draining his glass.

"For all your long absence, you seem well acquainted with these matters, I must say! You have had an exciting time in France, Quinn, and cannot complain of the dullness of life."

"Dull. My dear fellow, you talk rubbish!" Quinn said

curtly. "I have seen the most appalling human misery and cruelty; I have seen greed, wanton destruction, violence, and injustice, such as you cannot comprehend. We live in a country where law, order, and justice are so much part of our lives that we take them for granted. It is not so in France."

Simon walked toward the window and stared at the rolling parklands of Westhaven.

"England crawls with French spies, Quinn; there was such a man employed as tutor here. I rented a small cottage to him, at Uphallow. His name was Philip Janson."

"I have heard of him," Quinn said guardedly.

"He seemed an agreeable enough fellow," Simon continued. "After the soldiers took him away, I examined the cottage. The fellow left no documents by which he could be identified, but there were personal appointments of the kind only a wealthy man would possess. He has broken out of Dorchester jail and is still free, so far as I know. After his escape, he is said to have murdered an old woman in a cottage, whilst helping himself to her food and money. A dangerous fellow. I wonder what has happened to him? Ah, well, you have returned to your family and you seem well content with life. How is your grandmother?"

"In fair health, physically; mentally, her mind wanders at times," Quinn said dryly.

"And Mary? Still immured like a nun in a convent?"

Quinn shrugged.

"At her own wish. I cannot force her to be otherwise."

"You have a charming young companion to console you for the loss of Marianne," Simon murmured softly, and smiled, unabashed, when he saw a flicker of anger in Quinn's eyes. "I will detain you no longer; I am sure you have much to do," he murmured.

Quinn did not try to persuade him to stay; he was aware of a gap between himself and Simon that had not existed in the old days, when Simon and Marianne had been close companions, and Simon had been a constant visitor to Westhaven.

As for Simon, he rode back to Bellminster in a thoughtful mood; he had many weighty problems to occupy his mind. He was in a fever of impatience to wash his hands of Bellminster and begin to live the kind of life he loved best, but the time for him to do that had not yet come. He knew he needed to be patient, but for how much longer? he wondered bitterly. God, he was sick of the inactivity that circumstances had forced upon him!

Within an hour of Simon's departure, another visitor was announced; Sir Julius Margrave was ushered into Quinn's study.

Quinn greeted him with astonishment.

"I have penned a letter to you but a couple of hours since!" he declared.

"Then I have saved you the trouble of dispatching a letter. God, my bones ache! I left London, posthaste, yesterday, and spent the night in an uncomfortable bed in a most miserable inn that should be ashamed to take good money from unsuspecting travelers! I told mine host what I thought of his wretched beds and miserable food! They do not care, these days, so long as they can rob a man!"

Sir Julius was a tall, commanding man in his late fifties; he had piercing gray eyes, broad shoulders, and a massive, leonine head of thick gray hair. All his life he had scorned to wear a wig, declaring that no wig would sit easily upon his springy locks. He dressed with the utmost simplicity; he had as many enemies as he had friends; his mind was like a rapier, he was as wily as a fox, had the courage of a lion, and his tongue could be as deadly as a swordthrust.

"I will order you refreshment," Quinn said, "and hot water and a bed, for no doubt you wish to sleep."

"Sleep? Not yet, Quinn! Refreshment, yes, but I have business that cannot wait."

He waited until Quinn had summoned a servant and ordered breakfast for him before he spoke again. Beneath the beetling gray brows his eyes were kind, and his voice was quiet.

"I have heard of Miss Walton's death; I am saddened for you, my friend," he said simply.

"Ill news travels fast, they say!" Quinn replied curtly.

"*All* news travels fast—to *me*."

"Ah, yes! You have spies, informers, agents, everywhere!"

"Why so bitter, Quinn? We all work toward the same end—our concern is for the good name of our country. The count is safe. You are to be congratulated. Now that we can no longer use the northern ports of France, nor the route through Spain, we are greatly hampered in all future operations, I fear."

"We shall not even be able to take refugees through Italy, soon," Quinn agreed. "It is only a matter of time before Bonaparte takes Italy. The man bears a charmed life, I swear."

"Charmed, but not necessarily a long one," Sir Julius answered dryly. "Sir John Jervis has scattered the Spanish line off Cape St. Vincent—*what* a battle! What wouldn't I have given to have been there! As to the unfortunate matter of the mutiny in the fleet, the men's grievances have been settled and they have since shown their gratitude by acquitting themselves nobly against the Dutch at Camperdown. Nine out of sixteen Dutch ships captured! That miserable little rogue Bonaparte must be greatly disturbed by such news! In his desire to prove himself the savior of France, he crushes all Europe beneath his boots, but I tell you, Quinn, his time is running out!"

Quinn listened to the impassioned voice; his father, he remembered, had thought highly of Sir Julius as a fine soldier, but at this moment he could not share in the rejoicing. Sir Julius suddenly divined the cause.

"You believe that had you not been engaged upon smuggling a very valuable member of the French aristocracy to England, Marianne might be alive? Come—is it *that* thought which torments you?" he asked.

"I undertook the mission voluntarily—as I undertook all such missions," Quinn reminded him.

"You do not answer my question. Perhaps we should let it remain unanswered. Time heals all the pain of the most cruel loss—I quote an easy platitude for which you will have only contempt, but it is the truth!"

The voice was still gentle. Quinn sighed and asked brusquely, "What brings you here?"

"I have a favor to ask of you," the older man said persuasively.

"I will undertake no further missions," Quinn retorted. "It is time I looked to my own affairs. The stench of war is still in my nostrils; the marching French stain all the world with blood from the helpless flesh they have ground into the earth. I have seen the innocent and the beautiful, the helpless and the noble, all of them plundered, tortured, torn to pieces, brutally done to death. I tell you, I have had enough."

"What I have in mind will not take you far from home," Sir Julius told him. "We are searching for a criminal who is known to be in this part of Dorset. His crime is one that cannot go unavenged. Finding him is a matter of the utmost urgency."

Seeing that he had Quinn's entire attention at last, Sir Julius sat back in his chair, crossed his legs, and put his fingertips together, looking into the distance as he spoke.

"The man's name is Jackson Parnall. Have you heard of him?" he asked.

"No," replied Quinn.

"He has many other names and as many disguises. He is one of a number of ruthless and cunning men who offer safe conduct from France to important refugees. Such refugees never reach England; they are murdered and robbed, for most of them are carrying jewelry and personal possessions of considerable value. Parnall has amassed a fortune, and early this year he committed the most outrageous, brutal, and cold-blooded murder of them all, in order to steal the jewels of Marie Antoinette."

"The queen has been dead for more than four years!" Quinn said, astonished.

"I am aware of that. Before her death she entrusted her most valuable jewels to an Englishwoman whose French husband was at the court of Louis XVI. These jewels are unique and were given to the queen by an admirer whose name has never been revealed. I have not seen the jewels, though they have been described to me and I have had the details of them copied for you to see."

He opened the heavy leather satchel that had been fastened to his wrist since leaving his London home and took out a painting, which he handed to Quinn.

The artist had reproduced the jewels in fine detail, using a black background, the better to show them off in their splendor: a necklace, a ring, earrings, bracelets, brooch, and hair ornaments, worked in fine diamonds in the form of flowers, with rubies at the center of the petals and emeralds made into leaves on either side of each flower.

Quinn drew a long breath; they were exquisite. Sir Julius saw his look and said, "They are called the Flowers of Darkness. I am told there is a curse on the jewelry. The lady-in-waiting, Eleanor La Vanne, promised the queen that she would bring them to England; it was the queen's dearest wish that they should remain safely in this country until the time came for them to be returned to France, one day, when the Monarchy was restored. If, for any reason, the jewels could never be returned, then they were to be sold and the money used to assist those of her countrymen—and women—who had escaped the guillotine. A noble wish: one which Eleanor La Vanne had sworn to carry out.

"The queen went to her death—nobly and with dignity, as we know; but Eleanor could not leave France immediately. Her husband was in hiding. He was dying, and she nursed him at the home of two of her most faithful servants; after his death, she was compelled to remain in hiding still. Two attempts to smuggle her out of France failed—each time with the death of the courier who was to have brought her to safety."

"So the jewels are aptly named?" said Quinn dryly.

"It seems so. Eventually, Eleanor's servants were forced to flee from their homes, and—after a great many misfortunes—she met Jackson Parnall, who offered her safe conduct through France to England. Whether he knew, then, the nature of the treasure she carried, or whether he discovered, later, the richness of his haul, we do not know. Near their journey's end, he betrayed her—stole the jewels and left her to die horribly, stamped beneath the feet of a drunken mob in the barn where she had been hiding. He *must* be found and brought to justice; his deeds shame us and stain the honor of our country.

"How do you know that all this is true?" Quinn asked.

"My dear fellow, do you need to ask such a question?" Sir Julius said irritably. "My contacts are many; men and women from many countries and from all walks of life; the names of some of them would astonish you. Couriers returning from France have brought me bits and pieces of information which I have pieced together during the past months into this tale of greed and betrayal. Well, Quinn?"

"You are asking me to find a needle in a haystack!"

"I tell you, Quinn, he is in this part of Dorset; he landed secretly and alone, by night. The man who testified to that fact died honorably in France, weeks ago, gathering information about the movements of Napoleon's troops."

"Parnall could be *anywhere* by now," Quinn argued. "Out of the country, perhaps."

"No," the older man insisted. "He has been seen in Axminster; in Dorchester. Disguised as a vagabond; a soldier; a young man of means lately come into an inheritance."

"Why has he remained so long in Dorset?"

"*Ah!* Why indeed. That is an unsolved mystery. Some weeks ago we almost had him," Sir Julius said ruefully. "An unsigned note was handed to the man on duty at the gates of Dorchester jail, stating that a criminal named Jackson Parnall, wanted for theft and murder, would board the London coach at Axminster the following morning. The governor dispatched a party of men to intercept the coach, but Parnell was not on it."

"Who tried to betray him?"

"The note was handed in by a lady dressed in black, I understand. She did not speak, and her face was heavily veiled."

Quinn looked at him sharply; now his interest was well and truly aroused.

"It seems that Parnall was warned in time. How do you know he is *still* in Dorset?" Quinn asked.

Sir Julius replied smoothly, "A few months ago, a local man was picked up for poaching; he was sentenced to transportation, but he passed information that earned him his freedom. You know our methods, Quinn—they are unorthodox, at times, and the rewards we offer are not always monetary ones."

"Well?" said Quinn impatiently.

Sir Julius drew a deep breath, pleasantly savoring the news he was about to tell.

"This man said that he was one of several who had been paid to keep a constant watch on this house; his description of the man who paid him accurately matches our description of Parnall."

Quinn stared at him in outraged disbelief.

"Paid? To watch *Westhaven*? For what purpose?" he demanded incredulously.

Sir Julius shrugged, his eyes lit with sly amusement.

"One must conclude, my dear Quinn, that news of your exploits in France have reached his ears and he wishes to know when—or *if*—you are returning here. I have no better explanation to offer, but I *do* have a rough sketch of Parnall. The man comes of a fine old family; his parents are dead; thank God they have not lived long enough to be shamed by their only son, a dissolute and utterly dishonorable man."

Quinn looked at the sketch that Sir Julius took from his case; it was a head and shoulders drawing of an elegant young man with a narrow face, a thin, cruel mouth, and deep-set eyes; the artist had captured perfectly his look of fastidious disdain for the world around him.

"Well, Quinn? Do you accept the challenge?" Sir Julius murmured.

Quinn nodded briefly.

"Thank you," Sir Julius said quietly. "Is there any assistance I can give you in your task?"

"I shall require a letter of introduction to the governor of Dorchester jail," Quinn replied. "I need your authority before he will give me information concerning his prisoners. You will stay the night? Good."

"You shall have your letter; and now," Sir Julius said, with a sigh, "your softest bed, Quinn . . ."

* * *

Mrs. Farley informed Betty that there would be four people to dinner that evening.

"Four? There's the master and his visitor. Who else?"

"There's Miss Mary, for one."

"Never! She don't leave 'er room for no one!"

"The master has ordered her to grace the head of the dinner table. He *is* head of the household, after all," said Mrs. Farley primly.

"Who's the fourth to be, then?" Betty wanted to know.

Mrs. Farley smiled, anticipating the sensation her words would cause.

"The fourth one is the little urchin to whom you gave a good scrubbing when the master brought her here!" she said.

"Ah, now, you're 'avin' me on!" Betty protested.

"I assure you it is true. The master himself told me. He introduced that same little urchin to his visitor, as 'my grandmother's young companion.' *Some* people have come up in the world quickly, and no mistake!"

Mrs. Farley looked down her long nose and swept out of the kitchen with a great rustling of skirts, leaving Betty and her attendant kitchenmaids open-mouthed.

"You know how much I dislike meeting people!" Mary said stormily to her brother.

"Sir Julius is an old friend; besides, you shut yourself away as though you are misshapen and hideous. There is no need to do so; such solitude is not good for a young woman of your age."

His voice was gentle; he was fond of his sister, even though he did not understand the complexities of her nature. She shrugged and bit her lip, knowing it was her place to act as hostess until such time as Quinn had a wife. Well, at least he was not going to make Marianne his wife now, Mary thought bitterly; her hatred of the girl Quinn had loved went beyond the grave . . .

"I have asked Luella to join us, so you will not lack feminine company," Quinn added.

She whirled on him, furious.

"Are you mad? Asking a servant to share your table!"

His voice was several degrees cooler.

"She is not a servant, Mary; she is helping Emmie to look after our grandmother, and discharges her duties quite satisfactorily, I am told."

"I heard of the circumstances under which she arrived here!" Mary said scornfully. "A little guttersnipe, no more!"

He looked so angry that she thought he was going to strike her; instead, he held her arm in a grip that made her wince.

"Keep your comments to yourself!" he told her savagely.

She wrenched her arm free.

"Is she your mistress that you show her such favor?" she demanded.

She saw the white ring of anger around his mouth, the ice and fire in his eyes. With a tremendous effort at self-control, he turned on his heel and left the room.

Mary rubbed her arm where his fingers had held the flesh in such an iron grip. He could make her put in an appearance at the dinner table if he chose, she thought resentfully, but she was damned if she would acknowledge the presence of Luella March.

Quinn sent for Luella. She stood in front of the desk in his study, hands folded demurely in front of her. Her expression was anything but demure; she was remembering that only last night Quinn had flung her on the bed and torn the clothes from her. It was a memory that should have horrified and distressed her; she discovered that when she recalled the occasion it was with slow-burning pleasure tempered with curiosity.

He handed her a golden guinea, watching her closely.

"Your first month's wages," he told her.

Her glance was suspicious.

"A guinea for each month? That is twelve guineas for a year. As a servant, I should be fortunate to receive half that sum," she told him sharply.

He hid a smile, applauding her shrewdness.

"You are not a servant; as companion to my grandmother, your status here is entirely different," he told her, and added blandly, "You will not be called upon to provide any other services, I assure you."

"I don't know what you mean," she told him, frowning.

"In some households for such a handsome salary you might be expected to provide services for the master," he murmured.

"You mean, such as those you wished me to give last night when you came to my room?" she asked.

A clear, bright spring of amusement welled up in him; for a little while, he forgot Marianne, the horrors of France, the mission that Sir Julius had detailed. He smiled, and it made him look startlingly young and attractive.

"You didn't give a service!" he pointed out. "Instead, you bit my chin. Why?"

"I was afraid," she said, bright pink color in her cheeks.

"Of what?"

"Of—you," she admitted, confused. "I hope that you did not make me pregnant. If I have a child, how shall I go to London and earn my living?"

"*Make you pregnant*?" He stared at her, dumbfounded. "I realize you are a virgin, but how can you be so ignorant of the coupling that must occur between a man and a woman before a child is conceived?"

"I have heard—tales," she admitted uncertainly. "I have been told that once a man touches a woman in her most secret places then she will undoubtedly have a child. I have heard other, stranger, tales of how a man will tear a woman apart in terrible fury if he wishes her to have a child."

"I see. Who told you all this?"

Green eyes met ice-blue ones; there was not a glimmer of humor in Quinn's face as he studied the girl in front of him.

"We spoke of it at school, among ourselves," she said.

"Was there no woman to—advise you?" he demanded angrily.

"We were not supposed to ask questions. We were told that if a woman is chaste she will come to no harm, and that we had no need to concern ourselves further with such matters."

He thought of Marianne, worldly-wise, setting his blood on fire with the soft promises for the future that she had whispered on their betrothal night.

"Sit down," he said curtly.

Luella sat obediently on the edge of a chair, watching him suspiciously; he went across to the window and stood with his back toward her, hands clasped behind him, feet apart. Carefully, painstakingly, without mincing matters, he explained the basic facts of conception and childbirth to her.

She listened with grave attention; when he turned from the window, she was still sitting composedly with her hands folded in her lap.

"It seems a very complicated business," she told him candidly.

"I have no doubt that you will find it an agreeable one with a young man for whom you have an affection," he retorted.

What did she know of affection, he wondered? There had been no one in her life on whom to spend whatever emotion she possessed—no parent, brother, sister, or friend. She had known only how to hate Henrietta.

He said abruptly, "You cannot spend all your time indoors. You are free to wander in the grounds when my grandmother gives you leave. You will dine this evening with Sir Julius, Mary, and myself."

"I cannot possibly!" she cried, thrown into feminine panic.

He looked as haughty, as forbidding as ever.

"Why not?"

"I have never dined in such state as you keep here! I do not know what I must wear, what I must do and say!" she told him, shaking her head.

"I am disappointed in you, Luella," he said coldly. "I thought you had more spirit, yet you resist the first challenge that comes your way. Mary will tell you what you should wear; as to the rest, you will be required to behave with dignity and make very little contribution to the conversation."

Up went her head; out went her stubborn chin. His

words were a douche of cold water. She stood up, smoothed down her skirts, and said coolly, "I shall endeavor to remember all you have said!"

"All?" he said softly; one eyebrow quirked upward, a muscle quivered in his cheek, but he would not unbend sufficiently to smile. "Yes, remember it *all*, Luella; one day the things I have told you may stand you in good stead!"

She did not answer him; she walked toward the door, and he called after her.

"I have not given you permission to leave!"

"I know," she replied calmly, and opened the door, closing it behind her with quiet deliberation as she went on her way.

Quinn stared unseeingly at the chair in which she had been sitting; Luella had a strange effect upon him. He had known Marianne since she was a tiny child; he understood her, for she was wholly feminine and he prided himself on his knowledge of her heart and mind.

Luella, not yet a woman, defeated him. She was a mixture of maturity and innocence, pertness and meekness, he reflected; a child who had never played as other children play, who had known little of the warmth and all of the coldness of life.

For the second time that day, he snapped a quill between his fingers.

CHAPTER 5

Luella went to Mary's room and knocked on the door.

Mary's voice was sharp as she bade her enter; she stood with her back to the door, looking out of the window at the tumbling seas. She was without her veil, and thought it was only her maid, Janet, who had entered. Janet was old and nearly blind.

She turned and saw that it was Luella.

Luella looked at her with surprise and curiosity. Mary's eyes were not such a bright blue as her brother's, but there was the same hint of sensuousness about the full mouth. Her features were clear-cut, her look was one of authority; on the smooth flesh of cheeks and forehead and chin were the marks left by smallpox: small deep pits that nothing could erase.

"I told you never to come here again," Mary said sullenly.

"I know that. I am sorry that when I came before I asked if you wore a veil because you were ugly. You are not ugly at all."

Mary grabbed Luella's wrist, pulled her forward, and jabbed at her own cheek with her forefinger.

"Not *ugly*? Are you mad, or are you trying to win my favor by pretending that you do not see these marks? The mirror never lies—*you* hope to ingratiate yourself . . ."

"No!" retorted Luella. "I spoke the truth! If you were truly ugly then I would have said so! It is your tongue and your temper that are ugly, not your face!"

With an angry jerk, she pulled free. Surprise held Mary silent for a moment. *You are not ugly;* so Philip Janson had said. The memory had the agony of a swordthrust. She loved him with all the fierce intensity of which she was capable, and he was a French spy, who had escaped from Dorchester jail, murdering an old woman for her food and money.

Mary did not care what he had done; I would have helped him, she thought dully; I would have gone with him, wherever he has gone. Even to France.

"What do you want?" she demanded of Luella.

"I do not know what I should wear for dinner this evening. Your brother said you would tell me."

"Did he, indeed?" The full upper lip curled scornfully. "He has taken a fancy to you, I suppose; did you snare him with those witch's eyes of yours?"

"No," said Luella gravely, "but I once wished death on a woman who had treated me badly, and she died four days later."

It was said in a childish spirit of bravado; Mary stared at her, astonished at first, and then with contemptuous amusement.

"You are ridiculous," she said. "When you came here, you were a sorry little creature, I'm told—and now you think yourself good enough to sit at the table with us."

"It was your brother who thought so," Luella retorted.

"Oh, please yourself what you wear!" Mary said tartly. "Dress yourself up like a whore! Make sheep's eyes at Sir Julius; he will enjoy that. He is an old fool!"

Luella went out in an angry whirl of skirts, and Mary thought: Quinn will have his hands full with *that* little spitfire—serve him right.

She went back to her contemplation of the sea. Was Philip already across the Channel, out of her life forever? she wondered sadly.

She knew she would never see him again; the tears ran down her cheeks, and she beat her fists helplessly against the glass.

Luella went to Jessica Mallory, who sighed and said,

"I have no idea what young ladies wear nowadays; fashions change so fast, and have become so absurd. You will be sure to find a pretty gown in one of the cupboards! You are a good child, and I want to show you something. Help me out of this wretched bed—there is little enough wrong with me. The old grow lazy and bored, Luella."

Luella helped her employer from her bed and dressed her in the quantity of wrappers that she insisted on wearing when she was up and about; then Jessica Mallory firmly grasped the top of her silver-knobbed walking stick, and with Luella holding her other arm, they went to the sitting room of the sea tower.

There was no one about; the maids had cleaned the rooms, and Emmie had gone to the village on an errand for her mistress.

Following Jessica's instructions, Luella guided her across the room to a wall where there was a delicate little writing table inlaid with mother-of-pearl and ivory, and a gilt chair with a velvet seat; between the desk and the chair—which was placed against the wall—there was a distance of some three feet, and the damask that hung on the wall exactly matched the hangings of the rest of the room.

Jessica lifted the damask aside, with Luella's help, and there, to her surprise, Luella saw a small door.

Jessica suddenly let the hanging fall back into place; she sat heavily on the chair, annoyed with herself that she was out of breath and trembling.

"I have not half the strength I used to have," she muttered irritably. "You will find the key to that door inside my writing desk. Open the desk."

Luella obeyed; inside was a small key, which she took out and handed to Jessica, but the old woman shook her head.

"You will have to go by yourself, child; I can no longer climb the stairs to my treasure room. Oh, there is no secret, nowadays, about the existence of this door, and the fact that there is a staircase outside that descends to the outside of the house and goes on up to the very top of this tower; but once it was one of Westhaven's best-guarded secrets."

"Why?" Luella asked, fascinated.

"My husband told me the story; long before his parents were born, there was religious persecution in this country, and the celebration of Mass was forbidden to good Catholics. Priests were forced into hiding, and many of them risked torture and death to celebrate Mass secretly with the faithful; so great houses such as this often had hiding places for the priests and secret rooms for their ceremonies. The room above this was just such a chapel and a refuge. Now I keep all my treasures there. Marianne loved to be allowed to take the key from me and go there to look at them when she was a child."

Luella saw tears in the old woman's eyes; gently she put a hand on the thin shoulder. Jessica shook away the tears impatiently, as though she detested such signs of age and weakness in herself.

"You must go alone," she insisted. "Time was when I *ran* up those stairs. Ah, I wasn't so much older then than you are now, and there were not enough hours in the day for all that I wanted to do; now time is a heavy stone that I must carry everywhere with me. You are good, Luella— and kind; so you make the stone seem less heavy. Sometimes I tell myself that it is all a bad dream, and that Marianne will come back to me. I know it is not so; I saw her as she was when they took her out of the sea, and it was not a pretty sight. Marianne is not here to make me laugh with her nonsense and her coquettish ways, but *you* have come to me instead!"

The thin hand with its weight of rings and blue veins like a map of time itself lay over the hand that Luella had placed on her employer's shoulder. Jessica patted Luella's hand and then nodded toward the key she held, as though silently telling her to go.

Luella was deeply moved by the unexpected gesture of trust and affection. Like a frozen stream coming to life, all her emotions were awakening slowly; she felt the beginnings of deep affection for this old woman.

Jessica waved her stick, and her laughter rustled as dry as dead leaves scudding along the gutters.

"Go, then, child, and do not linger too long, else the ghosts of yesterday may come and spirit you away. The tower room *is* full of ghosts; I have sensed them often. You may choose one of my treasures as a present for yourself."

With a small shiver of anticipation—and with no idea at

all what she was going to find—Luella pulled back the damask, fitted the key in the lock, and opened the door easily
enough.

She stood on a small stone landing, from which a flight
of stairs spiraled downwards, just as a similar flight spiraled
upwards. The stairs were cut into the solid stone of the
thick walls, and there was a heavy rope handrail fastened
to the wall to guide and steady those who used the stairs.

From the steps that went downward—presumably to an
exit from the tower—came a cold draught of wind. It was
dim on the stone landing where Luella stood, as the only
light came from a small, barred window set high in the
wall.

Slowly, Luella went up the stairs, firmly clutching the
handrail, her heart beating fast; the place was full of an
unnatural silence that she did not like.

At the top of the curling flight there was another door;
Luella tried the handle, and it opened inward, with a pro-
testing squeak. The wood was heavy and had great iron
hinges and a latch; it would be a very safe hiding place, she
thought.

Luella found herself inside a small room with bare stone
walls. The light came through a window similar to the one
on the landing, set high in the wall.

She was right at the top of the house, Luella realized,
directly beneath the stone battlements; she could hear the
wind whining softly, like a prowling animal looking for
shelter.

Under the window was a stone altar containing two plain
wooden candlesticks with stumps of yellow wax in them;
between altar and window, a Crucifixion scene had been
painted on the wall in colors that had faded from their
original bright splendor to a muted softness.

Ranged around the walls were a few chairs, some of
them broken, and several dusty hassocks, split at the seams.

In this chapel, high above the rolling seas and windy
cliffs, prayers had been said to which only the wind and
waves had listened. It did not seem to be a place of peace,
as most such places are; Luella thought that some restless
and troubled spirit still lingered there, like the bittersweet

smell of incense, clinging long after the smoke has curled heavenward.

She moved quietly and breathed softly, because it was, after all, still a chapel in her eyes; she looked with curiosity at the shelves along the wall, and the big oak coffers where Jessica's treasures had been set out with such meticulous care.

Luella fingered exquisitely shaped shells, carved by the hand of the sea into delicate whorls; fossils with strange imprints and beautiful fernlike designs upon them, reminders of another, much older world than the one in which she lived. Such fossils were found in great numbers along the Dorset beaches, although she did not know that.

There were also curiously shaped pieces of wood, bleached and smoothed by the same hand of the sea; several birds' feathers, some birds' eggs, a child's rattle of silver and coral, a glittering shoe buckle, scraps of silk, and a broken necklace of amber beads.

Carefully, Luella lifted the lid of a coffer that had nothing on top of it; inside was a quantity of old-fashioned child's clothing, the silk and lace brittle and yellow with age. She closed the lid quickly, feeling like a trespasser; after some deliberation, she walked around the chapel and chose a large, smooth stone shaped like a crouching lion.

She was not sorry to close the door behind her and go downstairs to where Jessica sat waiting expectantly.

Jessica held out a hand as Luella locked the door of the sitting room behind her.

"Let me see what you have chosen," she commanded.

Luella handed over the stone for inspection, and Jessica nodded, a gleam of amusement in her eyes.

"I remember the day I found that; it was when Quinn went away on one of his secret missions, more than three years ago. I was walking on the beach with Marianne when we picked it up; she laughed and said it looked just like Quinn: a lion crouched ready to spring. I used to love sitting up in the old chapel, turning over my treasures, remembering when I had gathered each shell, each stone, each piece of wood. When the wind blew hard, up there, it roared like the sea, and I was a bird soaring high over the world. Time is almost done for me, and I am tired. Help me to my bed."

Back in bed, she lay against the pillows, looking frail and spent.

"Sometimes," she said sadly, "I know I hear someone up there, in my room. It is not just an old woman's foolish fancy, I *know* . . ."

The wrinkled lids drooped heavily, curtaining the faded eyes; Jessica was almost asleep when Luella left the room.

Emmie was in the sitting room; she had brought a pile of sewing and was opening an inlaid workbox, velvet-lined, full of small spools of silk and with a silver thimble and tiny scissors.

Her eyes were bright and inquisitive.

"Mrs. Mallory is asleep," Luella said. "She showed me the room up above this one."

"Oh?" The bright eyes narrowed. "Do you mean to tell me she climbed those stairs?"

"No; she gave me the key and told me to see it for myself."

Emmie threaded a needle with great deliberation.

"She gives you too many privileges," she commented shortly.

After much deliberation, Luella chose a dress from the nursery wardrobe of spotted yellow muslin, with a low neck and puffed sleeves; there were knots of pale green ribbon on the shoulders and threaded through the hem. There were gloves to match the dress, so Luella concluded that all rich young ladies wore gloves in the evening.

There were yellow silk slippers with green rosettes to match the gown; both fitted Luella as once they had fitted Marianne when she was a year younger than the girl who now wore them.

Luella made her preparations carefully; she stripped and washed, looking with dissatisfaction at her slim white body: Her breasts were not rounded enough for her liking, and her hips were too bony.

She found silk underwear, and the feel of it was as delightful against her skin as the stockings were on her long legs. She needed someone to help her, and there was no one to whom she could turn for such help. Despairingly, realizing she could never manage to produce the fashionable ringlets and curls, she brushed her hair back from her face and fastened it with a wide green bandeau around her forehead. Had she but realized it, the effect was startling and original; the green of the ribbons and trimmings exactly match her huge, excited eyes.

Dressed, she felt incomplete; she had no jewelry to wear, now that Quinn had taken possession of her locket. She went to Marianne's jewel box and selected a small string of seed pearls; doubtfully, she clasped them around her neck. In the box, also, were the bracelets that Marianne had been wearing in the portrait, but they did not match Luella's outfit. Finally, she chose a plain gold bracelet set with seed pearls to match the necklace she wore.

Looking at herself in the mirror, seeing her pink cheeks and glowing eyes, Luella shivered with delight. Oh, if only the girls at the charity school could see her now! If only Henrietta had lived to see her so arrayed! What if she *was* wearing borrowed clothes and was looked upon as a servant? She did not care, at that moment; she knew in her heart that she was a very different person from the cold, hungry little runaway who had been scrubbed in a tin bath by Betty Graddle.

Having dressed, and still having considerable time to spare before she was expected to make her entrance downstairs, Luella took down a slim book entitled *Social Graces That Should Be Learned and Practised by Aspiring Young Ladies*, which lay on Marianne's book shelf; she read parts of it with care, and when she replaced it, tried to remember all that the writer of the book had said concerning Behaviour . . .

Luella walked down to the long gallery and entered the sea tower, anxious to show her finery to Jessica; but Emmie, still sewing in the sitting room, told her sharply that Jessica was asleep and not to be disturbed.

Emmie's eyes roved over the outfit; she sniffed disdainfully. Quinn was going to give this chit ideas, and no mistake; how stupid men were! Grudgingly, she admitted that

Luella looked outstandingly attractive. More to the point if she plied her needle, though, Emmie thought resentfully. She would speak to Mrs. Mallory about Luella making herself useful by doing some of the sewing; all that fine work made her eyes and her head ache, now that she could not see so well as she once could.

"Do I look—suitable?" Luella asked, needing approval from someone.

"Suitable for what, may I ask?" Emmie demanded, with another sniff.

"To sit at the dinner table with Mr. Mallory and his sister, and Sir Julius."

"Oh, you'll do well enough. Don't go getting ideas in that head of yours, though; you are not Miss Marianne, nor ever will be."

"I do not wish to be Marianne." Luella's head went up proudly. "I am myself. I never want to be anyone else."

"You wear fine plumage, and it becomes you," Emmie admitted. "Would we not *all* strut like peacocks if we were arrayed like them? You are as frivolous as Miss Marianne; her head was full of nonsense, she was greedy for clothes and pretty things and attention from young men, even when she rejected such attentions and loudly declared herself to be true to Mr. Mallory."

Luella looked at the older woman in astonishment.

"Did you not like her, then?" she asked.

The eyes were suddenly veiled; Emmie had a place at Westhaven that she did not wish to lose, and she wondered, vexed, what had made her speak out so foolishly.

"I have not said that I disliked her," she retorted, rubbing her aching eyes. "She was young and beautiful, and everyone spoiled and petted her. That was her right; it is not *yours*. Go and enjoy yourself while you may; time for pleasure is all too short. *I* had little enough."

"I am sorry," Luella said gently.

"Oh, be off with you," Emmie muttered, embarrassed.

At the door, Luella turned, struck by a sudden thought.

"Which rooms were Marianne's?" she asked curiously. "I have looked in many rooms, but not seen those that belonged to her—at least I do not *think* I have seen them."

"I doubt you have seen all the rooms in a house so vast as this one," Emmie commented dryly. "Miss Marianne had her rooms in the wing way behind this sea tower; you will find them in the corridor leading from the far end of the long gallery. Go and see for yourself, if you are so curious; they are not locked."

She gave Luella precise instructions, with a gleam of amusement in her eye.

Marianne had lived in a splendor that put the rest of the house to shame, richly though the other apartments were furnished; Luella discovered that fact when she opened the door into the sitting room, bedroom, and dressing-room whose windows overlooked the wild moors and the road leading away to Dorchester and London.

The walls were hung with satin, the gilded chairs upholstered in velvet, the small gilded tables and stools decorated with mother-of-pearl that had the soft shimmer of moonlight. The ceiling cornices were painted and gilded; the curtains looped back with tassels of gold; everywhere there were miniatures of silver and gold, coral and carved jade, displayed in walnut cabinets. There were small tables of papier-mâché with whole scenes of Chinese life elaborately inlaid in rich colors; beneath her feet the carpet was thick and soft, and all around her was the sensuous feeling of utter luxury.

The bedroom was even more splendidly decorated and appointed, with a bed that matched Jessica's for sumptuousness, and a mirrored dressing table, draped from head to toe in soft pink silk.

Fascinated, Luella examined the contents of the dressing table. There were flasks and bottles of red and white Nailsea glass and rich blue Bristol glass, many of them containing eau-de-cologne, rose water, and orange-flower water. There were small silver and enamel boxes full of patches and powders and hair ornaments; silver-backed hairbrushes, crystal pots of creams, figurines of ivory and alabaster.

Half-fearfully, Luella unstoppered one of the flasks and rubbed some of the liquid upon her wrist; it was honey-water, sweetly scented. She lifted her wrist to her nose, feeling a purely sensuous pleasure and marveling at the luxury that had surrounded Marianne.

All at once she had a frightening conviction that she was not alone in the room.

Sharply, she looked around her; she could have sworn that one of the thick velvet curtains moved slightly, as though someone was concealed behind it.

It was not Luella's way to run from fear. She braced herself to meet whatever waited for her, but as she moved, her arm caught one of the glass flasks, and it toppled over and shattered into fragments on the top of the dressing table.

Horrified, she stared at the wreckage and smelled the sweet scent of spilled liquid; she had no idea of the value of the flask, but she imagined it to be considerable. She turned and ran from the room, through the sitting room, and out into the corridor beyond, her heart beating apprehensively. The breaking of the flask had seemed like a warning that she should not be in the rooms of the girl who was dead, and who had once filled them with her glowing personality. If someone lurked behind the curtains, it was probably no more than an inquisitive servant, Luella reflected, dismayed.

Unhappily, she went downstairs; Quinn, standing in the hall, saw her pause under the great stained-glass window, and caught his breath at the sight of her. He thought she looked like sunlight, a golden girl against the somber background.

He was alone in the hall; he watched her slow progress, waiting for her to join him, and when she reached the bottom step, he saw the pallor of her face, the misery in her eyes.

"What is it?" he asked sharply.

Falteringly, he told him what had happened; he drew his breath sharply.

"A broken flask? The cause of so much distress? Come, you have no need to fear punishment. The flask is of no great value, in any case."

"I should not have been there." She did not add that

101

Emmie had told her how to find the rooms, for she had no desire to bring down any wrath on the old woman's head.

"You should not have been in her rooms, certainly," he agreed levelly. "Why did you go there?"

"I—I was curious," she admitted honestly. Her eyes glowed suddenly. "They were so beautiful, so splendid. In all my life I have never *seen* such splendor. Then suddenly, I was frightened; I thought I heard someone."

"Your imagination plays you tricks. Don't trouble yourself any further with what has happened. The rooms shall be locked until I decide what is to be done with them. It will be better that way."

He spoke half to himself. Wanting to lead his mind away from sad reflections, Luella said, "Do my clothes please you?"

"They become you very well," he told her gravely.

She gave a great sigh of relief.

"Then I do not look like a whore?"

He stared at her in utter astonishment.

"In heaven's name, Luella March! I doubt you know what a whore is! Do you, now?"

She shook her head.

"Who suggested that you might look like a whore?" he demanded.

"Your sister said I could dress myself like one if I pleased; from the way she spoke, I believed it to be something—bad."

His lips quivered; he looked young, easy, and relaxed. Luella stared at him, marveling at his changing moods.

"You must not place too much reliance upon Mary's remarks," he said. "She has suffered a great deal as a result of her illness and is unhappy, lonely, and troubled in mind. A whore, my dear Luella, is a woman who pleases men with her body, for whatever reward she can get; do you understand?"

She nodded.

"There was a girl at school who told us about women who do strange things to please men," she said unthinkingly. "She said that gentlemen expect women to parade before them quite unclothed except for such things as a crown of feathers and a pair of gloves, and then demand that they take part in acrobatic feats."

Quinn's eyes danced; he threw back his head and roared with laughter.

"By heaven, Luella, you never cease to surprise me! That is a naughty tale indeed to come from such pretty lips, and not one to be repeated at the dinner table! *I* never required such services of *my* mistresses!"

"Did you have many?" She asked innocently.

"Not by the standards of most men of my age and situation," he replied dryly. "Those I took had need only to warm my bed when nights were cold, and cheat the dark thoughts that come to torment a man in the small hours of the morning. Now, Luella, what of these acrobatic feats of which you spoke? Tell me of them!"

She realized that he was teasing her, and her lips remained obstinately pressed together; her reflections on the old story she had heard was given new significance by the facts that Quinn had explained to her in his study, and they made her aware of him in a way she had never before been aware of any man.

Quinn looked at her and reflected that it was cruel to ruffle the plumage of such a fledgling; her untouchedness had the sweet taste of early morning. One day, a man would come to take that morning freshness from her— some farmer, rough and bawdy, or a pale young man with dark appetites, perhaps.

He was surprised to discover that he found the idea distasteful.

The dining room looked splendid, candles curtseying and fluttering in all the chandeliers, the great table set with fine linen and crystal and silver. Mary had seen to the table decorations: clusters of small china figurines following an outdoors theme of river gods, nymphs, shepherdesses, and little china trees, with leaves of glass, all of it delicately colored. Luella remarked delightedly how pretty it looked, but Mary scarcely acknowledged the compliment Sir Julius paid her on the artistry of her arrangements. She was wearing her veil and had to lift it with one hand in order to put food into her mouth, much to Quinn's annoyance. He wished she was not so morbidly sensitive, but anything he said on the subject seemed to drive her further into herself, and it was his opinion that she had something on her mind other than her smallpox scars.

Luella thoroughly enjoyed herself, with two footmen to wait upon her and hand her a great deal of rich, strange food such as she had never eaten in her life: fish, lobster, roast beef with a great many condiments, apricot tart and jelly and syllabub, all accompanied with wine served in glasses that sparkled like diamonds.

At first Mary did not address a single remark to her, in spite of Quinn's frown of annoyance, and she spoke little to Sir Julius; the two men discussed the affairs of the day, of the mixed blessings of the Enclosures Act, the factories that were sucking in people like hungry monsters—people robbed of things that were their birthright.

Luella listened attentively, sharpening the edges of her mind on all she heard, and Quinn was aware of her rapt curiosity. The female sex was not expected to take an interest in such things, and he found it a novelty to discover an inquiring mind in a young woman.

"No good will come of all this change," Sir Julius prophesied.

"They call it progress," Quinn told him ironically.

"I would sooner call it a monument to human greed; besides, change makes men restless and dissatisfied, it claws their very roots from the ground. It is the same when they are allowed too much learning; it is no kindness to them, for it makes the laboring classes discontented; of what use to *them* is the fact of being able to read and write?"

Quinn, watching attentively, saw the look on Luella's face; Sir Julius turned to her and said apologetically, "A dull conversation for your ears, m'dear!"

"No," she said eagerly, "I am enjoying it greatly. I think that people should be allowed to learn to read and write. It is a sad thing not to be able to read books or write down one's thoughts."

"Bless you, ma'am, what thoughts do *they* have that are

worth writing down?" Sir Julius demanded with genuine astonishment.

"How shall we know the answer to that if they are not able to write their thoughts?" she challenged.

He looked at her with interest, deciding that Quinn had taken himself an excellent mistress to share his bed and ease the misery of Marianne's death.

Mary's voice was clear and cold.

"Luella was educated at one of the charity schools of which we hear so much these days!" she said scornfully.

She turned to Luella, her smile thin and cold behind her veil as she addressed her for the first time.

"What were *you* taught, Luella?" she asked smoothly. "We are all most anxious to hear."

Quinn gave her an angry glance, but Luella, whose wits and tongue had been sharpened by a fair quantity of unaccustomed wine, rose splendidly to the occasion.

"We were taught meekness, piety, humility, obedience, and thrift," she announced.

"Which of those precepts do you consider you should follow?" Mary demanded.

"I do not think much of meekness, for there is little pleasure in subjecting oneself to the ill temper of others," Luella observed. "As for humility, we were taught that we must be humble to our betters and those in authority over us, but I do not think I care to be humble, either. Thrift I have practiced because I have been unable to do anything else; I have had enough of both obedience and piety, for I never could please Henrietta, no matter what I did, and she quoted the Scriptures every time she took her cane to thrash me."

"Who is Henrietta?" Sir Julius demanded.

"She was my mistress. She grudged me even the time I spent in sleep and that was little enough. She was so cruel that I wished her dead. My wish came true, so perhaps I am a witch. Witches *do* have green eyes, I have heard—and mine are green."

The eyes of the footmen were almost bulging from their sockets; it was the finest tidbit they had picked up in many a long day to retail to the rest of the servants.

Something that might have been a smothered laugh escaped Quinn; Mary sat like a ramrod, angrily aware that, far from making Luella look foolish, she had made Luella the center of attention.

Quinn, who was watching Luella indulgently, commented, "It is obvious that you have not been taught the lesson of sobriety. You are a little drunk, Luella. I think it is time you went to bed. Sir Julius and I have much to discuss that can only bore both you and Mary, so you are excused for the remainder of the evening."

With the last of her dignity, Luella bade Sir Julius goodnight; he was leaving for London early next morning, and expressed his regret that he would not see her again. He remembered Quinn's description of how he had found this child, sitting in the cemetery and brushing out her hair, looking like a landlocked mermaid, calling herself Marianne Walton; an extraordinary tale indeed, he told himself.

Luella, however, was in no mood for sleep; the night was young, and the moon was up. She felt restless, having been cooped up too long inside this great house; she had an overwhelming desire for fresh air and freedom.

She decided that no one would miss her, so she took off her finery and put it away with a faint sigh of regret, wondering whether she would ever wear such clothes again or dine in such state.

From the wardrobe Luella took the dark dress that she wore by day, and a dark cloak; hurriedly, she dressed in them.

There were several exits from the house; she chose the most unobtrusive and went into the grounds, drawing in great breaths of sharp night air to cool her head and her senses.

She did not yet know her way around the grounds and would have been sadly lost without the moon's lantern hanging in the starry heavens; the light it gave was clear, cold, and beautiful. It was a calm night, and beyond the high walls the sea ran quietly. It was not a night for those who smuggled in spies or contraband, for the moon that gave them enough light to see by also aided those who came in search of them.

Luella moved light-footed down the formal walks of the gardens, between thick green hedges of clipped yew and box, past white statues that gleamed with ghostlight under the moon. Somewhere an owl called mournfully and was answered by an equally sad cry, almost as though it was a signal. The gardens seemed peaceful enough, yet Luella had an awareness of being watched by unseen eyes, the same awareness that had alerted her when she stood in Marianne's bedroom. She knew that dark and dangerous forces were gathering themselves together around this house, waiting to be unleashed.

She walked close to the hedges, in the shadows and out of the moon's brilliance, as though trying to become invisible, but the eyes followed her, she knew, so where the gardens broadened out into parkland, she turned and walked swiftly back to the house.

Luella had come around to the front of the house, where it faced the sea, and the sight of it took her breath away; it was like a fairytale castle, its walls silvered, many of its windows blazing with golden light. Her gaze traveled upward toward the tower in which Jessica lived, and up still further to the small window of the chapel.

Her heartbeats quickened; she could have sworn that she saw a faint light in the window. It was done in an instant, and then returned, an uncertain flickering light, as though someone moved there with a candle.

Perhaps Jessica had got out of bed and, in one of her strange moods, had made her way up to the old chapel.

Luella ran indoors, thankful enough to be out of range of eyes that she felt had marked every step of her progress. She went on tiptoe past the study where Sir Julius sat listening to Quinn's story of his grim journey home to England, up the stairs, and into the sea tower rooms.

There was no sign of Emmie; a lamp burned low in the sitting room; softly, Luella opened the door into Jessica's bedroom.

Jessica was propped against her pillow, sound asleep,

snoring gently, her mouth half-open. In the light from the lamp on a nearby table she looked as brittle as a dead leaf.

Luella listened intently, hearing no sound; she tiptoed back to the sitting room and carefully opened the small writing desk.

The key to the chapel was still there, where she herself had replaced it hours ago.

Luella went to bed, troubled and uneasy; she lay awake for a long time, thinking. She knew she should tell Quinn what she had seen, but he would be angry if she interrupted him now, and would he not tell her that her imagination played her tricks, just as he had when she had told him she thought someone was in Marianne's room?

Once she got out of bed and looked at the ghostly moors; they were wild and savage and cruel, she thought somberly. Beyond these sheltering walls there was no safety for the poor, the hunted ones, the people who did their business stealthily by night.

She thought of the fugitive who had given her his food; she hoped he was safely over the Channel to France. She had heard the gossip between Jessica and Emmie, with Jessica expressing astonishment that the pleasant young tutor should turn out to be an enemy agent; Luella had no doubt at all that the man whose leg she had bandaged *was* Philip Janson. He had said he was innocent; well, he would scarcely say otherwise, she reflected, with a sigh.

As soon as Luella had reentered the house, the owl hooted again, twice, and was answered; the man who had kept watch on Westhaven crouched low against the concealing wall as he ran toward the farthest end of the grounds, where there was a handhold of ivy, the stems grown thick with years.

He was a small, wiry man, and he swung himself over the wall, dropping with a soft thud on the turf on the far side. He was joined immediately by another man, tall, thin-faced, with a cloak wrapped tightly around him.

"Well?" said the second man curtly.

"I saw her, sir," the first man panted. "Walking by herself in the gardens. I kept her in sight all the way, sir, till she went in."

Jackson Parnall swore furiously.

"Damn you for a fool, Hines! You could have taken her easily! Why the hell didn't you?"

The man hesitated.

"We was close by the house, sir. She kept moving very fast and then she went in; there was activity aplenty inside. What if she'd made a fuss, and brought the servants out?"

"One of these days you will hesitate a second too long," Parnall raged, "and that will be the end of you, my friend. I will not do business with men who hesitate and fumble and show cowardice. Get on your way! You have not earned your promised reward this night, and you will not get it."

The man looked angry as he turned in the direction of Axminster, but he knew better than to argue with him. He was ruthless: When he was pleased, his rewards were high; when he was angry, it was as well for a man to get out of the way with all speed. Especially a man like himself, wanted for half a dozen crimes, Tom Hines reflected; Mr. Jackson would have no compunction in betraying him, if he displeased him too much.

So he returned to the hovel on the moors that had recently sheltered Philip Janson, cursing both his ill luck and the speed at which Luella had moved.

Parnall, filled with savage disappointment, walked to where his horse was tethered, some distance away, and rode off in the opposite direction to that taken by the man he had sent on his way. He, too, cursed his ill luck in having to use men without wits or courage for his more menial tasks. Still, he would have her yet, he vowed to himself; and when Quinn Mallory came searching for her, he would have him, too, a double victory to recompense him for all these miserable weeks of waiting.

Having promised Sir Julius his support, Quinn wasted no time in getting to work.

As soon as Sir Julius had left for London, he rode over

to Dorchester jail but was unable to see the prison governor, who had taken to his bed with a severe chill, so Quinn called at an office in the winding High Street of Dorchester before returning home on his big black horse, Kalidas.

The offices he visited were those of the agents who managed the estates of one Andrew Peirse, a flaccid young man, owner of Dunbury House. Andrew hated the place and was busy dissipating his father's fortune by dividing his time between whorehouses and gaming clubs in London; he left his affairs to be managed by agents and had no interest in his estate, apart from collecting rent for it.

The chief clerk at the agents' office, a long, bony man who looked as though he suffered from a permanent cold, could tell him little, except that a man had called some months ago, saying he was the nephew of a Mrs. Cazelet, who desired to rent a house by the sea; Mrs. Cazelet, it seemed, was not in the best of health, being lately widowed, her husband having been killed in France. The man had produced references and handed over several months' rent in advance.

Quinn suspected that the agents had been only too anxious to get the property off their hands; he took the sketch of Jackson Parnall from his leather satchel and handed it over.

"Did the man who conducted Mrs. Cazelet's affairs look like this?" he asked.

The clerk studied the sketch and shook his head decisively.

"No sir. He was younger, more pleasant-looking, not so sharp-featured."

Quinn replaced the sketch and handed the clerk a guinea; he did not expect an easy and early victory where Parnall was concerned, he reflected, as he went on his way, choosing the route that took him past Dunbury.

The house was considerably smaller than Westhaven—no more than a fair-sized manor house, neglected and seedy-looking from the outside. The shutters were firmly locked across its windows, the garden was rank with weeds and overgrown with tall grasses. Outbuildings and stables were in a sorry state of repair, with holes in roofs and breaks in the walls. Mrs. Cazelet had obviously decided that there were better places in which to take advantage of the health-giving sea breezes.

Checking up on Mrs. Cazelet was probably a waste of time; however, he could not afford to leave any stone unturned, he reflected, as he remounted Kalidas and turned toward Westhaven.

He considered all the people he knew who might prove useful: Like Sir Julius, Quinn had his own list of contacts who rendered good service, even on affairs that took place on the far side of the Channel—people who had met and talked to the French agents coming stealthily to the coast, people who knew all that passed in the farms and cottages around Westhaven.

Like Jackson Parnall, Quinn used people—with one difference. He paid well for services, never used physical violence, and collected knowledge, not for his own ends, but solely to bring criminals to justice.

He wanted Parnall very much, for the shame and dishonor his acts had brought upon the name of England; so, at the last moment, he turned away from Westhaven and made for a small, derelict cottage in a clearing on the very edge of his lands, while Luella, tired of being confined to the grounds, set off to explore the country outside the sheltering walls of the house where she worked.

CHAPTER 6

In the clearing stood the cottage where Shep Tulley lived alone in the indescribable filth to which he had long since been indifferent. When he earned money, he drank himself into oblivion; when he had none, he stole or begged and found both activities fairly profitable. The local people treated him with a mixture of fear and indulgence, for it was said that in his drunken state he had the gift of prophecy; whether or not that was true, Quinn had no idea. What he did know was that Shep missed nothing in the way of local gossip and had a mind as sharp as a needle.

Quinn halted his great black horse several feet from the broken door of the stone-walled, one-story building; a curl of smoke issued from the chimney on the sagging roof. He heard the sound of pots and pans being rattled and a man's voice singing a bawdy sea shanty in a rich baritone of surprising quality.

Quinn drew a breath of relief; it sounded as though Shep was sober enough to be of use to him. When the singing stopped, Quinn gave a high-pitched whistle and called loudly to Shep to come out at once.

There were several seconds of complete silence; then the man came, with surly reluctance, to the door and opened it cautiously. He was small and thick-set, his clothes no more than a bundle of rags tied about the middle with a worn leather belt. His hair was prematurely gray, verminous and unkempt about his shoulders, and thick stubble on his face almost masked the heavy features; his eyes were deep-set, bright and cunning.

"What 'ee want?" he demanded.

"A word with you!" challenged Quinn. "Come on out,

113

man! Have you forgotten that I am the local magistrate and the penalty for poaching is hanging or transportation? How many of my rabbits and hares have found their way into your cooking pot? How many game birds of mine have you smuggled out to the London markets? Remember it is by *my* grace that you stay instead of having this hovel pulled down around your ears!"

The man came into the clearing, pale sunlight shining on his dirty, sullen face.

Quinn leaned forward in the saddle, his voice soft.

"Have you heard of a man called Jackson Parnall?" he demanded.

"No," retorted Shep.

"Are there strangers in the village, Shep?"

"In the village—no. In Dorchester, aplenty. Out o' touch with news, then, are thee?" the old man taunted.

He saw the look on Quinn's face and added reluctantly, " 'Tis a profitable line o' business: getting the Frenchies out of jail for a handsome sum, and finding boats as'll take 'em home. 'Tis more rewarding than fishing for a living, I hear; them same boats comes back wi' brandy and laces and silk, so 'tis twice profitable to them wot does it."

"Have *you* had a hand in any of it, Shep?" Quinn demanded.

The man spat fiercely into the dust at his feet.

"I be many things, mister, but I bain't a traitor."

Quinn took the sketch from his satchel.

"Did you ever see a man who looked like this?" he asked.

Shep stared at it thoughtfully.

"I did," he said finally.

Quinn's pulses quickened with excitement; with difficulty he controlled his features and voice. It would not do to let Shep know the importance of his mission.

"When and where?" he demanded.

"What's it worth, mister? Times ain't easy . . ."

"Don't whine, Shep Tulley; it ill becomes you. There's a guinea in it that you'll no doubt spend on drink. Remember, man, you could hang or serve the rest of your life in the penal settlement in Botany Bay."

114

Shep said sulkily, "I see 'im in Dorchester. 'E was in a little street behind the market and talking to my cousin Tom Hines, that's 'ow I noticed 'im. I dunno what passed between 'em. I don't see Tom so much now, since 'e's married to a fancy woman with fine airs who says I'm too dirty to come into 'er bloody kitchen," Shep concluded bitterly.

Quinn tossed him a sovereign; the gold coin lay gleaming at his feet, and Shep picked it up with a deep sigh of satisfaction.

"Bring Tom Hines here tomorrow morning," Quinn commanded.

" 'Ow can I do that? I told you, I don't see 'im no more!"

"I don't care *how* you get him here," Quinn retorted.

" 'Ow much?"

"Another guinea."

"Tain't enough!" cried Shep.

"Damn you, two guineas, then!" cried Quinn, enraged. "Don't drive too hard a bargain, Shep Tulley! Else you may kill the goose that lays the golden eggs! You're a waster, a drunkard, and a thief! If you got some decent food into your belly, scrubbed the filth off you, and worked like a man, you'd be the better for it!"

Shep made no attempt to argue; why should he, when he knew that all Quinn said was perfectly true?

Luella, well wrapped against the chill breeze that blew off the sea, followed one of the winding paths that led from the clifftop to the beach.

The tide was out; clusters of rocks were embedded like jewels in the glistening golden sand, and the seaweed was spread out to dry in the sun. Overhead the gulls swooped and cried, their wings scything the pale sky. The restless sea tumbled over itself in its eagerness to return again and swallow up the shore.

Where the cliffs had broken away there were great piles of shale and stones. Luella picked up some of the stones and examined them with interest; they bore the imprints of fossils and were similar to those she had seen in Jessica Mallory's room.

There were caves at the back of the beach, some of them little more than holes scooped from the cliffs, some of them accessible only by rocky ledges and standing above high-water mark. Luella peered in at one of the caves; it smelt dank and sour.

She became so absorbed in examining stones that she was unaware of anyone else on the beach until she rounded a small headland, made where a shower of rocks and stones had fallen and lay piled at the foot of the cliffs. On the other side of the headland the sands were deeply indented to form a small, curving bay with a large, open cave at the back of it. There a man was standing, apparently lost in thought.

Disconcerted, Luella lost her balance and stumbled to her knees, dislodging a pile of small stones that rattled noisily. The man turned his head sharply and, seeing her, walked across to help her to her feet.

"Are you hurt?" he demanded.

"No," she said breathlessly and, remembering her manners, added sedately, "thank you."

"We have met," he said. "At Westhaven. You are Mrs. Mallory's companion."

"Yes, and you are Mr. Simon Corbie from Bellminster," she said. "This is the first time I have been out of the grounds of Westhaven."

Involuntarily, she glanced upwards; it was quite a climb to the top of the cliffs, even for the agile ones. She thought of Marianne, falling from the path, to lie amongst the rocks, dead or unconscious, until the tide carried her away.

"Did you know Marianne Walton?" she asked, still obsessed by thoughts of the girl who had grown up at Westhaven and whose bright, vivid personality still seemed to linger there.

"I knew her very well. We played together as children," he said lightly.

Luella glanced toward the great cave that dominated the small bay. Simon saw her glance, and said swiftly, "Caves are most unpleasant places, Miss March!"

"Are they? They fascinate me."

116

"One can become trapped in caves such as that, at high tide."

"The tide has ebbed," she pointed out, watching his face and seeing a sudden look of strain in it that puzzled her.

He said, with a smile, "Will you not walk along the beach a way with me? Around this next headland there is a fine view of the coastline all along to Weymouth. Do you know Weymouth, Miss March? It has become a most fashionable place since the king goes there to bathe in the sea. I have heard much of the benefits of bathing in the sea, though I have not yet tried it . . ."

Adroitly, skillfully, he steered the conversation and Luella's footsteps away from the danger that the cave represented. She allowed him to walk her to the headland and admired the long coastline stretching away toward the great Chesil Bank and Weymouth. Then he insisted on taking her back to the very gates of Westhaven, where she bade him good-day and watched him step out briskly in the direction of Bellminster.

She was not deceived; she knew that Simon Corbie did not want her to look inside the great cave.

Very well, she would explore the cave come other time, she decided. In the meantime, she had no intention of returning to the house. Jessica Mallory had told her she might use the day as she pleased, and such freedom was a great novelty.

She walked all day upon the moors, while the sun climbed the heavens and warmed the air sufficiently for her to throw open the cloak she wore. Her hair streamed behind her in the breeze as she trod happily over the springy turf or rested in a sheltered hollow, blissfully happy because she was alone with no one to harry her. Until coming to Westhaven she had never, in all her life, tasted such freedom as this, and it was headier than wine.

A little wind whistled jauntily among the grasses, the scrub and crouching furze; paths crisscrossed one another, and occasionally she passed cottages where women came to their doors to eye her curiously, saying nothing. She got lost, and did not care, for she knew if she turned her face seawards she must, eventually, come back to Westhaven.

In the distance she saw the road that ran between Devon and Dorset; a few farm carts rolled sluggishly along it, then a private carriage with drawn curtains and high-stepping horses. Behind the carriage came the London-bound coach, its driver sitting high in state, whip curling above the backs of the team of horses. There were passengers sitting on the outside seats; it seemed centuries ago that she had sat there, crying to the driver to stop because she had lost all the money she had in the world. Now she had a golden guinea safely tucked away among the chemises and stockings in her bedroom, and the prospect of going to London to work was becoming less attractive as the days passed.

She walked and rested, and walked again, thinking about all Quinn Mallory had told her of men and women and the begetting of children.

She had moved in a complete circle and came at last within sight of Dunbury. She was unaware that Quinn had visited the house only a few hours earlier; unaware, also, that Tom Hines, whose task it was to watch the comings and goings at Westhaven, was on his way back to the wife who had no idea how he earned the money he spent so freely.

He saw Luella approaching Dunbury and hid in one of the looseboxes; she would have to pass right by its walls to get back to the path leading to Westhaven.

Luck was with him, such luck as he had not expected. Luella was curious enough to step through a gap in the wall to take a better look at the crumbling house. What a sinister place, she thought.

The name was cut in the wrought iron of a great arch over the main entrance: "Dunbury." This was where the mysterious Mrs. Cazelet had lived, the woman Marianne had taken pity upon and visited, much to Jessica's annoyance. Mrs. Cazelet had been a recluse, rarely going out, heavily veiled, still in mourning for a dead husband: Luella had pieced together a vivid picture from the gossip she had heard at Westhaven.

There was no one living in the house now; it looked not

118

only desolate but sinister. A flurry of gray clouds had ridden up out of the west, obscuring the sun, and the afternoon was growing late. It was time for her to return to Westhaven, and Luella knew she would not be sorry to do so; she was tired after a day spent in the fresh air.

The wind was rising, moaning in the shivering grasses, and the incoming tide, running strongly, thundered along the shore. Luella had a sense of being utterly alone out on moors that were no longer friendly, but savage and cruel as the sea; yet not alone, at all.

Uneasily, she turned to go; the heavy front gate was locked and barred, so she retraced her steps to the gap in the wall, near the looseboxes and the broken, moss-patched cobbles of the stable yard.

She was within sight of the gap when Tom Hines sprang at her from behind, dragging her to the ground. She screamed, and his hand, grimed, smelling of dirt and tobacco, was rammed in her mouth, almost choking her. She spluttered, fighting him off furiously. As she rolled over on the cobbles, she saw his face, thin, foxy. He was a small man, but he was like a steel hawser, gripping her flesh, forcing her head back against the cobbles.

Her head met the stones with a heavy thud. Tom Hines's face dissolved into blackness, and she felt herself spinning away down a long dark tunnel that had no light at its end.

Luella went limp, and Hines grunted with relief. He dragged her across the stable yard and found the small door at the rear of the house that was the quickest way in and out. He opened the door without much difficulty, for he was familiar with the place. Then he pulled the still unconscious Luella over the threshold and through the kitchen toward a door that led down to the cellar below.

He opened the door leading to the cellar and heaved Luella over his shoulder as though she were a sack of coal. A shallow flight of rotting wooden steps led down into the cellar with its thick stone walls, its piles of accumulated rubbish, and its single window. The air whistled coldly through the window; there was no glass in it, and one of the rusted iron bars set into the stonework was missing.

119

Panting, Tom Hines dumped Luella with her face against the wall. He took the greasy kerchief from around his neck and tied her wrists together behind her back. Then he went in search of the man who employed him.

It was a long haul to Dorchester, he thought resentfully; unless he got a lift on a farm cart, it would be several hours before he could reach Mr. Jackson.

Grumbling, he went on his way; he reached the main road, passing within only a few yards of Quinn, who was riding toward Bellminster to talk to Simon and discover if he could give him any information that might help him in his task.

Tom Hines was fortunate; the driver of an empty farm wagon, creaking and lumbering its way home to the outskirts of Dorchester, willingly gave him a lift.

Reaching the town, Tom made his way through a maze of streets to the high, narrow house where Mr. Jackson, scholar and gentleman, had his rooms.

He was angry when he saw Tom.

"I told you not to come here," he said.

"Unless 'twas a matter of the greatest urgency," Tom reminded him.

"Well? I hope for your sake that it is," retorted Jackson Parnall.

The soft gray dusk came in as swiftly as the tide, but it was still light enough for Luella to see her surroundings when she regained consciousness.

She moved her head carefully; it ached as though it was one giant bruise. She tried to move her hands and found they were tied behind her. Then she remembered what had happened, though she had no idea where she was. She could hear the sea roaring in the distance and felt the cold pulse of night air throbbing through the window.

She looked with horror at her surroundings; there were piles of rubbish around her: old boxes, broken and split, dirty straw, broken furniture, pieces of driftwood, as though all the jetsam of other people's lives had been cast down here haphazardly.

Luella realized it was some kind of cellar, for it was similar to the one at Henrietta's house. Henrietta had once locked her in the cellar for several hours for staying too long at the market. Luella remembered how frightened she had been when it grew dark and rats began to scurry beside her on small, whispering feet. She had been near-hysterical when Henrietta had finally opened the door, and Henrietta had whipped her all the way to her room for making such a noise.

Soon it would be dark. She wondered if she was in the cellar at Dunbury. Why had she been left here, tied up? It would soon be dark, and the thought of being alone here in the darkness was unendurable.

Frantically, she tried to loosen the kerchief that bound her wrists. Tom had done his work competently, but the kerchief itself was rotten; she felt it give considerably under her frantic and persistent tugging. Hope blazed high within her.

The hope, however, was short-lived. She loosened the bonds, but could not get her hands free; exhausted, her head throbbing, she lay back on the floor, tears running down her cheeks.

The wind was rising; she could hear it howling outside, driving the sea into a frenzy against the cliffs.

After a while she gained enough strength to pull herself into a sitting position, grazing her elbows, bumping her shoulders until she felt sick and her head spun giddily. She tried to rise to her feet, but could not, hampered as she was with her hands still fastened behind her back; she lay sprawled against the wall, panting, weeping, utterly spent.

The last of the light was ebbing as the tide had ebbed down the beach that morning; Luella heard faint rustling sounds in between the gusts of wind that were growing in strength. That small, evil noise brought reminder of the horror of Henrietta's cellar, the scampering rats, the thick, terrifying darkness.

She began to scream aloud; her screams became shuddering sobs, and her head felt as though it was going to burst. The pain behind her eyes was intolerable; she moaned and fell sideways, lapsing again into unconsciousness.

* * *

Jackson Parnall had moved with the stealth and speed that had saved his life on many occasions. Hines was an encumbrance to him, and he would be glad when he had no more need of the man. Parnall had little time for stupid men who could not think for themselves, nor anticipate a move like a chess player facing an opponent.

However, he reminded himself, his days of hide-and-seek were almost over. He would soon no longer need to dice with danger and death, nor hide behind disguises, skulking in Dorchester when all he wanted to do was shake the dust of England from his feet forever.

He would be content, he thought, even if he did not take Mallory, although the capture and death of the man who so bedeviled him would give him tremendous satisfaction.

He wondered, fleetingly, what had happened to Janson; he knew that the escape from jail had been made days ago. Janson had not been recaptured, so by now he was probably safe at the other end of England or across the narrow strip of water dividing him from France.

Parnall looked up and saw the stars twinkling above him; their brightness was not one quarter as great as the brilliance of the *true* Flowers of Darkness, he thought, with sudden yearning and hunger.

He remembered the barn and Eleanor La Vanne, beautiful even in the depths of misery and degradation. He thought with contempt of the drunken rabble of peasants, surging like a fetid sea, bent only on the destruction of a fellow human being.

"May the winds of fate blow coldly about you."

Damn it, why did he remember those words *now*? Why did he feel again a breath of wind so icy that it chilled him to the marrow? He would not have said that he was chilled to the soul, for he liked to boast that he had long since sold his soul to the devil.

The winds of fate had not blown coldly upon him—until he landed in England. It was one of his boasts that the winds of fate blew people about like leaves—*if* they were weak and soft and foolish; but since the night he had betrayed Eleanor La Vanne, nothing had gone right for him.

122

Well, much of it was his own fault, he admitted bitterly; rage and hatred rose like bile within him, a red tide that momentarily blotted out all reason and almost drove him mad.

However, he had long since learned the value of keeping a cool head and clear judgment in times such as these. He thrust Tom Hines ahead of him, in case there was a trap or ambush waiting. The man stumbled, cursing weakly under his breath, and Parnall smiled to himself in the darkness. Once Hines had ceased to be useful—and he had been of little enough use so far—then he would be dispatched to his death by whatever means were most readily available.

The two men entered the house. Not until the door was safely barred behind them did Parnall light his lantern and curtly order Tom Hines to do the same with *his* lantern.

Luella had returned to consciousness, slowly and painfully. She lay on her back with only the faint light of the moon for comfort, completely defeated for the first time in her life; the ordeal had almost broken the spirit that Henrietta's cruelty had been unable to crush.

Almost, but not quite. As she lay, wondering whether she was going to be left here to die and whether it was punishment for wishing Henrietta dead, she heard bolts being pulled back from the door at the top of the stairs.

Her heart leaped high with joy and relief; then the same sixth sense that had sprung to life in Eleanor La Vanne suddenly quelled the joy in Luella, making her suddenly still. *This was not help*; it was danger more deadly than she had ever known, lurking in the darkness at the top of the stairs.

All her senses were alerted as the small, frantic signals stabbed her brain; she did not know *why* she closed her eyes again the instant she saw that two men had entered the cellar. She lay very still, scarcely breathing, feigning unconsciousness.

"There!" whispered Hines triumphantly, pointing to the huddled figure against the wall.

Every nerve in Luella's body was tensed; she wanted to scream, to lash out, to rend with her nails and stab with her teeth at these men with their lanterns; instead, after the first flickering of her eyelids on their arrival, she kept her eyes firmly closed.

A lantern was held above her while one of the men bent and peered into her face; she could feel his breath, smell eau-de-cologne and the clean sweetness of new-washed linen.

She was quite unprepared for what happened next.

The man who had bent over her straightened up; Luella felt the light move away from in front of her closed lids as he swore a dreadful, blasphemous oath and then whispered savagely,

"God rot you, Tom Hines, for the fool that you are! You have blundered yet again, and, I swear, for the very last time . . ."

"Sir, she came from Westhaven!" The second voice was coarse, not educated like the first one. "She was the one in the grounds! 'Twas moonlight, and I seed her clear, and 'tis the same one . . ."

The flight of words, pitched high with fear, ended in a sudden, strangled cry; Luella heard the sound of flesh meeting flesh as Parnall rammed home his fist. Then she heard the sickening thud of a body sliding to the floor.

Cautiously, fearfully, she opened her eyes; the man with his back to her was tall and thin; he wore leather boots, breeches, and the clothes of a gentleman; on the floor, writhing in pain, lay a roughly dressed man who looked like a farm laborer; in the light of the lanterns Luella saw blood running from his nose and mouth.

She felt sick; she was terrified half out of her wits, and only rigid self-control kept her immobile.

"Damn you!" whispered Parnall again. "You slobbering half-wit, you have brought me here on a wild-goose chase! I have never set eyes on this creature before! Either you have fed me on lies with the hope that you could escape me before I discovered the truth, or you are a greater fool than I believed. *You* have brought me nothing but ill luck, and I am no nearer the truth now than I have ever been!"

She heard the despair and frustration in his voice; cold beads of sweat broke out along her forehead. She could not lie here much longer, she thought, without betraying that she was conscious, for great, silent screams of terror were rising up within her and it was with the greatest difficulty that she kept them from breaking into sound.

She peered from under half-closed lids; what she saw horrified her even more. Jackson Parnall bent over the man who lay on the floor, pulled a pistol from his belt, and held it to the man's temple.

"You will make no more mistakes, Tom Hines!" he said bitterly, and Luella had the feeling that all his emotions were penned into such savage hatred because she was not the person he had expected to find.

Whom had he expected to find in the cellar? Luella wondered.

Mary?

There was no other possibility; for one wild moment she thought of Marianne, but Marianne was dead and lying in her grave.

Perhaps he did not know that. The idea made her blood run cold. Her brain was too confused to try to make some pattern from the fragments of knowledge she held . . .

The report from the pistol was deafening. Tom Hines jerked convulsively, twice, and fell back into a heap of rotting boxes and a pile of moldy straw.

Luella jumped violently but forced herself not to retch; it was a superhuman feat. The man with the pistol had his back to her, but she realized, grimly, that if he suspected she was alive, she would probably meet the same fate as Tom Hines; if he thought she was dead, might he not go away and leave her there?

Only the knowledge that her life hung by the thinnest thread kept her as still as if she was clamped to the floor. Her heart was thundering like galloping hoofbeats, and she felt sure that the man who had killed Tom Hines must hear it, but the cellar was dim, and the light of the lantern he held barely pushed back a handful of shadows.

As he turned toward her, she closed her eyes again. She heard him come over to her, felt his nearness as he bent over her, his breath on her cheek as he swung the lantern

125

to and fro. Burning sickness rose in her throat and filled her mouth, but she lay still, the instinct of self-preservation strong within her.

He turned away and walked toward the foot of the stairs, deep in thought. She heard him fumbling with the catch that closed the face of the lantern Tom Hines had carried.

"No witnesses!" he said aloud, to himself. "So long as only *one* can testify, there is danger. . . . There must be no sign that anyone has been here."

He spoke the words as though repeating a well-taught lesson; Luella heard curious sounds, but dared not open her eyes. The man in the cellar seemed to be moving boxes and piles of straw and rubbish toward the foot of the stairs.

Then she hard an ominous new sound: a hiss, a crackle, and a soft splutter. Footsteps mounted the stairs two at a time, and the heavy door to the house was slammed home and bolted on the far side.

With a final, frenzied jerk she tore the kerchief free and heard the rotten material rip apart as it tore away from her wrists. Luella struggled to her feet, and screams broke from her in wave after wave of sheer horror as she saw flames racing through the dry rubbish and rustling straw that had lain snug and dry in the cellar for months.

She hurried to the foot of the stairs, kicking aside burning rubbish, her throat dry and sweat like a mist of fine rain chilling her body. It was too late. The door was thick, the cellar soundproof, and Jackson Parnall had already hurried on his way out through the door that was kept unlocked for him. He went, unseen, into the night and back to Dorchester to resume the role of Mr. Jackson, gentleman of letters and scholar.

Luella beat on the door with frenzied fists; her head throbbed, and the cellar seemed to whirl in a kaleidoscope of fire.

She was going to be burned alive; there was no escape. The full horror of the situation engulfed her in a black, sickening cloud. If she had not feigned death, the man who had held the pistol to Tom Hines's head would have dispatched *her* with equal coolness into the next world, but such a death would have been quicker and cleaner than being roasted alive.

Already the heat and smoke were unbearable, making her choke and splutter for breath. She looked wildly for something with which to batter at the closed door, but she knew she had not the strength to attempt such a task, even if the means to do so had been at hand.

She ran down again, bending to look at the body of the man with blood on his face; she wept for him, tears mingled with those of utter despair at her own hopeless plight.

Luella glanced around her, trying to rally her almost broken spirit; the steely will that had sustained her so far gave her fresh strength as she assessed the situation.

The rubbish was now burning fiercely, the little flames dancing gleefully in every direction to gather fresh fuel for the insatiable appetite of the fire. She had no means of quelling the growing blaze that would soon engulf her, but as she glanced toward the window, she noticed the gap made by the broken bar.

She was small and thin; even so, she knew it would require an almost superhuman effort to squeeze through the gap. She drew a deep breath, found a chair with a broken back, and dragged it forward to stand upon.

By standing tiptoe on the chair, Luella discovered she could just reach the bars.

She looked at the humped body near the wall. She could not leave the body there to shrivel on a funeral pyre; she dragged it inch by inch, slowly and painfully, toward the window. The effort of heaving the dead weight, in such heat and with her head still throbbing, made the sweat pour down her face again. Gasping, sobbing, she got the body underneath the window and then realized the utter absurdity of trying to lift it, unaided, to the opening; even could she have done so, Hines had been heavily built and she could never have got his body through the small gap.

So she left it by the wall under the window; Hines was long past her help, and she was still doubtful that *she* would escape. A small flame licked at the hem of her dress and she stamped it out fiercely; the air was full of the scent of smoldering cloth, and that scent spurred her on to fresh efforts.

She climbed on the chair again and grasped two of the bars, grimly swinging herself upward like a small, agile monkey.

Once, twice, three times she made the upward swing. Just as she was certain she would never make it to freedom, she managed to retain her grip on the bars and haul herself to the sill, balancing there precariously while she wriggled herself into the gap between the rusted iron columns.

The bars on either side of her held her firmly, giving her support and respite, but she knew it was going to be a tight squeeze, even for someone as small and bony as she was. She wriggled desperately, inching herself through, wincing as the unyielding bars bruised her body, making her feel as though the flesh was being remorselessly scraped from her very bones each time she moved.

Inch by painful inch she made it. When she felt she could stand no more, she was suddenly free, and she fell heavily into a small paved area near the stables.

Fortunately, it was a fall of only a few feet, but in Luella's already exhausted condition it was enough to leave her helpless. It was several minutes before she could struggle, winded and bruised, to her feet.

Above her the stars twinkled coldly and frostily. Freedom had never looked nor tasted so sweet. Behind her the fire roared fiendishly, its red glow lighting up the window and giving her some means of checking on her surroundings.

With the need for iron self-control finally removed, she began to shiver and sob violently; her mind seethed with confusion, bubbled as furiously as a boiling cauldron with fears and strange fancies, all of them like broken fragments of a nightmare.

She was running away from Henrietta, she told herself wildly; Henrietta was in full pursuit, demanding justice for the theft of five golden guineas, and the upraised hand holding the supple cane turned into a great black cloud from which Luella knew she *must* escape with all speed.

She stumbled out through the stable yard; she, who had been in a fever of heat, now ached with the cold. Somewhere there was a place that offered shelter from Henrietta—if only she could find it. She had been there before, she knew; Quinn's face bobbed in her mind, briefly, and was gone, to be supplanted by Jessica's face, kind and concerned.

She stumbled on, falling, pulling herself to her feet, her mind veering between madness and sanity like a seesaw. She missed the path that would have taken her straight to Westhaven. Her feet bled from contact with the rough ground. During her desperate bid for escape she had shed her shoes, and one lay in the stable yard, though she did not know that.

She was walking into blackness; only when the voice of the sea sounded very loud in her ears did an awareness of danger briefly penetrate the fog in her mind, like a shaft of sunlight through mist. She crouched against a furze bush, trying to make sense of the nightmare she found herself in.

Luella knew she was near the cliff edge. The pulse of the sea was strong and full, its voice supplemented by other, smaller voices: the sound of a boat scraping on shingle; muttered words floating indistinctly between one pulse of an incoming wave and the next. She thought a lantern bobbed far below her, its pixy light dancing feebly in the darkness; it was suddenly obscured at the sound of an angry command.

She knew there were people below her, people who had business that could only be conducted under the cover of night and the cloak of secrecy. She heard the sound of footsteps coming up the path and crouched low under the bush, her sixth sense telling her that she must not be discovered.

Those who had climbed the path passed within a few feet of her and went their ways. She had heard the talk of French spies. This was a new boatload of them, she thought vaguely, and they were going about their work, preparing the way for the invasion from across the Channel that everyone expected . . . everyone was going to be killed by Boney's soldiers . . . someone had said so . . .

The mists closed around her again. She knew she must reach the great house on the cliffs that would shelter her in safety if she could only find her way to it.

She missed her way and came around the back of the house, where the gate in the wall was locked. Quinn had swept out through the great front door mounted on Kalidas, to go in search of her, sending a party of servants inland, never dreaming that she was anywhere save out on the moors between Devon and Dorset. One of the kitchenmaids, returning that afternoon from a visit to her father, had reported seeing Luella making toward Dorchester, so the band of men fanned out, armed with sticks and lanterns, wondering at the master's concern for his grandmother's companion, and putting their own interpretation upon it.

Luella came upon the gate. The late-rising moon, peeping coyly from cloud wrack that littered the sky like the wreckage of the day, gave a faint, misty light, just enough for her to see the gate.

She rattled and beat upon it, and called aloud with the last of her strength, but the same breeze that sent the moon into hiding behind the scurrying clouds carried her words away. This gate was some distance from the house, a short cut to the park, and there was no lodge beside it.

Luella looked up and saw the lights in the windows of the house; they seemed as far off as the lights of paradise. She would never again find rest or shelter anywhere, whispered a small, malign voice in her tired, wandering mind. She had glimpsed paradise, but now, like Adam and Eve in a great colored picture she had once seen, she was doomed to wander outside its shelter forever.

Her hand slid down the bars of the gate and fell despondently to her side. She went on because she did not know what else to do, her progress slow, the last of her strength rapidly running out.

She went on for a considerable distance before her knees finally buckled beneath her. She slid in a heap to the path, as exhausted as though she had been walking through all eternity. She wanted only to sleep . . .

Her mind still hovered between light and dark, now

plunged into depths approaching madness, a result of the ordeal she had suffered, now surfacing for a few seconds to hold small, coherent thoughts.

She thought of Marianne; her cloak and bonnet had been found, and her death was presumed to be an accident. Ah, how easy it would be to fake such an accident and send her dead body down into the arms of the sea. Perhaps Marianne had known something she should not have known . . . perhaps the man who killed her had not expected the sea to give her back again.

Luella thought, briefly, about Mrs. Cazelet, the mystery occupant of Dunbury, now many weeks departed from the place; but *had* she departed, or had she, too, met with a sinister accident? Would she be discovered, dead, one day, just as the man in the cellar would be discovered . . . ?

Much later that night, Simon Corbie, his night's work done, rode along the path where Luella lay. His horse reared up suddenly and neighed with fright, refusing to move, so Corbie slid from the animal's back and investigated.

She was lying on her side. He lifted the lantern and turned her over on her back, with a small whistle of shocked surprise as he recognized the girl he had escorted earlier in the day to the gates of Westhaven. Her face was pale and still, streaked with dirt and tears; he felt through the torn bodice of her dress for a heartbeat and discovered that she was alive—just . . .

He was only a short distance from Bellminster; he moved her to the side of the road, covered her with his cloak, and rode home furiously.

His thoughts were in a ferment as he let himself into the house and called loudly for the two remaining menservants who—with his old nurse now turned housekeeper—made up his staff.

Nanny, who had nursed him in his youth, came grumbling from her bed; meanwhile, Simon sent the servants to bring in Luella. They went armed with a makeshift stretcher and blankets.

Simon, supervising the lighting of a fire and preparation

131

of a bedroom, wondered at the wisdom of sheltering Luella March under his roof; would it not have been wiser to have dispatched someone to Westhaven, in order that she could have been taken there? However, she had been lying almost outside his gates. There had been little choice for him in the matter; after all, Quinn would come with all speed and order her return to Westhaven.

He was not a quick-thinking man; the twists and turns and complexities in the dangerous game in which he was involved troubled him at times.

So his servants brought Luella in, and Nanny undressed her, getting her between the blankets with commendable speed, considering that she was old, deaf, and rheumatic. Finally, she forced some brandy between the chilled lips. When Luella coughed and spluttered, Nanny said tersely, "She'll do, Master Simon!"

Relieved, Simon set off for Westhaven.

Dunbury House was gutted by the fierce-raging fire that clawed its way through the cellar door to fasten upon dry timbers and feed hungrily on old furniture in the rooms above. Not all the efforts of a band of hastily summoned firefighters could save it. From every window fierce red flags of fire waved jubilant banners as the house died in the flames. Dry weather and the incidence of accumulated rubbish everywhere only added to the size and ferocity of the conflagration; by the time the villagers and tenants from Westhaven and Bellminster estates came crowding to look, the whole place was a massive bonfire, and the blaze could be seen far out to sea, toward the French coast, like a blazing beacon.

The crowds watched and murmured, keeping their distance from the heat and flying sparks, saying that no doubt tinkers and gypsies had been living there and were responsible for the night's mischief. It gave them an hour's excitement to watch the spectacle of a gentleman's house being reduced to ashes. It made a change from speculating in smoky inns and at hearthfires as to the possibility of England being invaded by the Frenchies, discussing the expected arrival date of the next consignment of spies and contraband from across the Channel, or asking one another whether or not the soldiers would ever catch the man who had murdered an old woman and made law-abiding people afraid to sleep in their beds at night.

Quinn came late to the scene. He had seen the glow from far inland, where he had ridden Kalidas hard, circling endlessly over the same ground, calling Luella's name.

He dismounted, tethered Kalidas well back from the crowd, and walked toward the house. The groups of people, recognizing the master of Westhaven, moved back respectfully to let him through.

"Was there anyone inside the house when the fire started?" Quinn demanded.

"We don't rightly know, sir." It was a tenant from one of the Bellminster cottages who answered him, a small, bent, middle-aged man. "I did 'ear that Jack Dowsett picked up a lady's shoe in the stable yard."

"Where is Dowsett?" Quinn demanded sharply. Without waiting for an answer, he strode past them all, around to the stable yard that was clearly lit by the raging fire.

He called the man's name loudly, and eventually Jack Dowsett appeared, basking in the attention he was receiving because he had found something the master of Westhaven considered to be important.

Quinn almost snatched the shoe from him, snapping question after question at the man as he examined it. It was a stout leather walking shoe with a silver buckle upon it, the kind women wore for walking out-of-doors, firm and well made to withstand the rigors of stony paths.

There was nothing to prove that it was Marianne's shoe, he told himself, nothing to state that this was the shoe that Luella had worn when she left Westhaven that morning.

Holding it tightly in his hands, he walked back to where Kalidas stood, restless, pawing the ground. The three men who had been sent to search the beach came back and spoke to him.

"No, sir; nothing. No sign; but the tide is in . . ."

The man who had spoken, paused; they were remembering the night they had searched for the girl who was to have been the future mistress of Westhaven.

"Very well," Quinn said wearily. "Go back to the house. You will search the beach again at first light."

What would they find, he wondered, in sudden agony? Nothing. He was a fool. He, who had so lately mourned the death of one girl, to be now so shaken by the disappearance of another: Luella March, an odd, fey little creature, a blend of innocence and shrewdness, so different, so alien in every way from Marianne; aloof and lonely, with a quick tongue and a mind of her own, an air of independence, a tough spirit that had survived months of ill treatment . . .

He swore loudly and furiously. Still clutching the shoe, he mounted Kalidas and rode hard back to Westhaven, telling himself, with conviction, that Luella March had simply run away, eager to see London, and unwilling to remain a captive to his grandmother in the house by the sea.

He didn't believe it; he believed she had died in the inferno of the blazing house, and the thought roused a storm of anger and despair within him that stunned him by its ferocity.

CHAPTER 7

Quinn sat staring into the heart of the fire, his thoughts turbulent. He had eaten little, fending off the chill in his veins with brandy. He was not a man used to inaction; the thought that Luella might have died in the fire at Dunbury was an agonizing one, and there was nothing he could do, at the moment, to avenge whoever was responsible. He felt as though a chill wind blew desolately over his heart. A ragged little mermaid, combing out her golden tresses in the morning sun, had come into his life unexpectedly, and gone again as suddenly . . .

He was startled when a sleepy manservant announced the arrival of Simon Corbie.

Simon swept into the room, his face pale and strained, his whole manner nervous and agitated.

"I found Luella March on the footpath almost outside Bellminster gates," he declared brusquely.

Quinn drew a deep breath. He sprang to his feet, composing himself with a superhuman effort.

"Is she—alive?" he asked.

"Just. I took her in. Nanny has put her to bed. She appears to have had some kind of shock and also to be suffering from exposure."

"I will ride back with you," Quinn said quietly. A huge wave of thankfulness rose and broke within him.

"What was she doing abroad at such an hour?" Simon demanded curtly.

"My grandmother told her she might have the day to herself. Apparently she went over the moors; no doubt she enjoyed both the freedom and the fresh air."

"This morning I met her on the beach. You should take

better care of her, Quinn, and see that she does not wander from Westhaven. These are strange times, as you know."

Quinn made no reply; he was already calling for his horse to be saddled. Simon followed him from the room, deep in thought.

Nanny padded into the room where Luella lay shivering in spite of the fire's warmth. When Luella saw Quinn bending over her, a vague flicker of recognition lit her eyes for a moment and then was gone. She stared at him vacantly.

"Dead," she whispered, her eyes going fearfully around the room. "Shot . . . Tom Hines . . . the man in the cellar shot him because I was not the person he wanted me to be . . . *dead* . . . and burned in the fire . . . I *cannot* bear it! . . ."

The words came like beads scattered from a broken string. She was in a state of shock, shivering violently.

Luella's face was like marble. She looked beseechingly at Quinn, as though asking him to take the nightmare from her, and her limbs jerked convulsively as she whispered the word "dead" over and over again.

"Send for the physician," Quinn ordered Nanny in a loud voice.

"At this hour, Master Quinn?" she cried, outraged. "He'll not come!"

"He will—if I have to ride over and drag him from his bed!" shouted Quinn furiously.

Nanny shrugged philosophically and shuffled off in search of one of the two menservants who comprised Simon's entire staff.

"Are you not being overzealous on Luella's behalf?" Simon demanded sharply. "Little ails her beyond exhaustion."

"She is deeply shocked. I wish to know the extent of the damage to her mind. If her presence causes you inconvenience, then I will see you are repaid for your trouble," Quinn replied sharply.

"My dear fellow, she is welcome to my inadequate hospitality," Simon answered smoothly. "If I have given the impression that she is unwelcome, I apologize."

Quinn was silent. When Nanny returned with the news that one of the servants had ridden for the physician, Simon suggested to Quinn that they should repair to the study to seek refreshment.

He clattered noisily down the stairs ahead of Quinn, talking loudly, while one of the doors on the floor above opened a fraction and a silent watcher applied both eye and ear to the crack.

The top floor of the house was unused; Nanny never climbed the stairs to it, for they were too steep for her stiff old legs.

Simon took Quinn to the study and blew on the dying fire with a pair of bellows. Quinn thought how dusty and neglected the room seemed.

"Well!" said Simon, rubbing his hands briskly together, "Luella certainly tells a strange tale! Someone killed Tom Hines and fired the cellar. She seems to have escaped by a miracle!"

Quinn was silent, reluctant to divulge details of the task on which he was engaged. Simon added casually, "It appears, from what Luella said, that she was mistaken for someone else. She wears Marianne's clothes, does she not? Then could her attacker believe she *is* Marianne?"

Quinn stared at him in astonishment.

"Marianne has been dead these many weeks!"

"True enough. I saw her in her coffin—I attended her funeral," Simon agreed. "Yet it *could* be that the man who attacked Luella was unaware that she is dead."

"Even supposing you are right, why should he wish to attack Marianne?" Quinn demanded.

"*I* cannot answer that question; perhaps *you* can," Simon replied.

Quinn shook his head. The idea seemed preposterous; what information could Marianne have possessed that a man might need so badly that he was prepared to kill for it?

"Or could it be that Dunbury is haunted by Mrs. Cazelet's ghost?" Simon said casually.

"*Ghost?* Is she, then, also dead?" Quinn asked.

"How should I know?" Simon countered quickly. "One

assumes things, my dear Quinn, in the absence of facts. The lady left Dunbury very suddenly. Marianne was constantly in her company—much to your grandmother's annoyance, for she did not like Marianne to be far from her side. It is rather like the games of blind man's bluff that we enjoyed as children."

"A much more deadly game," Quinn commented dryly.

Dr. Curtiss arrived, grumbling and cursing at being prised from his bed at such an hour; however, he examined Luella painstakingly and pronounced that she was in a state of considerable shock.

"She is young and resilient," he said. "I do not think there is permanent injury to her mind from her experiences, but she needs rest. She should not be moved for several days."

Simon stifled his dismay and fury.

"Naturally, she will remain under my roof until she is fit to return to Westhaven," he assured Quinn.

"I will send a servant from Westhaven to assist Nanny in her task," Quinn said.

"Certainly not!" Simon said swiftly. "Nanny would resent the suggestion that she needs help!"

Quinn looked at Luella before he left. Dr. Curtiss had given her a sedative, and she was sleeping, but she still moved uneasily and jerkily as though she relived, in all its detail, the horrors of the time she had spent in the cellar at Dunbury.

When he rode home to Westhaven, he told his grandmother only that Luella had lost her way on the moors and had been found exhausted, and suffering from exposure, at the gates of Bellminster, where she would stay and rest for a time.

Quinn told Mary the same story; she received it with disinterest.

After he had breakfasted, later that morning, Quinn rode over to Dunbury; the place looked eerie and forlorn, a blackened and disfigured shell, with plumes of smoke still mounting lazily on the morning air.

Quinn questioned the grimed and weary men who were still working to kill the last vestiges of the fire; he was told that a body, charred beyond recognition, had been found in the cellar of the house.

He rode on to the cottage in the clearing and whistled for Shep Tulley. The old man appeared at the door, bleary-eyed and blinking in the sunlight; it was obvious how he had spent most of the money Quinn had given him.

"Where is Tom Hines?" Quinn cried.

"I dunno, Mister Mallory. All I know is 'e bain't been 'ome all night," Shep retorted, surly at the loss of the two guineas he would have received for producing his cousin.

Quinn did not wish it known that he was aware of Tom Hines's death. He merely said, "Perhaps he has met with an accident?"

"Like as not," Shep replied indifferently.

Quinn hid his bitter disappointment. Tom Hines could have led him straight to Parnall, he reflected.

He took the sketch from his pocket and held it out for that the old man to see.

"Look at that, Shep Tulley!"

"For why? I seed it yesterday," Shep grumbled.

"Look again—so you'll know the face next time you see it in Dorchester! Watch for this man, and tell no one. If you breathe a word to a soul, Shep, I'll see that you hang from the gibbet at the crossroads! Find the man, and I'll give you, not two golden guineas, but *ten*! He *must* be found—and *soon*!"

Shep looked at him in astonishment. He knew that Quinn was neither mad nor drunk and that he was a man of his word. His eyes glittered; *ten* gold coins? It was more wealth than he'd ever had at one time in his whole life.

"I'll look out for 'im, mister," he promised.

Quinn rode to Dorchester jail after he had seen Shep. The governor, recovered from his chill, was up and about again.

He was a small, harassed man who complained bitterly of the conditions under which he was expected to work. There was unrest among the prison officers, he declared,

due to the overcrowding caused by having a high propor-
tion of French prisoners. Indeed, he added acidly, it was
almost a relief when some of the prisoners escaped, for it
eased the situation—until the arrival of a new batch.

"They should be taken inland, away from the coast," the
governor said wearily. "For we are too near the sea here.
'Tis easy enough to get them across the Channel. There's
plenty here who'll pay well for the service, and traitors
aplenty on the outside who'll take the money for the journey—why, they're touting for custom, you might say!
Those same boats that take the Frenchies home come back
loaded with spies and contraband. What a flouting of the
law! What a mock of those who administer it! Now, sir,
what can I do to assist you?"

"I wish to see the records of all your prisoners," Quinn
said calmly.

The governor's eyebrows rose, though he said nothing.
He offered the services of a clerk, pointing out that Quinn
had a mammoth task ahead of him.

So far as Quinn was concerned, it was a monotonous
task, and one he could not hope to complete in a day. The
report yielded little of help or interest—until he came to
the papers concerning Philip Janson.

Philip Janson's arrest had followed the receipt of a note
handed in to the officer on the gate one evening. The note
stated that Janson was a French spy, wanted also for smuggling valuable jewelry into the country.

The note that had been handed in was attached to Janson's papers; Quinn studied it thoughtfully. The printing
was educated and legible, the paper of good quality, and
there was neither address nor signature.

Quinn sent at once for the man on duty who had accepted the note.

"The note was handed in by a lady, sir," the man told
him.

Quinn's eyebrows rose sharply.

"A *lady*?"

"Yes, sir; at about eight o'clock one evening, a few
weeks ago now. I can't recall the exact date."

Quinn checked the report. The date was late in August.

"What did the lady say when she handed you the note?" Quinn demanded.

"Nothing, sir. Never a word. Just passed it to me and went on her way."

"Was she alone?"

"So far as I could see, there was no one with her, nor did she come in any kind of conveyance."

"At that time of night, it would have been light enough for you to have seen her face. What did she look like?"

The man smiled faintly.

"*Seen* her, sir? Not likely. In black, she was, from head to toe, and with a thick veil over her face."

Quinn hid his astonishment, remembering what Sir Julius had told him: that a note had been handed in by a woman dressed in black, and veiled, stating that a criminal named Jackson Parnall would board a coach for London at a certain time.

Parnall had not boarded the coach, nor been found. The woman who had handed in the note had not spoken on either occasion; was she afraid her voice would betray her?

Quinn dismissed the man and sent the clerk in search of the note that contained the accusations about Parnall.

The clerk brought the note to him. It was attached to a brief report, penned in neat copperplate, stating that the allegations contained in the note had been investigated but that no trace of the man named had been found, though both coaches leaving for London on the day in question had been searched.

Quinn put the two notes side by side and studied them carefully. They were identical.

He questioned the officer again, painstakingly. Had the bearer of the note been short or tall? Fat or thin? Did she walk like a young woman or an old one?

Oh, she was fairly tall. Thin? Ah, who could say, in these days, when concealing cloaks were so fashionable? One thing the man was insistent upon: she had walked upright, not bent and slow.

Quinn remarked on the fact that Janson had been kept in jail merely on the evidence of an unsigned note; the governor replied resignedly that they lived in strange and difficult times, and were dealing with traffic in human lives between countries at war. Janson had made matters difficult for himself by refusing to say where he came from or where his relatives lived. His behavior had cast grave doubts upon his innocence. Again, Janson had made a daring escape, after being a difficult and troublesome prisoner. As to the murder, he had been seen near the house of the old woman who had been killed; what more conclusive evidence of his guilt could there be?

It was all too neat, Quinn thought, reflecting on the governor's indictment. He turned it over in his mind while he dined alone in Dorchester.

After he had eaten, he rode with all speed to Bellminster. Simon was out. Nanny took him to see Luella; to his surprise, she fitted a key into the lock on the bedroom door.

"Why is she locked in her room?" he demanded angrily.

The old woman blinked at him from tired, rheumy eyes. "Master Simon's orders. I haven't eyes in the back of my head, Master Quinn, and the young lady is strange—she is not herself. If she was to get out of bed and wander about and fall down the stairs, where 'ud we be, then, eh?"

"It is unnecessary!" Quinn retorted curtly.

Nanny shrugged and muttered that he should take up the matter with the master of the house.

Luella lay propped against the pillows, golden hair spread over her shoulders. She seemed immeasurably weary, drained of all vitality.

Quinn looked down at her with concern, and she thought how much younger he seemed than the grim-faced man who had swept her so unceremoniously into Westhaven, such a little while ago. There was no arrogance in the handsome face, only anxiety. The lines of his mouth were softened and relaxed. He looked splendid in his leather boots and caped coat, the sun shining on his crisp, curling hair. There was a tremendous magnetism, for her, in the broad, muscular shoulders, the set of his head, the narrow hips, and air of whipcord strength, controlled but powerful. A man who would love a woman as fiercely and ardently as he fought for a cause; a man with a rapier wit, quick

142

humor, sudden, savage gusts of anger, gone as quickly as they had come.

Unthinkingly, Luella put out a hand, the first spontaneous gesture she had made toward him.

Gently he took her small hand between his, holding it captive.

"Well, Luella—are you recovered?"

"I am much better," she said gravely, but the horror of what had happened lay at the front of her mind, still, and her eyes filled with tears.

"I never before saw a man shot," she whispered.

He gently disengaged her hand. Then he drew up a chair and sat down beside the bed, taking her hand in his again, looking at her with a compassion that was something new to Luella.

"You need not speak of it if it distresses you," he said gravely.

"I would *like* to tell you about it, Mr. Mallory," she insisted.

"Quinn," he corrected softly, and when she did not reply, he spoke his name again.

"Quinn," he said. "You say it, Luella."

"Quinn."

"That sounds much better," he told her. "You have had an unhappy experience. In time, the memory of it will go away, as a nightmare vanishes at daybreak."

"I have remembered many unhappy things," she told him, with a frown. "At school, I felt a strange loneliness deep inside me. I felt prisoned. I was not free, as I long to be free, to run over the moors."

Suddenly, she touched her neck and her frown deepened.

"My locket! I wore it always . . ."

"Do you not remember?" His eyes held hers. "It was— broken. I shall have it repaired for you. When this sorry business is over and done with, then I will take you to London town and we shall see if we can trace your parents, with the help of the locket. That is a promise I make you for the future."

She was silent, remembering how the locket had been

143

broken. Color filled her cheeks and she looked away from him.

"No one shall harm you, Luella," he told her quietly. "Do you remember you once told me you were a witch?"

She nodded.

"It was very wicked of me to wish Henrietta dead," she replied ruefully.

"It was understandable, but you had nothing to do with her death. Such things are not in our hands."

"Then I am *not* a witch?" she asked sadly, and his lips twitched.

"In that sense—no."

"I do not understand you."

"When you are older you will understand what kind of witch you are. You will one day be a very attractive woman."

"I feared Henrietta," she admitted. "I feared her cane and the pain it could inflict, but I would not tell her that; to acknowledge fear is to admit to its power over oneself."

"Luella, you are but sixteen . . ."

"Almost seventeen!" she cried.

"As you will. Almost seventeen. There are many days of freedom and happiness ahead of you."

"*Yesterday* was a happy day," she said reminiscently. "I was alone and free as a wild bird. I went to the shore; I saw Mr. Corbie there and he walked with me; then I went over the moors. I did not think about the *time*!" she whispered. "Always, before, I have had to think: it is time I did this, I did that. Yesterday, I did not care!"

"Were you not hungry?" he asked gently. "You were out all day in the fresh air."

"I began to feel hungry as I was walking back, and then I came to Dunbury . . ."

Her mouth trembled. He touched it gently, to stop the quivering of her lips.

"Hush! Dr. Curtiss says you must not trouble your mind with such things!" he said softly.

"I shall no longer be troubled if I tell them to you," she answered. "For when I have said it all, it will be like opening a cage to let a wild bird fly out."

144

He was deeply moved and felt a fierce protective instinct rise up within him. This child needed his protection. He did not feel a man's love for a woman for *her*, he told himself; his action in trying to take her by force shamed him. He wanted to make her laugh, teach her to be young and happy, spoil her, take care of her.

However, there were other things to be done before he could allow his thoughts and feelings a free rein; he listened carefully while Luella told him, slowly and haltingly, of all that happened to her on the previous evening.

"You showed great courage in escaping as you did," he told her. "You must not grieve that you had to leave Tom Hines lying there; he was dead, beyond all hope of help. You could do nothing for him."

He reached into the deep, inner pocket of his coat and took out a sketch.

"Look at this, Luella. Is *this* the man you saw in the cellar? The one who shot Tom Hines?"

She blinked at it, uncertainly, then nodded.

"Yes. Yes, I am sure of it. Who is he?"

"He is a man I am commanded to find and bring to justice. Would that *I* had been in that cellar!" Quinn said yearningly.

She shivered, looking at him with enormous green eyes.

"There is something else that I have not told you," she admitted.

"What is it? You do not need to fear me," he said gently. "Is it something you have done?"

She shook her head.

"I promised him I would not speak of it to anyone . . . but perhaps it will not matter now," she said. "For I do not know where he has gone; I only remember that he was kind to me, that night . . . he had escaped from Dorchester jail."

He listened as she pieced the story together, telling him anxiously that she did not believe him to be a man who had committed a murder.

"Did he tell you his name, Luella?"

"No," she said.

"Can you describe him? Are you too tired to go over the tale once again, for me?" he queried.

She smiled and shook her head. This man, Quinn Mallory, was kind, kinder even than the fugitive on the moors had been, and there was nothing she would not do for him. How strange that she had ever thought him formidable!

The memory of the night he had tried to take her came back, and yet . . . and *yet*, she thought, though I was afraid and angry, some memory of sweetness and longing remains, so deep inside me that it will never go free, as the bird from the cage is free.

"Why did you not tell me this before?" Quinn asked her, when she had finished telling her tale for the second time.

She hesitated.

"I did not want him to be caught," she said finally.

He felt a flicker of jealousy, swift as a flicker of summer lightning, gone within seconds, surprising him.

"He has probably returned to France," he told her brusquely.

"Is he a spy, then?"

"I cannot say. I do not know yet."

"You think that he may be?" she asked sadly.

He evaded the question, saying, "I have persuaded you to talk at great length, and Nanny will not allow me to see you again!"

"I shouldn't like that!" she said, quickly, and added, "I wish to return to Westhaven."

"So you shall, when you are strong enough; it must be done secretly, so that I can keep you hidden until the criminal is caught. It is not so long since you wanted to leave Westhaven and go to London to seek your fortune!"

She saw that he was teasing. He stood at the foot of the bed, and the mischief in his eyes gave him a boyish charm that made him seem as young as she was.

When Luella was silent, he asked lightly; "Can it be that you do not now wish to leave us?"

She nodded, half-smiled, and closed her eyes; she was almost asleep by the time he left the room. At the door, he paused for a last backward glance at the small figure in the big bed.

He knew that she would no longer be troubled by the nightmares that had bedeviled her.

Quinn had much to think on as he rode to Westhaven; he went by way of the shortcut through the cemetery, but this time he did not ride through on horseback as he had done in the past, to tease the rector. He dismounted and led Kalidas past the quiet gravestones, moss-encrusted and ivy-ribboned, nestling in grasses that sighed in the wind from the sea.

He stopped by Marianne's grave and stared at the inscription: "Whom the sea took from us." Below the inscription, someone had placed a fresh posy of late flowers.

He wondered who had put the flowers there. His thoughts went back down the years to a younger Marianne, still a child when *he* had grown to be an adult, for he was ten years older than the girl who had died. He remembered half a dozen of her youthful escapades, and the wind echoed his sigh.

Suddenly aware that he was not alone in the cemetery, he turned sharply and was just in time to see a veiled, black-clad figure move from beneath the church porch into the church itself.

A woman. Watching him, yet not wanting to be seen. Mrs. Cazelet, perhaps! Quinn frowned; *he* believed she had never left Dunbury alive, but he could not be sure.

Quinn walked to the gate and tethered his horse; then he returned to the cemetery, threading his way between the humps of the graves to the church door.

He hesitated for a moment before lifting the heavy iron latch. The wooden door, old and scarred, creaked its soft protest at being disturbed for the second time in such a short while, and Quinn knew that whoever was in the church must have heard the sound of the opening door.

Quinn stepped over the worn stone flags and looked down the long rows of oaken pews, each with the carving of an apostle at its end; past the polished brass candleholders to the simple stone altar, with its cross and candlesticks; and up the the great east window with the Crucifixion scene painted in tapestry-rich colors that the fading sun of an autumn afternoon repeated in splashes of vivid red and blue all over the cold stones.

He looked at it all for a moment, savoring its peace and beauty, setting it, in his mind, against the horror, the filth, the bestiality he had seen during the past months. Then he stared gravely at the solitary figure kneeling in one of the front pews, head bowed, hands clasped, clad in funereal black, from the velvet bonnet with its thick, face-concealing veil to the matching cloak of black velvet tied with ribbons of the neck. Even the plumes that quivered slightly on the bonnet were of the same somber black.

The figure knelt unmoving, head bowed. Quinn withdrew to the porch and sat on the worn, stone seat, waiting; there was no other exit by which the woman could escape.

After he had waited what seemed to him a considerable time, the door creaked softly open. The woman came out cautiously, and seeing Quinn, tried to withdraw, but he grasped her wrist firmly.

"I should like to talk to you," he said firmly, indicating the seat on which he had been sitting.

"Oh, Quinn!" said Mary's voice, angry and despairing.

Astonished, disappointed, he lifted the veil in one quick movement that she could not forestall. Her face, blotched and tear-stained, looked back at him. Her eyes were red-rimmed, and she was a sorry sight.

"What are you doing here?" he demanded.

She pulled free of his hand and dropped the veil over her face again.

"That is my affair!" she said angrily.

"Sit down!" he commanded.

Reluctantly, she obeyed, sitting stiffly upright, gloved hands in her lap, staring straight ahead of her.

He sat beside her and said bluntly, "You have not been inside a church since your illness; you swore never to go inside one again after you had the pox. I know there has been little understanding between us, we are so different, you and I, but . . ."

"Yes, Quinn, we *are* different—*you* are arrogant," she interrupted.

"You have your share of arrogance; remember I am

master of Westhaven, responsible for many people, for farms, cottages, land. I am the local magistrate. I have also been entrusted with difficult and dangerous missions across the Channel. Meekness and humility do not sit well upon a man engaged in such activities."

She sighed and said bitterly, "We used to talk together when we were young. Now it is all changed."

"Because you have become embittered."

"Have I not cause enough to be bitter?"

"Learn to live with your scars. Look into your mirror each day and tell yourself that those who care most for you notice least the ravages of illness and time. You are a woman in mourning; *what* is it you mourn so deeply? The loss of a little of your beauty? Your eyes, your voice, the shape of your features, the presence we all know—these things remain the same, and are still loved!"

She was silent; Quinn had never spoken to her in such a manner before. Something had happened to change him, under all that arrogance of his, she thought.

His words lay in her mind like stones dropped into a deep pool. She was reflecting on them when Quinn added, "When I first saw you here, I thought you must be Mrs. Cazelet; you are dressed like her."

She looked startled.

"She has been gone for many weeks!" she pointed out.

"Did you know her, Mary?"

"No. She disliked any contact with people. She entertained no visitors—save Marianne—and turned her head away when addressed out of doors. She was a strange woman. Once I saw her in the market at Axminster, looking for all the world as though she was watching for someone—though I could not see her face."

"Why did Marianne visit her so often?"

"I daresay she saw herself as the privileged visitor, the only one to penetrate the fortress of Dunbury!" Mary retorted scathingly.

"Why do you hate Marianne?" Quinn demanded, and when she would not reply, he pressed the question upon her again.

"Because she was beautiful and everyone sang her praises!" Mary retorted at last, with bitter reluctance.

"Was there any other reason than that?"

She looked at him fiercely.

"*No!*"

"You lie, Mary; you never *could* lie to me. Your whole manner always betrayed you—remember?"

"Very well, then!" He voice was still low and fierce. "I will tell you, but you will not like what you hear! Philip Janson was infatuated with Marianne, and she basked in his admiration like a cat sunning itself. They say he is a French spy and has murdered an old woman! It is not true. It is *not*!"

He saw the tears running down her cheeks.

"You were in love with him," he said quietly.

"Yes, Quinn! And still am! Though he never showed anything but friendship and kindness to me. I love him with all my heart and soul. He was a gentleman!"

"A gentleman can still be a murderer," he replied crisply.

"I will never believe that *he* is a murderer! Oh, God, that I knew what had happened to him. . . . I am sure he is dead and I shall never see him again!"

She put her hands to her face, and Quinn made a sudden decision.

"If I have your word that you will not repeat what I say, I will tell you something," he said.

She nodded, astonished, and listened while he repeated what Luella had said. He saw, with pity, the flicker of hope in her eyes.

"My prayers are answered!" she whispered. "I believed that Philip was taken as retribution for my hatred of Marianne!"

"Is that why you put flowers on her grave?" he asked, and she nodded, shamefaced.

Silently, they left the porch; Mary was trembling and glad of Quinn's arm. He unhitched Kalidas, and together they walked back to Westhaven, closer to one another in spirit than they had been for many a long day.

* * *

The events that had been set in motion with the betrayal of Eleanor La Vanne in a derelict farm in northern France were moving slowly but surely toward their appointed end as the tinkers foregathered under the shadow of Tarberry Hill, at Horcastle, for the last of the annual fairs held in the western counties.

. Their wagons were within sight of one of the charity schools that were the subject of argument and speculation among those who could afford to have their children expensively educated; it was the school in which Luella March had spent the greater part of her life.

Three days within the boundaries of any parish was all the tinkers were allowed; after that, they would be sent remorselessly on their way again. For them, it was a brief respite at a time when the weather was cold and sullen rain fell relentlessly, turning the waste ground on which their wagons were parked into a sea of mud.

There was not much comfort to be had, even in the shelter of the wagons, but they were not used to comfort and so they were cheerful. Winter did not last forever, they reminded one another; spring came, and—with luck—summer, with the country fairs, and housewives eager to have their old pots and pans mended (if they could not afford new ones), and newlywed girls willing to buy bits and pieces for their freshly cleaned kitchens. Ah, it was not such a bad life, when the sun shone and people spent money, the tinkers said.

Philip Janson sat on a makeshift bed in the back of the wagon in which Seth and Kyra and their two children lived. His quarters were cramped and lacked any kind of privacy, but he knew very well the size of his debt of gratitude to the woman who squatted on her heels in front of him, rearranging the thin blankets with grimy hands and looking anxiously at him.

She had saved his life, nursed him through the delirium of high fever, dressed his wound, fed him when he was weak and in pain.

The wound had been a deep and jagged one; now it was

clean and almost healed, thanks to Kyra's secret remedies. Even the clothes he wore had been given to him; they were rougher and coarser than anything he had worn in his life before, but he had been glad enough of them. There were days when his body had seemed to be afire, other days when he had been drenched with sweat, shivering uncontrollably, cursing fate and crying that the Flowers of Darkness should have been fashioned as a gift for Lucifer's bride. . . .

Kyra had listened, marveling at the fine flow of language, understanding little of it, while her husband, grumbling furiously, had taken the wide-eyed children from the wagon. . . .

Now, in response to his request, she handed Philip his own clothes. The blood and dirt had been washed from them and they were neatly mended.

"Thank you," he said, and he unfastened the leather belt that he had been wearing when Kyra first saw him.

He looked at the prematurely aged face, careworn, only the eyes still bright and full of humor. He saw the thin shoulders move beneath the patched old dress she wore, and smiling, he found the secret compartment cunningly concealed on the inside of the belt.

" 'Tis all right, mister," she said dryly. "*I* found the secret purse that's inside the belt, long since. There ain't no secrets like that *us* don't know on, but we steal naught from those we shelter."

From the belt he took ten golden guineas, the same amount Quinn had promised Shep Tulley if he found Parnall, though Philip did not know that.

Gravely, he counted out nine of the guineas, and taking Kyra's hand from the blankets she was tidying, turned it palm upwards and laid the coins upon it.

"Take them," he said. "You have earned every one. I am not a poor man. One day our paths may cross again, and I will repay you much more than this; but for *you*, I would have been dead or recaptured long since."

She looked at the money with respect; she had never held so much in her hand before. It would clothe them all

152

and put food in their bellies for the long cold weeks ahead; it would effectively silence Seth's grumbles about the cost of caring for a stranger and the risks they had run.

Philip saw her look of gratitude. His present plight was the result of his own folly, he reminded himself bitterly. It was knowledge that he must live with forever, that would harm others as well as himself.

"I have kept one sovereign for myself," he told Kyra, "to take me on my way."

"Where 'ull 'ee go?" she asked fearfully.

"Seaward; to Dorset."

"Ah, not back there!" She shook her head vehemently. "They'll get 'ee, for sure!"

"No," he argued, with more confidence than he felt. "They will have called off the search by this time!"

"Not *they*, mister! They never lets go. Like leeches, they be!"

"Nevertheless, I *must* go; I have business to attend to."

She shook her head sadly, knowing that his decision was part of the strange things he had muttered in his delirium.

"Thee's still as weak as a babby," she insisted. "Get some strength in 'ee first."

"I am well enough, and the matter is one of great urgency."

"Thee's a spy for the Frenchies; is that so, mister?" she asked flatly.

He shook his head.

"No, I am not," he told her positively.

"There's French blood in 'ee," she retorted.

"How do you know that?"

"I ain't *sure* it be French," she admitted, "but it weren't in English, not what 'ee shouted aloud in the fever."

He did not reply. She shrugged and closed her thin fingers tightly over the precious coins. The rain sounded like a great sighing of seas on a lonely shore as Philip sat and made his plans.

Two days later, when the rains had stopped, he left the encampment and turned his face toward the sea.

The world is not a kindly place when you stand alone,

with your face to the sea and the open countryside at your
back, like a hunted stag.

He remembered that he had said those words to a skinny little waif who had bandaged his leg and eaten his food. He wondered how she had fared and whether she had found work at Westhaven.

CHAPTER 8

It was a novel experience for Luella to be waited upon; she was dismayed, however, to find that the door of her room was kept locked, making her feel like a prisoner.

When she questioned Simon, he was soothing.

"You have been most unwell," he told her. "Your mind had been upset by the shock you sustained. You might have had nightmares or frightening dreams, and wandered in your sleep, perhaps injuring yourself."

She looked at him steadily.

"I have had no nightmares, Mr. Corbie."

His eyes avoided the challenge of her glance.

"Nanny is old; it was she who made the request," he said placatingly. "You will be returning to Westhaven soon; you must not fret so about such a small matter!"

He gave her his charming smile and went on his way, while she puzzled over his words. Nanny was kind in her slipshod, grumbling way. Simon did not seem to be in the house very often, and once or twice Luella thought she heard him leaving Bellminster late at night, but she could not investigate, because the door remained locked.

She disliked Bellminster. Something about the place chilled and dismayed her. She was eager to leave, but Dr. Curtiss, in his ponderous way, insisted that she should not do so for two or three days.

Her presence was a confounded nuisance, Simon thought; if he did not ensure that her door was locked, Luella March might take it into her head to leave the room and wander about the house. Such a risk was unthinkable!

He rode over to Westhaven and talked to Quinn.

"Have you discovered the identity of Luella's attacker?" he asked.

"I think I know the identity of the man," Quinn replied guardedly.

"*Was* it Janson?"

"No," said Quinn.

"Do you think you will find the man?" Simon asked casually.

"I shall endeavor to see he is brought to justice," Quinn replied.

Quinn was being his most formal self, giving away nothing, Simon thought, exasperated. If only he knew how much Quinn Mallory had discovered since his return to Westhaven!

Simon had no doubt that Parnall had attacked Luella, which meant he was still in the neighborhood . . . waiting—and dangerous. He wished he had never got mixed up in the whole business; the glittering prize he had been promised, an end to all his financial embarrassments and the key to the door of a luxurious life, had never seemed so far away.

"Well, I wish you success in your pursuit of the criminal!" Simon told Quinn lightly. "As for Luella, she continues to make progress. Dr. Curtiss is hopeful that she will be back with you in a day or so."

Quinn frowned at him.

"Does Nanny still lock the door of her room?" he asked.

"I am afraid so. She is old and obstinate and persists in thinking that Luella may wander off and come to harm if she is not so protected."

"Absolute nonsense!" said Quinn arrogantly. "You will please tell her to leave the door unlocked. To a girl of Luella's temperament, imprisonment is frightening."

"Come, Quinn! It can scarcely be called imprisonment!" Simon protested.

"Nevertheless, I do not wish her to be shut in," Quinn retorted.

"I do not like this house," Luella told Quinn when he called to see her.

156

"It is shabby and neglected. It lacks servants to keep it in good heart. Simon has never realized that land is a proud heritage, Luella. A trust. To be cared for and well husbanded. I do not like the drift away from the land that is taking place these days."

"If you say I am to stay here, then I suppose I must do so," she said, sighing.

"It is only your safety that I have in mind," he pointed out.

She looked at him coquettishly from beneath her lashes.

"Is that important to you?" she asked, with pretended innocence.

He laughed delighted.

"So you are learning to flirt, Luella? You *are* growing up quickly! Yesterday, a child; today, a young woman!"

His words pleased her. She remembered the time he had told her the facts of life, and she blushed. There had been little significance in those facts when he had first given them to her; now she felt shy with him, without knowing why, and looked over the top of his head.

He reached in his pocket and drew out something that gleamed in the pale afternoon sunlight. She saw that he dangled a fine gold chain from his fingertips, at the end of which hung her locket.

"It is mended!" she cried delightedly.

"Indeed it is. I brought it from Dorchester this morning," he told her. "Let me put it around your neck, where it belongs."

She bent her head, holding aside the heavy masses of golden hair with one hand. He leaned over her and fastened the locket on the nape of her neck. His fingers brushed the warm, soft skin. Something leaped wildly in his pulses. He loved this child, he told himself, as he would have loved a favorite daughter.

"There!" He watched her shake her hair into place again and lightly kissed her forehead as she lifted her face to express her thanks.

"No one ever kissed me before," she told him. "At least—"

She bit her lip, coloring furiously.

"Go on," he said calmly.

"You kissed me the night you came to my room," she whispered, "but it was angry and cruel and fierce. Not gentle like this."

"I should not have kissed you so," he agreed gently, his eyes never leaving her face. "It was the kiss of a man who desires to possess a woman's body. I explained that to you when I told you how children were conceived."

She said slowly, "You wanted me to be Marianne. You were unhappy, and I reminded you of Marianne. That is easy to understand."

"But you still prefer the kind of kiss I have just given you?" he suggested, watching her intently.

"Yes," she said.

"Well!" His voice was suddenly brisk. "I have work to do, Luella. I will return later."

Quinn rode over to Dunbury and searched the cellar from which the remains of Tom Hines had been removed. He found nothing. Systematically, he went through the whole house, to no effect. How unlike his missions to France, he thought dryly! There was no sense of high adventure in tracking down Parnall—it was monotonous, a painstaking business that needed patience rather than skill and cunning.

Late that afternoon he rode to the cottage in the clearing.

He was in luck. Shep had wasted no time; while Quinn had sat in the governor's office, patiently sifting information concerning Philip Janson and Parnall, Shep had been busy about his own business.

He grinned slyly at the man sitting so proudly astride the great, black horse.

"Give me ten golden guineas, Mister Mallory!" Shep demanded, his eyes gleaming.

"Why? Do you have the man I seek, trussed like a guinea fowl, waiting for me inside your cottage?" Quinn demanded, with a laugh.

Shep's eyes narrowed.

"I bain't. I seed him but once, talking to my cousin Tom,

like I said. Well, now, it bain't easy, for that's not much to go on, but I found out summat, and many a weary hour it's took me, Mister Mallory. The man you want is called Mr. Jackson, and it's by good fortune 'e's living in the same street where I saw 'im with Tom. They're saying poor Tom died in the fire at Dunbury . . ."

"Yes," interrupted Quinn impatiently. "What of this man Mr. Jackson?"

"Gentleman and scholar 'e calls 'imself, and 'e rents rooms at number seven Abbot Street. Well, now—where's ten guineas I were promised for me trouble?"

Quinn took five golden coins from his waistbelt and tossed them at the man's feet.

"Mr. Jackson is not yet in my hands," he said grimly. "When I have him, *you* shall have the remainder of your fee."

"Then I'll not tell 'ee what else I found out, mister!" Shep taunted.

Quinn looked at him with narrowed eyes. He knew Shep Tulley well enough to be aware that the man was not bluffing and had another piece of information to be bargained for.

"Does it concern Mr. Jackson?" Quinn wanted to know.

"It does," Shep said with relish.

Quinn tossed him another coin; Shep caught it adroitly. He stood licking his lips and smiling, as though enjoying the brief power over the man who paid him.

Quinn's lips twitched. He hid a smile; Shep was a wily old rogue, who had given him good service.

"Your information had better be worth my guinea," he said.

" 'Tis worth more, Mister Mallory."

"Damn you, I'm in a hell of a hurry! Come on, man."

" 'Tis to do with stuff that's landed along the coast."

"Contraband? That's a matter for the preventive officers!"

"Aye, and a right lot o' thickheads they be!" Shep jeered. "Outwitted every time, and serves 'em right. Can't catch 'em, can they? No wonder—they got all the dullards in the country wearin' the king's uniform these days!"

"Don't be too sure of that. Get to the point. How is Mr. Jackson concerned with all the silks and brandy, laces and tobacco that comes across the Channel?"

His voice was skeptical. Such work would be very inferior stuff for a man of Parnall's talents, he reflected.

Shep's voice dropped an octave; he moved closer to Kalidas, who showed the whites of his eyes and moved restively.

"Tain't the stuff itself. 'Tis what's been hidden inside. That's all Mr. Jackson's interested in, I'm told. The men that brings the stuff over and them that unloads it can share it out among theirselves, Mister Mallory, so long as Mr. Jackson gets the packet o' goods that's been taken from the aristos wot 'ave 'ad their 'eads cut off."

"Jewelry?" said Quinn sharply.

Shep nodded triumphantly.

"Aye. Worth a bit, see? I mean, they wouldn't be just strings o' beads and gewgaws like you'd get off the travelin' peddler, would they? Not when you thinks on 'ow rich them aristos was."

"Where did you get your information, Shep?"

The eyes were bright slits, almost sunk in the stubbled flesh of the cheeks.

"Thee knows better'n to ask *that*! Though I'll not deny Tom told me a deal. Until he got a wife, 'e made himself a tidy sum—*she* stopped 'im. I'm glad I never got wed; a man should be able to call his soul his own."

"Have *you* ever helped unload the stuff?"

"Chance 'ud be a fine thing! Those that divide it, sell it. Price they asks is too 'igh for me. I'm a poor man, Mister Mallory."

Shep looked hopeful; Quinn missed the look and said thoughtfully, "How long has this business been going on?"

"I dunno. As long as Mr. Jackson 'as been in Dorset, I suppose you could say."

"When and where do the boats come in?"

"Wherever they're told. Word's passed on."

"Do you know when the next consignment is due?"

"It just so happens that I do, Mister Mallory."

Quinn waited. The old man waited, too, his face baby-innocent, his hand held out. Resignedly, Quinn took another coin from his pocket.

"Damn you, Shep, you drive a hard bargain!"

"Next unloading, this day week, if the weather be reasonable," Shep said briskly.

"Where?"

"Sea cave, an hour from full tide."

"Will Mr. Jackson be there?"

"Can't say. Reckon so, if he wants 'is bits and pieces. The rest of it 'ull be shared out. I won't be there, Mister Mallory, not if *you're* expecting to pay 'em a visit, and I won't tell a soul, I promise 'ee."

Shep chuckled wickedly as the coin spun through the air toward him.

Quinn touched the horse's flanks, and the animal wheeled away as though glad to be gone from the cottage in the clearing.

Quinn rode to Dorchester in a thoughtful mood. Shep's words had given him a great deal to think over. It was a diabolically clever—and repulsive—plan to smuggle to England the possessions of men and women who had gone to the guillotine. Such a traffic would explain Parnall's continued presence in Dorset—except for the fact that he had a treasure worth a king's ransom and did not need to trade in jewelry of much lesser value.

At Dorchester, Quinn stabled Kalidas near Abbot Street, with instructions that the animal was to be fed and watered and cared for until his return.

Abbot Street was little more than a winding lane, old and dark, the houses huddled close together, giving it a secretive look. The sun scarcely shafted through the patched roofs, the cobbles were rough underfoot, and it was such a narrow street that no more than two people could walk comfortably abreast.

Apart from the houses, there were some shops and a few solicitors' offices with brass plates outside their doors.

Number seven was a house, high and narrow. Quinn rapped on the door, and it was answered by a small, scared-looking maid with hair sliding awry from beneath her grubby-looking cap.

She blinked at him like a sleepy owl. Quinn smiled at her, one hand fastening on the pistol he always carried on such missions. He desired, fervently, that there would be no bloodshed. Knowing Parnall's cunning and ruthlessness, however, and the prize at stake, he was not hopeful.

"I have called to see Mr. Jackson," Quinn said.

The maid shook her head, sending more tendrils of hair escaping from under her cap. She had big, mournful eyes and a permanent look of being chilled, as she rubbed her red hands together.

"Mr. Jackson's not here, sir," she said.

"Then I must wait until he returns," Quinn said crisply. "I have to see him on a matter of some urgency."

"Mr. Jackson won't be back, sir. Not an hour since, he came in, packed his luggage, paid a month's rent, and said he was getting the four o'clock coach to London."

Quinn consulted his timepiece; it was just three o'clock.

"Why was he in such a devil of a hurry?" he demanded.

"Oh, sir, I dunno!" She looked helpless in the face of the obvious anger of this big, dark-browed man.

"Where is your mistress?"

"Out, sir; gone for the day to Weymouth, to her sister. I dunno what she'll say when she comes back and finds Mr. Jackson gone."

Quinn took the sketch from his pocket.

"Is this Mr. Jackson?"

"Oh, yes, sir, 'tis indeed! Ever such a nice gentleman, quiet and polite and no trouble. 'E was out quite a lot, gathering information 'e said, for a book 'e was writing all about Dorset."

Quinn's lips twitched, but his humor was grim. He asked, curtly, if he might see Mr. Jackson's rooms, and reinforced his request with a coin that sent the maid scuttling up the narrow stairs ahead of him, holding her skirts in her hands, her hair bobbing wildly.

The house was old and smelled of stale food. The windows were all sealed, and there was no fresh air anywhere. The rooms that Mr. Jackson had occupied were as sparsely and austerely furnished as most furnished rooms. As Quinn had expected, they yielded not a clue to the man he sought.

He felt bitter disappointment as he went out again into the sunless street. Either Jackson Parnall had been warned, or the acute sixth sense that serves criminals equally as well as it serves honest men had been alerted.

He doubted very much that he would find Parnall anywhere in Dorchester; the maid had assured him that "Mr. Jackson" had very little luggage and had carried it himself. The inn from which the London coach left every day was only a few minutes' walk from Abbot Street.

Though he had little expectation of finding the man, Quinn skirted the inn cautiously, coming to it by the back entrance. In the big, cobbled yard at the front was the usual bustle of activity that preceded the departure of a coach: shouting ostlers; sweating porters; excited children jigging up and down; giggling young women, bonneted and furred against the chill of the day, clustered together in groups; old men, irascible and important; young men, pompous and preoccupied, busy with quantities of luggage, consulting their timepieces, making a great show of telling one another that the London coach was never known to be late in departing, and vying with each other in exchanging experiences of rides during the worst snowstorm, the fiercest thunderstorm, the most excruciating heat of all time. Inside the inn, the landlord was taking last orders for refreshment from those who were waiting for the coach to arrive, his raucous voice telling them that there was little time left, and a long road in front of them.

In the shadow of the thick stone walls, Quinn remained unmoving, all his six senses alert, and not one of them bringing back the message that "Mr. Jackson" was near at hand, waiting to board the coach.

With a great flourish of horns, a clatter of hooves, and the sound of wheels turning, the coach, freshly cleaned and well turned out, came from the stables, where the horses had been groomed and fed and watered. The groups broke up and re-formed as travelers exchanged good-byes with those who had come to see them on their way, some of them tearful, some of them ribald. The noise grew louder and the confusion greater, but no one remotely resembling the man he sought boarded the coach, though Quinn scrutinized each intending passenger with an eagle eye.

The luggage was loaded; the outside passengers clung like birds to their frail-looking perches and made jokes about the possibility of bad weather; the crack of a whip sang through the air, and the horses galloped forward, almost jerking the outside passengers from their seats; there was a flurry of waving hands from the window; good-byes were called from the occupants and from those who had come to see them go; the sound of the horn died on the afternoon air, the coach disappeared from view, and it was over.

Quinn, in a fury of anger and disappointment, went into the inn for refreshment and information, but no one had seen anyone resembling the sketch he produced.

He returned to the stables and mounted Kalidas. Riding home as though the devil were at his heels, he considered his next move. He was certain that Parnall was still somewhere in the vicinity. He also considered the possibility that the Flowers of Darkness had been left at a hiding place in France, to be smuggled back to England one by one, and over a considerable period of time.

Disappointment had wearied him. He swept through the gates of Westhaven and rode to the stables, where he dismounted and handed the horse over to the waiting groom. Once indoors, he went upstairs to the long gallery.

He looked at the portrait of Marianne and then turned his gaze seaward to the restless waves running for the shore like a little fleet of white-sailed ships. Marianne was lost to him forever; Luella had eased some of the loneliness and desolation of his homecoming, and now, suddenly, he wished that Luella were here waiting for him. He needed someone to talk to; he would be glad when Luella was well enough to come back to Westhaven.

Meanwhile, there was Mary, coming from the sea tower. She paused when she saw him, and then, to his surprise, she hesitantly lifted the concealing veil and let it lie back from her face.

"That is much better," he said gently. "You are still a handsome woman, Mary, even though you bear scars."

Her smile was as hesitant as her action had been. She said slowly, "I am not given to premonitions nor fancies, as you must well know, Quinn, but this strange feeling of hope persists within me. I believe that Philip Janson is safe, somewhere, and that his innocence will be proved."

"How can I quarrel with such convictions?" he asked wryly. "I hope, with all my heart, that you are right. Meanwhile, my search for the man who stole a queen's treasure continues without success. I confess I am a disappointed man."

Briefly, he told her of his search in Dorchester. She listened gravely.

"You believe, don't you, Quinn, that Parnall and Philip Janson are connected in some way? That their stories are intertwined, and that one holds the key to the actions of the other?" she said.

"That is true. I trust Janson's innocence will be proved, but until Parnall is caught, I cannot unlock the door to any of these mysteries."

"I pray for your success, Quinn. Meanwhile, Grandmother is asking for you, complaining that she has all too little of your company. She has a head full of fancies; she vows that Marianne comes to the sea tower and goes to the room above hers. She swears she feels Marianne's presence."

Quinn went into the sitting room, where his grandmother was sitting, shrouded in wraps, by the window, looking bored and lonely. A fire burned brightly in the grate against the chill of the afternoon.

Quinn went across to her and took hold of her hands.

"Grandmother," he said quietly.

She turned a tired, querulous face toward him. Her eyes did not have their usual brightness, and he asked, alarmed, "Are you feeling ill?"

"No. I am lonely, Quinn. When will Luella be back to amuse me and keep me company?"

"Soon, I hope."

"You will not banish her again? You will not send her away?"

"I did not banish her; Doctor Curtiss felt it would be better for her to rest at Bellminster for a few days."

"I suppose Simon enjoys her company in that lonely house of his? He does not need her as *I* do! It is always the same with young people!" Jessica shrugged her thin shoulders. "Marianne was as restless as a butterfly, running away to Dunbury to visit the wretched Cazelet woman. Now Dunbury is burned to the ground, Mrs. Cazelet has gone, and Marianne is dead."

He had rarely seen her in such a doleful mood.

"Where is Emmie?" he asked.

"Taken to her bed with rheumatism. It plagues her so much these days that I fear you will have to pension her off, Quinn, and let Luella be my companion!"

"Gladly," he said happily. "We will ask Luella to stay, and if she agrees, I will give Emmie a cottage and enough money to keep her comfortably."

Suddenly, wistfully, his grandmother laid her head against his arm, in a gesture of surrender that touched him deeply.

"I am growing old, Quinn. When my time comes, I shall not be afraid, but I wish to see you wed, with a wife and an heir for Westhaven. Marianne has come back, Quinn. She will not show herself yet, but one day soon she will. I am glad that she has returned to me, but I wish that I could *see* her."

He heard the deep sigh and looked searchingly at the woman who clung like a child to him. By the cloudiness of her eyes, the vagueness of her expression, he realized that she had once again slipped quietly over the borderland between fact and fantasy.

"I am sure if Marianne had returned, *you* would be the first person to see her," he pointed out.

"She hides from me! I *know* she is here. I listen for her footstep on the stair; I hear it, light as a feather."

"How would you hear footsteps? These walls are thick."

"Ah, but I *do* hear them, Quinn! I, who knew and loved

her so well—I *know* when she is about! She goes up to the old chapel. It was always her favorite room; she loved the view from the window. I call to her to come down to me. Once I unlocked the door and called up the stair, but no one came. I cannot manage to climb the stairs now, and Emmie will not do so, for she declares that the place frightens her, silly woman that she is."

Gently, he disengaged her hand.

"Tell me where I may find *your* keys, and I will see if Marianne is in the chapel," he suggested.

She told him, without hesitation, to take them from her desk. He did as she asked and, lifting the hangings, opened the door that gave on to the landing and stairs.

Quinn stepped through. The place smelled cold, and there was a faint suggestion of sea breezes in the coldness, as though the lower door had recently been opened.

His search was thorough. He went down to the outer door that led into a tiny, cobbled courtyard. It was a private place, where his grandmother—and Mary and Marianne, in happier days—liked to sit and sun themselves in summer. He remembered how often he had joined them. Here he had sat with Marianne, making plans for their wedding . . .

None of the servants was allowed in the courtyard. There was an iron gate set in the wall, and beyond the gate were the grounds of Westhaven.

He walked forward and lifted the latch; the gate was not locked. It never had been, for the servants had respected his commands. In any case, none of them could have entered the tower and the chapel, to which only he, Mary, Marianne, and his grandmother possessed keys.

He returned to the tower and went slowly up to the little room under the stars. Like the courtyard, it was full of memories. Simon and Marianne had loved to shut themselves away there as children, playing their games of pretense, dressing up in the clothes they found in the coffers; to them, it had been a besieged castle, a beleaguered fortress, a secret cave, a lair that no one ever surprised.

Quinn smiled faintly, his sharp eyes noting every detail of the treasures carefully laid out everywhere. Nothing appeared to have been disturbed. He lifted the lids of the coffers and smelled the peculiar, musty odor of stale old clothes kept too long from the fresh air. He even reached down beneath the clothes, a wild idea forming in his mind that there might be a clue to the mysteries that bedeviled him, but he found nothing of value.

There was little wind today, just a sea breeze humming softly to itself under the battlements. Only Marianne's ghost was there, an echo of laughter, the faded scent of the sweet, flowery perfumes she used, the faint rustle of a skirt. None of those things existed outside his imagination, he knew. Abruptly, he closed the door and went back to his grandmother.

"There is no one in the sea tower," he told her. "Everything is just as it always has been. In a little while, Luella will be back to cheer you and make you laugh. Then you will forget your fancies."

For a long time after he had left, Jessica sat staring at the sea. Once she spoke aloud, trying to reassure herself.

"I *know* that what I have done would have given you great joy, Marianne; so why do you come back, a ghost to haunt me? Why do you trouble me so?"

Quinn went to Mary's room.

"Do you still have your keys to the tower?" he asked her.

She looked at him in surprise.

"I have always had them, Quinn. Why do you ask? Do you, too, share grandmother's strange fancies?"

"No, but keys may be taken and used by other people," he pointed out. "I wish you to search Marianne's rooms and see if *her* keys are there."

She nodded, still surprised, thinking that his behavior seemed odd.

He went downstairs to his study. Much later that evening, Mary came to him, looking puzzled and faintly uneasy.

"I have searched diligently, Quinn. I have looked in every place where keys might be, but I cannot find Marianne's. Do you wish me to question the servants?"

"No," he said. "Her rooms have not been locked, have they, since her death?"

She shook her head.

"There seemed no need to lock them. Grandmother went there, sometimes, and wept and made herself unhappy, but then, after a while, she seemed to accept what had happened . . ."

She paused.

"*Someone* has a set of keys," Quinn said softly. "Someone has Marianne's keys."

Mary shivered.

"Why would anyone wish to come and go from the tower?" she asked.

"I have no answer, yet, to that question. I shall set two men to watch the entrance to the courtyard, night and day. Marianne's keys must have been stolen by someone in this house."

Nanny shuffled away, bearing the empty bowl that had held the rather dubious broth she made. Luella looked around the chill bedroom and sighed.

She was dressed and had brushed her hair; she did not feel weak or ill or troubled in her mind. She wanted more than anything in the world to return to Westhaven and had Dr. Curtiss's promise that she should do so the following day.

That thought was cheering, but she still felt uneasy. She looked at the grate, with its pyramid of gray ash, the furniture with its patina of dust; the room had an air of complete neglect, as though no one cared about it.

The view from her window was depressing: the stable roof needed repairing, and a broken weathercock lay in the yard. A groom took two horses out for exercise some mornings—a sullen-looking boy in shabby clothes, the only person she had seen apart from Nanny and Simon.

Simon came to see her, hard on the heels of Nanny's departure. She heard him turn the key in the lock and enter the room.

Suddenly she was angry.

"I will *not* be locked in!" she declared passionately.

169

His eyebrows rose.

"My dear, do not get into such a pother! I am out a great deal. Nanny is old and deaf. What if the man who tried to kill you came seeking you here?"

She was silent, unable to argue that particular point. She sighed, smoothing down the skirt of her dress.

"This room is gloomy," she told him.

"I regret that it is. The house is in a deplorable state," he replied, with complete frankness. "My father was not a rich man, and an estate of this size demands a bottomless purse!"

She looked at him thoughtfully, head on one side.

"Also, you do not care for the country, Mr. Corbie!"

"That is true. My mother had a taste for gaiety that I have inherited. I like the gaming tables and enjoy the pleasures of life in civilized cities. There is *nothing* here: no witty or amusing conversation, no scintillating company, no balls and parties and gatherings, no coffee houses in which to while away a morning. Have you ever tasted life in a big city, Luella?"

"No. Quinn has promised to take me to London when his work here is done," she replied frankly.

"What a treat is in store for you! I assure you, you will find it delightful."

"Life does not seem dull to me at Westhaven. Why do you stay if you dislike Bellminster?"

His eyes had a veiled look.

"One needs resources to pursue an elegant life. I shall seek a buyer for Bellminster; I know that Quinn would like to add my lands to his. Then I shall have sufficient funds to take me where I please. I should like to visit Italy. Florence and Venice are beautiful cities, and the sun shines more warmly there than it does here!"

She listened, fascinated. He watched her eager little face and thought cynically, she has no idea of money. She does not know that the price of Bellminster and its lands would never pay for the life I intend to lead. Poor little simpleton!

"You will be happy, then?" she asked, when he had finished.

170

"Of course; and now, my dear Luella, I must leave you."

"May I not come and sit downstairs with you?" she pleaded. "It is lonely here."

He looked rueful.

"Alas, I am expecting a visitor, a dull fellow whose conversation would bore you. Tomorrow, Quinn shall take you back to Westhaven. You look pale, and I think you need to sleep."

It was a dismissal that made her feel like a snubbed child; however, it was no use arguing with him, she realized. After all, it was, as he had said, her last night in this house, and she knew she would be glad to leave it.

Gently, Simon turned the key in the lock, but his face was moody and bitter as he went, not downstairs to his study, but up to the top of the house.

Luella slept fitfully. She dreamed that Quinn did not come to Bellminster for her and that Simon appeared, his face cold and gray like the face of a dead man, telling her that she must remain in this room, a prisoner, forever.

She cried out in her sleep, and the scene changed. She thought a woman looked down on her, with pity; a beautiful, sad-faced, dark-haired woman, whose lips moved as though she was speaking, but no words came. There was a great cold wind blowing about her, blowing about all the world, scattering the stars in the heavens, and as they fell, they became flowers . . .

Luella woke in the small hours, clammy with sweat. She felt for the candlestick by her bed, but the candle had burned itself out into a stump of wax. She was very cold. As she lay there, pulling the covers around her chin, she faintly heard the crowing of a cock and saw a thin finger of light pulling the darkness apart, beyond her window.

It was today, and she was going back to Westhaven; her dreams were fragments of sadness, like the memory of her life with Henrietta. Tears of thankfulness rolled down her cheeks.

More than anything in the world, she wanted Quinn—wanted him to hold her and comfort her. He was a refuge

171

and a fortress, a thousand candles burning in the darkness of a frightening world.

She wanted his love, needed to lose herself in it, drown in it. She wanted the exultation of his mastery over her, she wanted to be taken as he had almost taken her in the old nursery. Most of all, she wanted his child. The very thought was exciting, frightening; it was full of ecstasy—and it was a dream forever out of reach. She would stay at Westhaven as long as he needed her there, but when his grandmother died, and there was no more need of her, then she would turn her face toward London, but never forget him. . . .

Luella was up early. She washed and dressed and brushed out her hair. It was still barely light, and far below her she heard a door slam, as though someone had come into the house.

She was sitting by the empty grate, hands folded in her lap, when Nanny brought in her breakfast. She ate it sedately, but inside, her heart and her soul burned with a fever of impatience.

Simon came to bid her farewell.

"I am sorry that you are leaving us," he said. "I trust you are fully recovered?"

"I am well enough, Mr. Corbie. Inactivity frets my soul, for I am unused to it."

"You should learn the delights of doing nothing at all," he told her gaily. "I can recommend it!"

Simon escorted Luella downstairs to wait for Quinn, two eyes watching them on their way. Simon was aware of the watcher, and it was with a considerable effort that he kept his attention wholly concentrated on Luella.

Quinn thought how pale she looked; only her green eyes were brilliant in her face. He held her hands and looked at her searchingly.

"Is there something wrong?" he asked.

She shook her head, her eyes full of tears. Good-byes were formal on Quinn's part, lighthearted on Simon's. Outside, one of the small carriages from Westhaven was waiting; Quinn was driving it himself.

172

He helped Luella into the seat and laid a rug over her knees, then he climbed up beside her. He was so close to her that their shoulders touched, and she felt the bitter-sweetness of the contact.

The horse stepped out smartly at Quinn's command. Luella did not turn to look back at Bellminster. Her face was toward the sea.

I am glad to be going home, she thought.

CHAPTER 9

This entry into Westhaven was so very different from the first one she had made, Luella thought. She wondered if Quinn remembered how he had dragged her into the hall, a small, scared urchin with her pitifully few possessions bundled into an old basket.

She had been frightened, hungry, bewildered, her clothes ragged, her future grim. Now she stepped into the hall, wearing the plain dark dress and cloak that had belonged to Marianne; both suited her small, slim figure. Good food had begun to round out the sharp angles of her body into softer curves. There had been time to brush her hair, so that it gleamed richly gold in the light. She walked with her head held high, for she no longer felt like someone of no account.

Sefton, the footman, inclined his head slightly, his face impassive. Two of the maids, waiting at the back of the hall, looked at Luella with curiosity mingled with grudging envy. The tales that flew around the servants' hall were lurid; the most interesting was that Luella was the bastard daughter of a French aristocrat who had gone to the guillotine.

"Are you glad to be back?" Quinn asked.

"Yes," she said, with a radiance in her face that startled him.

"I am having your belongings moved from the nursery suite," he told her. "There are rooms near the sea tower that are more suitable for you. The nursery is lonely and too shut away."

His glance raked over her clothes, and he added matter-of-factly, "There is a woman in Dorchester, a dressmaker, who will make clothes for you; also a milliner, who will make you some bonnets. I have instructed them both to call on you next week."

"I have these clothes to wear," she murmured. "And there are others, in the cupboards. They will do . . ."

"No, they will *not* do," he retorted. "They were made for someone else. Do you not also realize that the man who attacked you could have believed you were Marianne, simply because you have been wearing her clothes?"

"Then he must have been out of the country if he does not know she has been dead these many weeks," Luella replied. "Besides, why should he wish to harm her?"

"I should like to have the answer to that question!" he told her wryly. "I thought you would be pleased to have new gowns."

"Oh, I *am*!" Her green eyes sparkled, her lips curved into a smile.

"I have never had a new gown in my life," she whispered.

"*Never*, Luella? Oh, come!"

"It is true!" she insisted. "At the school I had hand-me-downs. When I left, I wore a made-over dress that had belonged to a servant of one of the governor's wives. It was good, sound cloth, though very plain, and did not really fit me. Henrietta would not allow me to wear it. She took away the clothes I had and gave me some that were old and ugly. I did not mind the ugliness, but they were very thin and I was always cold."

"I see," he said gently. "Well, you will not have to wear castoffs any longer. You'll look like a fine lady when the dressmaker and milliner are done with you. Go to my grandmother, Luella; she is impatient for your return."

Obediently, she ran up the shallow staircase, pausing, as she always did, in front of the window on the landing, to put out her hand and stroke the richly colored glass to remind her that it was real.

Quinn, who had seen her make the gesture many times, watched her with a curious, brooding tenderness of which she was entirely unaware.

*   *   *

176

Jessica welcomed her delightedly.

"You have no idea how bored I have been, child! I am tired of playing patience, looking at the sea, listening to Emmie complaining about her aches and pains. The only excitement was the fire at Dunbury. A good thing the wretched house is destroyed; there was a curse on it."

"Whatever do you mean?" Luella demanded, her eyes dancing.

"Laugh if you will, Luella. There is something about the house I never liked. As though it was always cold and no fire could warm it. Houses must be loved—as this one is. It was the same at Bellminster. That was a cold, drab house. How did you like it there?"

"Not at all," replied Luella, with devastating truth.

Thin fingers closed tightly over her wrist; Jessica's face was beseeching.

"You will stay, child? You will not go away to London?"

"I will stay," Luella promised.

"Splendid! Then Quinn shall pension off poor, silly, forgetful Emmie, instead of my having to endure her grumbles! *You* shall look after me, read to me, fetch my cologne and brush my hair, and have your own sewing box with a silver thimble and silver scissors. I *have* been lonely since the sea took Marianne, so *you* were sent to comfort me. Marianne does not rest, though I did what I could to make her as happy in death as she was in life. She haunts the sea tower. I hear her walking there. She is displeased with me."

"I am sure you are wrong," Luella comforted. "You and Marianne laughed and talked together, and shared secrets, so . . ."

"Ah, yes! She loved secrets. She liked to hide things, as a child; she liked to find places in the house where she could creep away. She told me about them, and made me promise I would never tell anyone. I always kept my promises. She liked my secret room, you know; she was always hiding things there. I wanted to please her, very much, Luella. Now I think I did not do what was right."

"What was it you did, Mrs. Mallory?"

Jessica shook her head.

"There are some secrets that must never be told," she replied.

Luella gave in unwillingly to Quinn's command that she should go no further than the grounds of Westhaven.

"The grounds are large enough to provide you with ample exercise and fresh air," he told her dryly. "Hasn't your experience on the moors chastened you sufficiently to make you realize what dangers surround you?"

She sighed, unwillingly acknowledging the wisdom of his ruling.

"There was such a feeling of freedom out on the moors!" she said, with a sigh.

"There will be plenty of freedom in the future. I do not want harm to come to you," he pointed out.

They were in his study. He put down the pistol he was examining. With slow deliberation he came across the room to where she stood by the fireplace, warming her hands.

"Luella," he said quietly. "Look at me."

Unwillingly, she obeyed; blue eyes met green ones. Luella's face was very still; Quinn's was alert. It was that moment of truth and tenderness before any words of affection are spoken between two people, a no-man's-land of the heart. Luella's breath came unsteadily from between parted lips. Quinn was master of the situation; he took her hands in his and held them lightly.

"We have a journey to make," he reminded her. "When my work here is done, we shall go to London together, and I will take your locket to every jeweler in the city to see if we can find out who you really are. It may be that we shall discover you are the daughter of someone rich and splendid, with an old and honorable name; it may be that you are a bastard, with no claim to *any* man's name, the result of an alliance between one of those women you spoke of, and a man with sufficient money to pay handsomely for an evening's entertainment. Whatever your parentage, it will not matter so much to me as the fact that you are Luella March of Westhaven. Do you understand what I am trying to tell you?"

"I—I think so," she said uncertainly.

"I want you to stay here," he told her.

"I have already told your grandmother that I will do so."

"*My* needs are different. I need a wife, Luella, and sons. For what are a man's lands and possessions worth, if he has no one to whom they may be handed on, in trust for the future?"

"Marianne . . ." she faltered, unable to believe her ears.

"She is dead." Luella saw naked pain in his face for a moment, and her heart plunged downward in headlong flight.

"I do not love you as I loved her," Quinn told her bluntly. "I have tenderness, regard, deep affection for you. These things can be enough between a man and a woman."

Not for me! she cried silently.

"I will never again try to take you by force," he promised her.

I wish that you would! her heart cried wildly. Oh, to recapture such ecstasy, now that I know the meaning of love!

He misread her silence. He put a finger beneath her chin and tilted her downcast face up to his. Very gently, he kissed her forehead.

"Let that kiss be a token between us, Luella; you have no cause to be afraid. You are too young, yet, for us to think of marriage. Time enough when you are eighteen or nineteen and have become used to the idea of having me as husband!"

"Oh!" she choked furiously, "I am *weary* of being told that I am too young!"

She turned and whirled out of the room in a furious temper. He stared after her in astonishment that was touched with amusement. Women were unpredictable creatures. He remembered how she had fought him like a tiger and bitten his chin when he had tried to possess her, and now, when he showed consideration for her feelings, she was equally displeased.

He went back to the examination of his pistol, thinking that it would be pleasant to have Luella always in the house. He had no doubt that she would be a good wife, and a dutiful one. As for passion, and all its delights, there were women enough in London to minister to his deeper, wilder needs.

The following day, after an exhausting morning questioning prisoners in Dorchester jail, without result, Quinn tucked his pistol in his belt and rode to Shep Tulley's cottage.

It was a dour afternoon, with a cutting wind and cold gray skies. The sea looked cruel and cold as it drove relentlessly shoreward. It was still two days to the date of the next unloading of boats in the sea cave.

Quinn reached the clearing and reined the horse to a standstill. The door of the cottage stood open, but no smoke curled from the chimney, and there was something unnatural in the complete silence all around him.

"Shep!" he called.

There was no reply. The silence had a menacing quality. The trees and bushes seemed to close in around him.

"Shep Tulley!" Quinn cried. "Come out!"

He whistled loudly; still there was no answer. He dismounted and tethered Kalidas, walking warily toward the open door.

The cottage had one room and a tiny lean-to shed that served as Shep as a scullery. The inside was gloomy, for the one small window was thick with grime.

Quinn was so tall that he had to bend low to enter the door. The place had a fetid smell that nauseated him. It was furnished only with a cupboard, a table, a truckle bed, and a chair.

Shep was propped sideways in the chair. His mouth was open; his eyes had the fixed look of death. When Quinn touched his hand, he found it cold, and the blood had clotted around the hole in his forehead. He had been shot through the temple.

Shep's body had been removed, the cottage had been examined; there was no trace of the murderer. Now the door was locked and a redcoat stood on guard. What a waste of time to post a man there, Quinn thought; was it likely that

Shep's murderer would return to see if the body had been discovered?

Shep had died because someone in Parnall's pay had discovered that the old man had been in Dorchester asking questions about Mr. Jackson. Whether or not the person who killed Shep had also discovered that the assignment at the sea cave had been revealed was a matter for conjecture, Quinn thought. He would have to take a chance that the rendezvous would still be kept.

He felt the old man's death keenly, believing himself to have been responsible for it; he was sick at heart when he returned to Westhaven. He had faced danger coolly, used all his wit and cunning to extricate himself and his charges from capture, and had run with death at his heels many times. He had not failed in his task; every fugitive whose life had been entrusted to him had been safely landed in England. There was something different about this business, though; it reeked of evil, and the sooner he could capture Parnall, the better.

He was in this mood of mingled fury and despair when Luella came upon him, much later in the afternoon.

"The milliner and the dressmaker will call next week," she told him dutifully.

"See to it, then," he told her absently. "It is woman's business. Order whatever you please."

She looked searchingly at the tired face with its sharp-etched lines of bitterness.

"What is wrong?" she asked.

"A man is dead, and I am to blame."

"I do not believe that."

"Believe it, Luella, for it is true. I bought information from an old man, the fact was discovered, and he was killed."

"You did not compel him to reveal information to you," she pointed out. "It was a bargain, surely, and one that he accepted?"

"One that ended with his death."

She sat down on a small gilt chair, spread her skirts around her, and folded her hands in her lap.

"Tell me about it," she said. "If I am to be your wife, then I must share your burdens."

"Such burdens that concern the management and affairs of Westhaven and our domestic life—yes. Such matters as these—no."

"I do not agree."

"Damn it, Luella, I am in no mood for argument!" he retorted, exasperated.

"I think, perhaps, there is no purpose in marrying you," she told him reflectively. "I do not want to be merely the bearer of your sons, keep the household keys, and give orders to the servants—and that is all you offer me."

"*All!*" He glared at her, torn between amusement and anger. "What a perverse little monkey you are! I also offer you a life that many women would envy! I offer you ease, wealth, security such as you can never have dreamed of when you scuttled about under the lash of a cane or recited your Bible verses in a cold schoolroom on a winter morning! I expect you to be a dutiful wife!"

"I shall never be that," she promised him calmly. "Henrietta was angry because she could not break my spirit; I am not a submissive person."

"Then learn to be, my dear Luella," he murmured. "I make my own decisions in certain matters and you can have no part in them."

"Then I won't marry you," she said promptly—and she meant it, he realized, astonished.

"What do you suppose you will do, then?" he asked crisply.

"I can still be companion to your grandmother."

"Oh?" He smiled widely, forgetting his troubles for a moment. "Supposing I decide that you shall not stay?"

Green eyes met his defiantly and without fear.

"I will take my chance in London."

"By God, I believe you would!" he said, with raised eyebrows. "I would even predict that you could become the indulged and pampered wife of some silly old man who likes a woman to be disobedient and willful!"

"Do *you* not like a woman with spirit, Quinn?" She looked at him speculatively, eyes slanted upwards from under half-closed lids. "After all, you enjoy riding a spirited horse."

"True, but I can control Kalidas. *I* am master. By heaven, you are the strangest woman I ever met. I could have put your talents to good use during my journeys through France!" he admitted.

She looked at the handsome face, the vivid blue eyes, at the mouth that could smile so tenderly, softening the harsh lines, and promising such bliss.

You will never love me, she thought; Marianne's ghost will always divide us, keeping your heart secret from mine, even when we lie in one another's arms and our bodies are one, as you have described to me. If I cannot share your heart, and share your bed only that we shall have children, may I not know your mind?

As though in answer to her unspoken question, he said suddenly, "Very well; hear the tale of the beautiful Flowers of Darkness . . ."

He took the sketch of the Flowers from a drawer and placed it in her hands. Luella looked at it with a feeling of coldness around her heart. These were the flowers of her dreams; she was glad it was only a sketch, and that the artist could not reproduce the unearthly brilliance of the gems. Whoever looks upon these Flowers, she thought, will be filled with a terrible desire to possess them, and possession bring a curse. One I hear faintly in the wind . . .

She pulled back her wandering thoughts, listening to the tale he told. She knew that Quinn was glad to talk to someone.

"It will be only a matter of time before you find this man Parnall," she said, when he had finished. "So it was he who employed poor Tom Hines? It was he who shot him, without pity."

"He has a great many men who are paid to do his work," Quinn agreed. "Some are known to Sir Julius and myself. *I* have but a few men and must move with caution. I have a couple of faithful servants who watch the sea tower; Shep has died. Tom Hines, who might have led me straight to Parnall, is also dead. If only I had the entire militia in the county at my disposal, to comb moors and beaches, highways and byways! Such action would betray what Sir Julius is most anxious to conceal: that the man we seek has dishonored Britain—and is British, a member of an old and distinguished family. The Flowers must be taken from him and given into the keeping of those for whom they were intended, as soon as possible."

"Will the boats come to the sea cave tomorrow night?" she asked.

"I believe they may. Whoever killed Shep may only have known that he had led me to Dorchester and one of Parnall's hiding places—and not been aware also that Shep gave me a date for the landing of the contraband."

"I shall come to the cave with you tomorrow night," she announced calmly.

He threw back his head and laughed heartily. She saw the white gleam of his teeth, the movement of powerful muscles in his throat and shoulders. Her heart contracted with love and pain.

"You will do nothing of the kind. There may be violence; it will be dangerous."

"I am not afraid of danger," she retorted.

"I believe you." His voice was dry. "Nevertheless, it is no place for a woman."

"Not an ordinary woman, perhaps."

"What on earth do you mean by that?"

"I have not been gently reared," she pointed out simply. "I do not have the vapors, nor am I afraid to dirty a gown or tear my stockings or disarrange my hair. I am small and slight, and I can hide in places where a man could not hide. My eyes and ears are sharp. I am not easily frightened by things I see and hear."

He looked at her quizzically. Marianne he had loved because she was wholly feminine, sweet, willful, capricious, with an insatiable appetite for pretty things. They met on the only level on which Quinn had ever believed a man could meet a woman: a wholly physical one.

Now, here was a woman who had a mind and will of her own. It was a novelty that surprised and intrigued him. For the first time it occurred to him that such a woman would be a wonderful companion to a man—as she had insisted she wished to be—as well as satisfying the hunger and need for comfort that he had believed was the purpose of a woman's existence.

"Luella," he said gently, "I cannot take you, no matter how you beg and plead."

"I should never do that," she retorted.

"Indeed you would not," he agreed, wryly. "I had forgotten how independent you are. Your body is sixteen and a half years old—I beg your pardon, almost seventeen years old—and your mind is a hundred years old. It is a unique combination, Luella, one that will stand you in good stead."

"*Will* you let me come with you?" she asked, with a touch of impatience.

"No. I cannot expose you to such dangers as may be there."

"Then I shall come without your permission," she replied.

He looked angry; he was more concerned on her behalf than he cared to admit.

"Would you defy me?"

"Yes, if need be."

"By God, Henrietta Spencer must have found you a handful!"

"That is not fair or true. I was obedient, I tried to please, I gave her no cause for the ill temper she showed, and I worked hard," Luella pointed out.

"I shall lock you in your room!" he threatened.

"I will find some means of getting out," she retorted.

"Luella, this is not a game!" He stood up, so that he towered over her. "What if I told you that I should whip you soundly if you disobeyed me?" he demanded, exasperated.

"It makes no difference." She looked at him thoughtfully, eyes half-closed. "I do not think that you will, though."

"Oh, Luella!" he said helplessly. "*Why* do you want to come with me so much? Is it just a taste for adventure that prompts you?"

She shook her head.

"No. It is something I cannot explain. I only know that I *must* be there," she replied simply.

He looked into her eyes and knew that she spoke truthfully; she was driven by some force that she did not comprehend, and it came from outside herself, not within.

Quinn, who was not a superstitious man, felt the power of that same force; it was like a great wind that seemed to tear down all his deep-rooted instincts. Taking a woman on such a task as he was about to undertake was contrary to all reason. It mocked his will and judgment, but for the first and last time in his life, he bowed before what he did not understand.

"Very well," he said resignedly. "On condition, only, that you will do exactly as you are told, and keep away from any shooting or fighting there may be, then I will take you."

"Thank you!" she murmured, and her green eyes glowed with an almost unearthly fire.

Witch or mermaid, he did not know what she was. He felt the dark forces moving around him, events moving toward an appointed end, directed by a will of greater strength than his own.

On the morning of that same day, Philip Janson crossed from Somerset over the borders into Dorset and made his way toward Westhaven, driven not only by the same strange force that had driven Luella and made its presence felt in Quinn, but motivated by a desire for atonement that had tormented him ever since he had been in Dorchester jail with time to reflect on his folly.

He was innocent of the crimes with which he had been charged; guilty of letting his infatuation for Marianne Walton come between him and the dedication he should have shown for his purpose . . .

Well, he had suffered for it, he thought with a sigh. Now he had to do what must be done. He knew that Quinn Mallory, whom he had never seen, was reckoned to be honest, fearless, and incorruptible. He hoped it was true; Quinn's sister Mary had been kind, and Philip felt great affection for her. If he could reach Westhaven, he could seek out Mary, tell her the truth; if Quinn had returned from his latest mission in France, so much the better. At least he would have tried to right the wrong he had done.

Philip fretted that the journey was tiring him more than he cared to admit; he had never been physically strong and was not fully recovered from the fever following his leg wound. He had to travel cautiously, lie low, live rough— and the guinea he had so optimistically kept as being sufficient for his needs was melting away alarmingly.

His need for atonement and the force that he did not understand drove him on, and as though fate had always intended that he should reach Westhaven at a certain time, he got a lift on a farm cart going to Axminster. His spirits rose as the heavily laden cart creaked and grumbled along the country lanes, while he rested and remembered Eleanor La Vanne's vivid description of the Flowers of Darkness.

Luella went about her work as usual; within her there was a tense inner excitement. It was not an easy day. Jessica had slept badly and was querulous. Emmie declared that her bones ached so much she could scarcely bear to move. Mary sat in her room, restless and uneasy, huddled over a glowing fire; her thoughts were of Philip.

In the forenoon Simon rode over to Westhaven and saw Quinn. He came straight to the point.

"You have long cast your eyes toward Bellminster, Quinn. If we can agree on the price, then it is all yours. I am leaving Dorset, for I cannot endure the thought of another winter here, with the cold raking my bones and nothing to look at but sea and moors."

"This is a sudden decision," Quinn said, surprised.

Simon shook his head.

"You know I have always been discontented with the life of a country squire. I shall live in a better climate than this, where the sun is warm, there is good company to entertain me, the comforts of civilization to sweeten life, and soft living to soothe me."

He named his price. Quinn said, with truth, that it was too high, and they haggled for some time before coming to an agreement. Quinn promised to ride over to Bellminster within the next few days to inspect cottages, farms, lands comprising the estate. They were all in a poor state of repair, as he pointed out.

The price is still too high, Quinn thought, when Simon had ridden home, but I would rather pay it than see the place go to someone who will use it as little as Simon has used it and not care about the land and the people who look after it.

Back at Bellminster, Simon unsaddled his horse himself, because there was no one else to do it. One of the servants was sick, and the other had suddenly left him; there was only Nanny to minister to him. Wearily, he climbed the stairs to the rooms at the very top of the house, up the steep staircase that Nanny's old legs could no longer manage. He felt both relief and resignation, though he flinched from the storm about to break over his head. The decision was made; there would be no turning back.

He tapped three times upon a door. It was opened cautiously, and he was admitted to a room furnished with a degree of comfort that the rest of the house did not possess.

"Well?" said the handsome, sulky figure in breeches, silk shirt, and expensive jerkin.

He braced himself and said, "I have sold Bellminster to Quinn Mallory. In a day or so he will come here to conclude the business with me. You must either be gone before then or tell him the truth."

"Never, *never!*" The words were flung at him with searing contempt. "You would not have done that! You have not sold Bellminster!"

"I have," he said, with a quietness more telling than any anger.

"You would betray us both? Oh, you are a fool, a weakling! There is too much at stake!" The voice was full of venom and fury.

"There is *nothing* at stake!" he retorted bitterly. "No one knows what has happened to the Flowers of Darkness! They have vanished from the face of this earth. *I* shall not be rich as you have promised. I have listened to you, helped you too long. I will no longer go to the sea tower, for I tell you, the jewels are not there; *nor* at Dunbury. Sometimes I believe that *you* know where they are—that you are cheating, deceiving me, lying low until Parnall is dead, because he will kill you when he finds you. And what of Janson?"

"*He* is dead! I know he is! He must be, for he could not have remained uncaptured all this time!"

"He could have gone to France. I believe that is what he did. Well, it is out of my hands, now. In a little while this house and all my lands will be the property of the master of Westhaven!"

"Damn you, Simon! Damn you! What am I to do, where am I to go? You cannot betray us now, when we could be rich beyond all belief! Oh, if you would *only* have the patience that *I* have shown! Parnall has the jewels, I know he has! When he is dead, they will be ours. We shall be rich enough to buy up half of England!"

"I do not want to buy up half of England! I want to live in the sun," he said tiredly.

"You will be able to do that. Take your half, go your way, we shall never meet again! *How* can you be so foolish, when victory is almost ours!"

"Victory? How much longer will *you* be safe? He is like a tiger waiting to pounce. It is a matter of time only before he turns his eyes toward Bellminster."

"We have been careful, Simon! He will never find me!"

"Believe that, and it may comfort you," he retorted. "Shep Tulley and Tom Hines are dead; Parnall killed them because they would have led Quinn straight to him. He is cunning and wily and ruthless."

Darkness closed in early. A languid moon rose from her bed, giving a pale ghost light as though she had no liking for the events that were about to happen and did not want to look upon them.

The wind had veered, blowing coldly from the east and promising snow before Christmas.

At Quinn's command, Luella dined with him. She wore a dress of Marianne's, in a shade of rich, wine-red velvet that made her skin look creamy and put a richer sheen on the gold of her hair.

Quinn looked handsome in evening dress; they had both dressed for the occasion, as though there was something to celebrate. Luella had no idea what they should be celebrating. It was not at all certain that the night's business would end in victory for Quinn and the return of the jewels. There were a great many obstacles and uncertainties; they both knew that.

When the footman had gone, Luella asked quietly, "What time do we leave here, Quinn?"

"At eleven." He peeled a peach with steady hands, as though he were contemplating nothing more unusual than a visit to the sea tower.

"Supposing the preventative officers have been alerted and are there?"

"I must take that risk. In not informing them that a consignment of contraband is due tonight, I have neglected my duty as a good citizen." He smiled rakishly. "In this case, discretion is the better part of valor. It is important that Parnall shall not slip through my fingers in the heat of a raid, and so my methods—as often—are unorthodox. Wear your warmest and darkest clothing. Keep well behind me. Damn it, I am still unconvinced of the wisdom of taking you."

Shaking her head mutinously, she lifted her goblet, and the wine sparkled in the light from the great chandelier.

"To success!" she said.

He laughed, lifted his glass, and said mockingly, "How well you do it, Luella! One would imagine you had always been accustomed to the life of a lady!"

"I doubt you mean that as a compliment!" she retorted. "Nevertheless, I shall consider it one!"

They moved in silence, shadows in the deeper shadows of the night. Luella kept a fair distance behind Quinn, who was repenting his decision to bring her, and was beginning to feel that the compelling force urging him toward that decision was mere nonsense. Yet he still felt that force strongly, as though it was protective; even though he wanted to, he could not deny its existence.

The path that wound between the furze and scrub had smaller paths, like branches spreading out from a tree trunk, all of them leading to the beach. Quinn knew the best and easiest route; not a difficult one, even with only faint moonlight to guide him. He could not look back to help Luella. When he reached the beach, he sheltered himself from sight in the lee of the cliffs and heaved a great sigh of relief when she jumped lightly beside him.

They moved toward the sea cave, still keeping in the shadows so that they merged with them. He breathed another sigh of relief when they reached the cave. He put out a hand, then, and guided her in.

A ledge ran all the way around the inside, sloping up from the sandy floor and wide enough to accommodate two men. This ledge was above high-water mark. At the back of the cave was a deep recess, and the walls were seamed with fissures of varying thicknesses, affording hiding places that Quinn knew well, for he had often played in the caves as a boy, cheating the tide by remaining crouched on the ledge until the first waves came booming in, then racing down and splashing through the water along the bottom of the cliffs until he came to the path.

Now it was not a game. He pulled Luella into one of the fissures, just inside the cave. He had no mind to be trapped; from where they stood, it would be possible to make a dash for freedom.

"How long must we wait?" she whispered.

"It will be a while yet before the boat arrives. Parnall will not be so foolish as to wait here, risking a trap; he will come when the boat comes, to take what he wants and then go again. I shall follow him when he leaves this cave. Wait here for me, Luella."

She had no intention of waiting, but she did not tell him so. It was pleasant to be in such proximity to him in the darkness. His arm went around her shoulder, pulling her close; it was a no-man's-land between safety and danger, and she was content. She would be instantly aware when

191

the boat was near, for she already knew what Eleanor La Vanne could have told her: that in time of danger, every sense is a sixth sense for some people.

He whispered to her, his lips close to her hair—not of love, for it was no time for pretty speeches. He talked of his boyhood; of years of the kind of freedom that Luella had enjoyed, so briefly, on the moors; of his grandmother, who had taught him to care for the land and the people who were part of it. He spoke of Marianne, how she had loved the beach, and the moors, and grown up to be mischievous, getting her own way with charm and skill—feminine, illogical, beautiful, tantalizing. She had captivated everyone, he said.

Luella listened and sighed to herself, watching the moon delicately fingering the sea, leaving silvery trails, like ribbons tying up the dark gown of night. She wished she was Marianne, even though Marianne had been dead now for many weeks, for there had been nothing of misery and loneliness in *her* life.

How *could* she have fallen, Luella thought? Lissome and light of foot, and knowing every inch of the way to the beach? She could not have fallen—she had been struck down . . .

Suddenly, she tensed. Surprised, Quinn withdrew his arm and thrust her behind him well back into the deep fissure that sheltered them on the ledge.

Luella could see, by craning her head to look around him; she saw the outline of a bulky, dark shape moving rhythmically over the water to the dip and soar of paddles. The shape moved into the path of the moon, and then the moon, capricious and coy, moved behind a cloud; when she reappeared, the boat was already scraping softly along the beach.

It was an hour exactly to full tide, and the sea boomed along the beach, running strongly toward the cave; Luella felt the pull of a tremendous excitement within her. She knew fear, also, but she was able to keep it controlled, though her whole body trembled and the blood raced furiously in her veins.

There were men climbing from the boat. They came up

to the mouth of the cave, laden with goods, and they clustered there, for all the world, it seemed to Luella, like departing travelers waiting for a coach.

They waited in an agony of suspense. Luella clenched her hands until the nails bit deep into the flesh of her palms, and the resulting pain was some relief from the tension she felt.

The boat crew seemed to be looking along the beach, in the direction opposite the one in which Luella and Quinn had entered it.

The person they were waiting for was apparently coming toward them. Quinn and Luella could sense their anticipation, seconds before a figure appeared at the cave mouth.

The figure was dressed entirely in black, with a long cloak and a bonnet from which hung a thick veil, concealing the face below the bonnet.

Mary?

Shaken and confused, Luella almost cried out. It was incredible that Mary should be concerned in such business as this.

Or was it Mrs. Cazelet? She had worn widow's clothes and hidden her face behind a veil!

Still Quinn did not move; he seemed to be an extension of the solid rock around him.

The veiled figure did not speak. Two of the men from the boat crew detached themselves from the others, and then the figure lifted a hand, pointing along the beach, obviously showing them the route they must take.

As the two men hurried away, Luella thought: They are French spies, ready to begin their work of gathering information and taking it back.

The moon gave a grudging light as Luella tried to see what was happening. Two more figures appeared from behind the veiled one, and they joined the boat crew.

French prisoners being returned, Luella decided. The exchange had taken place in silence, so far as she could see, and had the macabre quality of a play being performed in mime before a hidden audience of two people.

Finally, the man who appeared to be leader placed a small package in the hands of the veiled figure, who then signed to them that they might put their contraband in the cave.

Luella drew a sharp, frightened breath and felt the warning pressure of Quinn's hand on her arm, but the men entered the cave on the ledge opposite the one on which she and Quinn were hiding, to her intense relief. She could dimly make out figures placing the packages in a fissure similar to the one in which *they* were concealed. Then the men returned hurriedly to the boat and pushed it down the beach. They waded into the breakers with it and clambered in. Luella saw it bounce on the silvered waves, then the oars rose and fell as it moved out into the bay.

Somewhere out at sea there would be a larger ship waiting, Quinn thought. He tried to see if any such ship was within range of his vision, but he was unsuccessful. The whole operation was one of great precision and simplicity, he thought, and worthy of such a man as Parnall, who grew rich on stolen jewels while those who acted as ferrymen, bringing him his treasure, received contraband as *their* reward. No doubt he also collected a handsome reward, also, for his traffic in agents and prisoners.

There was no time to reflect on the crass stupidity of human greed: The veiled figure, who had watched the departure of the boat, had turned away and disappeared. Quinn bent his head and whispered in Luella's ear.

"Stay here, until I return for you!"

He went, swiftly, with the speed and grace of a tiger, dropping to the sandy floor, bunched low as he ran across the cave mouth, held briefly in a sliver of moonlight before he was gone.

Luella hesitated. She knew she must follow him, but there was no joy in defiance. She felt driven or guided, she did not know which. She was frightened, realizing suddenly that she was now quite alone.

She reached the cave mouth and saw that the relentlessly inward-rolling sea was coming ever closer, leaving only a narrow strip of beach at the foot of the cliffs. The spray from the waves damped her face and her hair, salt and cold.

As the moon sailed into a clear patch of sky, she took

stock of her surroundings. It was difficult to detach two dark figures from the thick shadows clustering at the base of the cliffs. Her glance went upward, and she was puzzled, because the paths that seamed the cliffs were bare.

She looked downward again, restive, uneasy, sending up a silent prayer for some sign of either Quinn or his quarry. Her prayer was answered. She saw two figures, one just ahead of the other, moving against the bottom of the cliff, at some distance from where she was crouched, and going away from the direction of Westhaven, toward Dunbury.

Desperately, Luella tried to see what was happening in the thin, uncertain light. To her astonishment, the first figure seemed suddenly to disappear into the cliff face; seconds later, Quinn, inching his way cautiously along the narrowing strip of sand, also disappeared into the face of the cliff.

The encroaching sea broke on the beach noisily and spread itself into a wide, foam-edged cloth, silvered at the edge, coming so far up the beach that it swirled around Luella's feet. She was frightened, feeling the water foaming about her ankles; it was a sinister reminder that she had little time to spare. She glanced fleetingly over her shoulder and saw that the mouth of the sea cave was already sucking in water.

Hastily, she scrambled along the base of the cliffs until she found the spot at which both Quinn and his quarry had disappeared.

It was another cave—not a wide-mouthed opening, like the one they had just left, but a narrow cleft, a mere slit that seemed to have been cut in the cliffs with a giant knife, and was wide enough to admit only one person at a time.

The sea was swirling around its entrance, tantalizingly touching the hem of her skirts with its cold fingers, as she eased her way inside.

The floor of the cave was rocky and had an upward slope, narrowing until the damp walls almost touched her shoulders as she felt her way carefully along.

Surely, they could not both have come *this* way, she thought uneasily. It was not so much a cave as a rocky defile, and she had nothing to guide her, not even the certainty that the two she followed had actually come inside.

The light from the moon did not penetrate deeply enough to give her any help. By the continued upward slope she knew that she must be walking toward the top of the cliffs, but she could not imagine what or where the final destination would be.

Then, to her utter astonishment, she heard a curious low rumbling sound ahead. She crouched against the wall, trying to flatten herself, and saw what appeared to be a huge stone turning in an opening to reveal a recess lighted by a couple of lanterns.

A figure was silhouetted in the opening. The black veil was thrown back from its face, though she could not see that face clearly. The figure stood motionless, then raised its hand, and she saw the glint of steel.

"My dear Quinn," said a voice she recognized, "I *thought* it was you who was following me! Do come in. I shall be delighted to offer you hospitality. Or should I, more appropriately, quote an old rhyme: 'Will you come into my parlour, said the spider to the fly'? In your case, a most welcome fly, I assure you!"

She heard the laughter, cold and chill. To her horror, she saw the dark bulk of Quinn's figure step forward into the opening, without fear, slowly, as though he had all the time in the world; but the black-clad figure, whose voice had betrayed him as the man who killed Tom Hines, held a pistol against Quinn's neck.

As Quinn stepped through the opening, split now by the stone that had pivoted to open it, Luella put the back of her hand against her mouth to stop herself from screaming out her fear and horror.

The stone slid into position again, shutting both men from view. Gathering all her strength, forcing her limbs to obey her will, Luella hurried forward and fell flat, bruising and shaking herself. She was on her feet in an instant, groping on the floor in the darkness to discover that the narrow fissure ended in a flight of rough steps leading directly to the door.

Cautiously, she made her way up the steps. At the top

196

she met smooth, blank rock face. The stone fitted perfectly and showed not a glimmer of light from the chamber on its far side. She longed passionately to claw the stone away with her fingernails, but she knew the folly and hopelessness of such action. Instead, she began trying to find the outline of the door, and it was a long time before she found it, a mere tracery in stone running up on her left-hand side, across the top of her head, and down the other side.

Having found it, her next task was to discover how it moved. Again and again her aching hands tried to make some impression, pushing, prising, searching for a clue as to how the door opened. The tears ran down her cheeks—tears not for herself but for Quinn, who was trapped on the far side. She could not hear their voices, so firmly did the thick door lie in its place, but far behind her she heard the triumphant roar of the sea as it entered the tunnel. Though she knew it would not reach such a long way into the rock as the steps on which she stood, she was aware of the sinister implications of a rising tide: It meant there was no way back for her. She could not swim, and nothing in her brief, uneventful life had prepared her for such a situation as this.

In an agony of mind beyond anything she had ever known, she thought of him trapped beyond the door that she could not open, with Jackson Parnall holding a gun to his neck.

CHAPTER 10

Quinn's eyes were ice blue, and every line of his face expressed his unutterable contempt for the man who held him prisoner. He was face to face, at last, with Parnall, and he was glad, in spite of the coldness of steel against the warm flesh of his neck.

He had been in situations just as difficult, just as desperate, during the times he had spent in France. He stared scornfully at the man holding the gun, then his gaze went beyond Parnall to the room in which they both stood, which was an exact replica of the cellar in which Luella had been trapped. It was empty except for a few boxes, some small packages, and the two lanterns, standing on a rocky shelf.

Parnall saw his glance and nodded, leaning negligently against the wall as though to express his contempt for Quinn, while his finger still held firmly to the trigger of the pistol.

"One of the cellars of Dunbury, my dear fellow," he said coolly. "The place is honeycombed with them. They are divided off into small cells like a beehive. I understand that many years ago there was just one vast cellar running under Dunbury, and the owner had it turned into a series of cells with thick stone walls in order to incarcerate those who displeased him. A man after my own heart! I soon discovered, when I took up residence at Dunbury, that one of the cellars led directly into the rock tunnel—*if* one discovered the secret of the turning stone! Of course, you do not know Dunbury well, do you?"

"No," agreed Quinn, in a voice of ice, his eyes never

leaving the other man's face. "So it is *you* who are Mrs. Cazelet?"

Parnall laughed. He nodded, moving away from Quinn, taking the pistol from his neck but keeping it trained upon him as he backed toward the wall on the far side, tearing off the bonnet with his free hand and tossing it to the floor. His eyes were narrow, brilliant, amused.

"Ask what you will, and you shall be answered this night! For as you will not leave this room alive, it is of no consequence what information you will take to eternity with you—certainly you will have no chance to use it! When *I* leave this chamber, *your* body will go rolling down the slope into the sea outside the tunnel, and *I* shall return to my lodgings at Axminster: Mr. Johnson, gentleman and scholar, occupying rooms there—just one of my many aliases!"

"Your traffic in jewels is even more odious than your traffic in spies and prisoners," Quinn said contemptuously. "You betray your fellow men and women, under the guise of friendship, in order that you may obtain their possessions! You are like a maggot feeding on dead flesh!"

Parnall laughed, showing pointed teeth that gave his smile a wolfish quality.

"Why do you stay in Dorset?" Quinn demanded. "You have the Flowers of Darkness. Do you consider *this* to be a safe hiding place? For I tell you, Parnall, *no* hiding place is safe. Kill me if you will. Another will rise up in my place to hunt you down, to the death!"

His voice had the ring of truth, but it was not Quinn's promise that cut the smile from Parnall's mouth and gave his face the chilling, brooding quality of intense evil.

His voice was like silk; it had undertones of menace.

"At this moment, the jewels are not in my possession! If you believe that fact gives you cause to rejoice, let me assure you that I intend to repossess them. I do not care how many die in order that I may achieve my objective."

"Just as you did not care how Eleanor La Vanne died?" Quinn retorted, with stinging contempt. "Do you remember how she died, Parnall? Butchered, by men worse than animals. Trampled into the mud of a farmyard. It would have been a more fitting death for *you* than for a woman whose only crime was that she sought to keep a promise to the woman her husband served."

The bright eyes of Jackson Parnall narrowed; his voice was still soft.

"The jewels have been stolen from me by a woman who was my mistress. I paid a high price for listening to lies from pretty lips, promising delights that set my blood afire! In a rash moment of folly, I showed her the jewels—decked her in them. She smiled on me when she knew they would make me the richest man in England, and begged me to take her with me when I left Dorset. I was living here only because I had business to do still with the French. I agreed that when it was done we would go away together. Then, soon after, she came to me and told me that my hiding place had been discovered, that men were on their way to have me put into prison, where I should be killed as a traitor. She told me that I must go at once to London, and she would hide the jewels so that there could be no proof that I possessed them. Then, she said, she would join me, bringing them with her once the hunt had been called off. Had I been less enamored of her, I might have suspected her plan. As it was, I agreed to it; I reached London and discovered it was all a trick. In fact, *she* betrayed me, hoping no doubt that with my death she would be safe forever with her prize!" The eyes were mere slits; a muscle quivered in the thin cheek.

"A very resourceful lady, by all accounts!" Quinn retorted. "Where is she now?"

"I believe she is being hidden in Bellminster, by Simon Corbie!"

"Oh, come!" said Quinn, amused. "I hardly think that Simon has any stomach for such doings!"

"No doubt she made promises to him, also!" Parnall fingered the pistol he held. "When I have found her, it will give me the most exquisite pleasure to tear the truth, slowly, from her. Until then, I wait and watch. Do you not wish to know her name, Mallory?"

"By all means, pronounce the name of this Delilah who has robbed you of your crowning glory, Samson!" Quinn replied sarcastically.

"Very well, Sir Galahad, knight errant, rescuer of damsels such as the little urchin who I thought was *her* . . ."

Parnall was laughing. His words were interrupted by a low rumbling noise.

Luella's frantically searching fingers had yielded nothing in the form of a handle or a key, and in desperation she slumped wearily against the wall, not realizing that the weight of even her slender body provided enough pressure to make the stone yield.

It began to give, grumbling as it moved inward with what seemed like agonizing slowness, revealing the cellar and the two men who stood there.

Parnall's surprise and dismay were of seconds' duration only, but even that sliver of time was enough for Quinn, whose heart leaped joyfully at the sight of Luella, causing him to breach the gap between Parnall and himself in one tremendous bound.

The two men went down together. Frightened, Luella crouched against the wall. Both men were tough and strong, and they were well matched. Quinn's advantage had been small, and Parnall retained an iron grip on his pistol. Quinn had him by the wrist, forcing his hand back, so that a shot was discharged, striking the wall and reverberating through the rocky chamber, making Luella jump almost out of her skin.

She looked longingly at the heavy wooden door on the far side of the cellar, wishing she could reach it, open it, and run for help, even though she did not know what was on its other side, but the two men who fought so grimly barred her way.

Then, suddenly, Parnall was scrambling to his feet, having aimed a savage blow at Quinn, who staggered back against the rocky wall, stunned for a moment.

The moment was enough; violently, Parnall wrenched open the door and was gone.

Luella ran across to Quinn and put her arms about him.

"You are hurt!" she cried.

"No!" he retorted grimly, shaking his head as though to clear the mists from his brain. "Go back to Westhaven, Luella! *I* shall hunt Parnall until I find him and kill him!"

He put her from him and was gone, through the door and up the flight of steps that rose on its far side.

Sobbing, she gathered up her hampering skirts and followed him as best she could.

When she reached the top of the steep stairs, she found herself in the gutted kitchen at Dunbury, lit by the faint light of the moon. The acrid smell of a burned-out fire was in her nostrils as she ran out through the space where the door into the overgrown garden had been.

Quinn was ahead of her, racing through the stable yard. There was no sign of Parnall. A little breeze blew softly, and the sea had cloth of silver laid upon it like a great carpet. Everywhere there was peace, and overhead a sky full of stars like scattered diamonds.

With his decision made, Simon felt a free man, no longer haunted by guilt, fear, and the ever-present need for caution that had so fretted him. He had been persuaded by promise of reward to do what he had done all these weeks; that promise now lay in the dusty fragments around him.

He went to the top floor of the house. The woman who had made it her hiding place for so many weeks, stared at him, bitterly angry. He was wearing his evening clothes.

"I am going into Axminster to dine," he told her. "I mean to celebrate the fact that I am a free man, no longer needing to trade in lies and deceit. In a little while I shall not be the owner of this house. True, I cannot live in luxury on the price Quinn will pay me, but who knows?"—his smile was more carefree than she had ever seen it—"I can try my luck at the gaming tables and perhaps win a fortune!"

"*You?*" she said, with a sneer. "You will squander all you possess and end up a pauper! If you pass the rest of your days in the poorhouse, it will be no more than your due! If you listen to me, you could become a rich man!"

"I am weary of your promises! You say you had the

203

jewels. *I* have never seen them! You sent me on many a fool's errand, searching for them."

She sprang across the room and dug her fingers into his arm as she clung frantically to him. He flung her aside as he would a troublesome fly, and she began to weep with rage.

"I *told* you where I hid them! It was true, I swear it was! I put them there, I thought they were safe! Someone has taken them!" she raged.

"In which case, how do you hope to find them again?" he demanded scornfully.

"I have told you, it is only a matter of time! We *must* be patient! It could have been Emmie or one of the servants who took them! I dare not search openly until I know that Parnall is dead. Oh, damn you, Simon, you *see* how I am trapped!"

She began to beat his chest with her fists. He looked at her without pity.

"I do not intend to share that trap any longer!" he retorted. "I am thankful that the whole wearisome business is done. I should have ended it long since, instead of listening to your lies and wheedlings and promises!"

He turned from her and strode from the room. Outside the front door, his horse waited. He mounted and rode away under the light of the climbing moon.

His decision to ride into Axminster did not seem significant to him, but the girl left behind, sobbing with rage and disappointment, was suddenly afraid of an empty house. It seemed a sinister place. It held only a deaf old woman sound asleep in her room. Every noise was magnified in a way she had never noticed before: every squeak in the wainscot, every creak of old wood, even the noise of the wind humming to itself as it roamed around the walls.

Behind the small sounds the night seemed to gather itself into a tangible presence, to become the figure of a woman—dark, beautiful, afire with jewels. A woman who moved slowly toward her and then was gone, a shadow against the shadows.

Her skin felt damp and clammy, her heartbeats were thick in her throat. She who prided herself on her coolness, her resourcefulness, was suddenly terribly frightened of an illusion conjured from loneliness and darkness. But it was *not* an illusion. Again she saw the figure, sparkling with jewels, the face sad, the eyes accusing.

She remembered how she had worn the Flowers of Darkness for Jackson Parnall, her white body naked except for the jewels. How his eyes had glowed as he had reached out to her! Oh, the fever and fire in his limbs as they had entwined themselves about hers!

She had lain in his arms, her body compliant, her mind detached, already laying the foundations of the plan to possess a priceless treasure.

Her plan had gone awry; worse, Philip Janson had deserted her.

She ground her teeth together and shuddered. Janson was dead. Parnall would soon be dead. She would find out who had taken her treasure, and then she would leave Dorset, free of them all forever!

So she made frantic promises to herself, trying to fight off the fear that gripped her, willing the figure in the shadows to go from the room, but the rubies that were the heart of the flowers glowed as red as blood . . . a glow that lit the room as the figure moved toward her.

She pounded from the room and down the stairs, into the night. The air was cold on her flesh, making her gasp and shudder. She would go to Quinn, she thought frenziedly, seek him out at Westhaven, throw herself on his mercy, tell him she had been held prisoner! Never mind the consternation her arrival would cause! Never mind that Jessica Mallory, who had all unwittingly helped her cause, would be denounced as a stupid old fool! At Westhaven she would be safe from the man who waited, patiently, for her to come from her hiding place so that he could kill her, as he had promised to do.

She would find the jewels, possess them forever. It must come true, this dream of herself, splendid as a queen! It would come true as soon as Parnall was dead!

Queen of the night, Parnall had called her when she wore the jewels. Never in all her life had she yearned for anything as she yearned to possess the Flowers. Parnall had seen the longing in her eyes and laughed, saying that such jewels should have been fashioned for Lucifer's bride, not the ill-fated queen of France.

A great fire raged within her, a fever burned in her mind. Her hands beat the air as she ran, stumbling, along the path to Westhaven. Simon's betrayal had been the last straw. She had made a bargain with him, he had broken it, and now her reason was crumbling . . .

Once, as she ran, she looked back to see if she was being followed; the path was empty, but still she felt driven onward.

She looked up at the sky, with its frostfire of stars that had never been so big or so bright, jewels in their own right, to deck the only queen of the night, the calm, silver-faced moon.

She decided to take the shortcut through the cemetery to Westhaven, but her hand froze on the latch of the gate. She knew she could not walk past the row of tombstones, gleaming as whitely as the bones they covered. She knew she could not look upon the one with its inscription to Marianne Walton, Whom the Sea Took . . . Whom the Sea Gave Back—or so a shortsighted, stupid old woman had believed, she told herself.

A figure barred her way as she stood there—intangible, darkness shaped out of darkness, not a human figure. Gone, even as she turned and ran despairingly along the path that was a longer route to Westhaven . . .

She heard the crack of a pistol shot. It seemed to split the heavens and made the stars tremble. She was checked as abruptly as though she had been tripped by a noose, but still she felt an unseen force hurrying her onward, along the path, beyond the great bulk of the house toward the small grassy knoll where she had often sat to look at the sea and dream of a life that was more rich and splendid than the one ahead of her.

The shot had also been heard by the man who was doggedly making his way toward Westhaven, impelled by an urgency that he could not explain. He was footsore and exhausted, he had eaten nothing all day, but the sharp bark of the pistol shot had the rallying effect of a bugle call on him. Afterward, he could never tell how he gathered strength to make the tremendous effort required for the last stage of his journey, but with the breeze cooling his damp forehead and his face turned toward the sea, Philip Janson struggled toward the place, just below a grassy knoll, where Jackson Parnall stood facing Quinn Mallory.

In Parnall's hand was the pistol he had just fired, but excellent marksman though he was, he had missed, for Quinn had ducked the shot with split-second timing.

Jackson was becoming unnerved; nothing had gone right. He had stumbled over a hidden root as he ran, and measured his length. Though he was on his feet again in an instant, the accident had winded him and betrayed his presence to his pursuer. Crouching low, he had flattened himself against a furze bush until Quinn was close to him, and then he had fired, but his hand was unsteady—something that had never happened before in his life. He was bedeviled, he told himself furiously.

Luella, several hundred yards behind Quinn, covered the intervening ground as fast as she could, her heart beating frantically. If *he* has been shot, if he is dead, then *I* will kill Jackson Parnall! she told herself wildly. She felt her love go out to Quinn, all the accumulated love, husbanded for years, with no one on whom to spend it, belonging now to this man she had known such a little while. I love him! she cried silently. I love him! Let love lend me wings and strength!

Long afterward, she thought: That night, we were all figures being moved on a giant chessboard, and the hand that moved the pieces was not an earthly one. The dead have no power over the living, so it is said; they cannot keep promises from beyond the grave.

Luella knew better than to believe that.

Quinn, hidden in the shade of a broken tree, held his pistol with a perfectly steady hand. Carefully, he took aim, but Parnall, with his animal sense of danger, stepped back into a patch of shadow.

The light of the moon was cold, clear, and brilliant; it lit the scene with unearthly beauty and might well have been a lamp placed especially to show the characters in a tableau.

On came Janson, as fast as his weary feet and still painful leg would allow him. Luella, reaching the clearing where Quinn and Parnall waited with their pistols, crouched beside a boulder, gripping the smooth, wind-worn stone with her hand, as though for strength. The air seemed charged with strange tensions; it seemed to vibrate with life. She did not look up to see the figure in the white dress standing on top of the knoll, a few feet above Quinn and Parnall.

Parnall was cunning; his groping fingers had found a small flint, which he tossed high in the air. It spun down on to the patch of grass that separated him from the man who hunted him.

Quinn did not move.

"An old trick, Parnall!" he called scornfully. "You have indeed lost your prowess—and your courage—if you must fling stones in the air, like a boy!"

Parnall never moved. His head throbbed. He thought he could feel someone behind him, and jerked his head sharply over his shoulder, but there was nothing except the moonlight with its footprints of black shadow. The voice of the sea was as soft as silk; it was murmuring something he could not quite catch, about the winds of fate . . .

He felt deathly coldness, like a mist upon him. It bit into his flesh, it was like icy breath on his cheek, it made his hands tremble. He felt afraid. He, who had nerves of steel and no imagination, was suddenly afraid of something he could not name.

The moonlight was so bright it hurt his eyes. No, it was not the moonlight, it was starlight, it was the flash of fire from a thousand diamonds, stretched across the heavens, with great drops of blood amongst them . . .

Quinn stepped into the clearing. Luella, seeing him, felt terror and exultation at the sight of the tall, splendid figure.

"Come out of hiding, Parnall!" cried Quinn. "Or shall I hunt you like the fox you are? For know this, I will follow you to the ends of the world if need be . . ."

The patch of shadow moved. Parnall stood up, pistol

cocked, his lips drawn back in a snarl. As Quinn fired, he dropped to the ground, twitched, and lay still.

It was an old a trick as the stone-throwing, and one that had often stood him in good stead.

Quinn stood motionless, undeceived by the act. The silence was unearthly; the sea seemed to have stopped breathing; the voice of the wind in the grass was stilled.

It was the girl on the grassy knoll who broke the silence.

"Quinn!" she cried.

Their eyes turned toward her: Parnall's, Luella's, Quinn's.

In the moonlight, she was like a beautiful ghost, a woman with rounded limbs and fronds of thick, reddish-gold hair curling over her shoulders. Her eyes were brilliant and huge, and her lovely sensuous mouth was curved into a smile as she held out her hands to the master of Westhaven.

"He is dead!" she cried, "and I have nothing more to fear! He has kept me prisoner these long weeks, ever since he cast down my bonnet and cloak to be found on the cliffs, as though the sea had taken me . . ."

"Marianne," said Quinn.

His voice was quiet, yet it seemed to crack like a whip around the starry heavens. The shock of recognition was the most soul-shaking experience of his life. This was the girl whose body he believed lay in the cemetery, the girl he had mourned as dead.

This was a trick of the moonlight. He stood unmoving, as she ran down the slope toward him.

The odor of her sweet, flowery perfume was all about him. She wound her arms around his neck and he saw the tears in her eyes as she pressed her lips against his cold mouth.

"Quinn, dearest Quinn, I am not a ghost! I am alive and warm!" she murmured.

"Your grave is in the cemetery, Marianne!" Quinn said, each word clear and distinct.

From the corner of his eye, he saw Parnall rising slowly to his feet; at that moment, the action meant nothing to him.

Luella, crouched in the grass, felt the warm tears rain down her cheeks. This girl, who clung to Quinn, was his lost love. She was more beautiful than her portrait. She was betrothed to the master of Westhaven, and now that she had returned, they would be married.

She wept, even while she rejoiced for him. She heard Quinn's voice, still clear and calm, each word measured.

"Where have you been, lost Marianne? Where have you been until this moment?"

Her breath came fast and shallow. She was afraid, and clung to him fearfully, even while she smiled up at him.

"This man kept me prisoner because I would not help him in his scheme to steal the Flowers of Darkness . . ."

Her voice died away. Quinn was looking at her with an odd expression on his face.

From behind her, Parnall spoke coldly. "You lie, Marianne! You lie, as always! You, who lay naked in my arms, decked in the jewels, plotting to steal them . . ."

Her gasp of sheer horror was clearly audible to Luella. Marianne whirled around, her face the color of the tombstones in the cemetery, as she saw Parnall standing in front of her, his pistol trained on her, a smile of lazy satisfaction upon his face.

"Oh, God!" she moaned. *"Oh, God, I thought you were dead!"*

"I am not, my pretty little whore! As you see, I am alive and well. I have searched high and low for you, and now, see my good fortune! I have found you! My bed has been cold without you and the delights you offered so freely. However, we have more important matters to attend to. Tell me where you have hidden the jewels, and you shall go free!"

Her lips moved soundlessly, and Quinn felt a quiver go through her as she pressed her back against him.

"I do not know where they are!" she stammered.

"Oh, come!" He shrugged, his eyes narrow and bright. "What a dilemma you are in, my poor Marianne! If you tell me where you have hidden them, you will go free—but Mallory will know you for the liar, cheat, and whore that you are! If you do not tell me, then I shall tear the truth

210

from you, rend your pretty limbs, teach you such a lesson as will have you praying for merciful death."

"Let her go, Parnall," Quinn said, with deathly quietness.

"No, my friend. Neither her—*nor* you. Move aside, Marianne! First I will dispatch *him*! Your death will be a longer agony than his, unless you tell me where I may pluck the flowers!"

Marianne leaned against Quinn, her eyes half-closed, her mouth dry. Her only hope, she knew, lay in the fact that if Parnall tried to shoot Quinn, he would kill *her* and he had no intention of doing that.

"Help me!" she moaned to Quinn. "Help me!"

"Tell me," said Quinn softly, "is all that he says true?"

"No. He lies!"

Parnell gave a great shout of laughter.

"Do you think *he* believes that you are the innocent young woman he left at Westhaven when he crossed to France? Shall I tell him the secrets of your body that only I know? The mole on your breast, the birthmark on your thigh . . ."

With one violent movement, Quinn thrust Marianne away from him. The action took Parnall by surprise. He fired, and the bullet grazed Quinn's shoulder. Blood streamed down his shirtsleeve, but with superhuman strength, Quinn wrenched the pistol from Parnall and sent it flying out of reach before he launched himself against the man who had betrayed Eleanor La Vanne.

Quinn caught Parnall by the throat. Luella, watching, sent up a silent prayer. The two men went down and scrambled to their feet again. There was blood on Quinn's cheek. Marianne, seeing it, crawled away, covering her eyes with her hands.

Now Quinn was on his feet. He dragged Parnall up after him with his hands around the man's throat and flung him as far from him as he could. Parnall staggered to his feet and came at Quinn, snarling viciously. As they rolled over and over, Parnall, weakening, tried to claw at Quinn's face, snarling still like a trapped animal.

They stumbled to their feet and stood circling one another. Parnall realized, too late, that he had his back to the sea. As Quinn sprang, he jerked sideways, lost his footing, and fell back, rolling to the edge of the cliff.

He hung there for a split second, poised above the calm, waiting waters. The last thing he heard as he plummeted down into the cold depths was the voice of Eleanor La Vanne.

Luella stood up, her eyes blind with weeping, her heart full of thankfulness. Quinn stood staring at the cliff edge, hearing the dying scream and the sound of a body hitting water. He felt no triumph, for he had no taste for death. Within him there was only a great weariness.

In an instant, Marianne was on her feet.

"Quinn!" She ran to him, weeping. "Oh, Quinn, it has been so dreadful! To be kept from you, to hear the lies he has spoken. . . . Say you do not believe them!"

He stared down at her somberly. Blood still oozed from his cheek. There was a spreading stain darkening his shirt-sleeve, and his face was as bleak as a December day.

"Marianne is dead," he told her flatly. "She is buried in the churchyard!"

"Foolish Quinn! She is *here*, alive and well! Look at me! *I* am Marianne!"

"Grandmother saw Marianne when she had been taken from the sea," he said, in the same expressionless voice.

"Grandmother is old and her eyes were blind with weeping! She could not be *sure* . . ."

"Have you ever seen the Flowers of Darkness?" he asked, abruptly.

She shook her head vehemently.

"Never!"

Slowly, Quinn turned his head. His voice rang clear and sharp as frost on the night air.

"Luella!"

She came forward reluctantly. Marianne stared at the disheveled figure with the disordered hair and tear-stained face.

"Who is this?" she demanded.

"Luella and I are to be married," Quinn told her, calmly.

Marianne turned to him and caught hold of him, standing on tiptoe and trying to reach his face with her lips. He

212

did not bend his head, and she drew back, puzzled and uneasy.

"Quinn, why do you pretend you do not know me? I *am* Marianne!"

"Yes?" he said. His face was expressionless. "With the mole on your breast and the birthmark on your thigh? Tell me, how did Parnall know such things?"

"He tried to take me, against my will. I *swear* it, Quinn! Let us go back to Westhaven. You are hurt. I will bathe your wounds, then we will talk together. We will tell grandmother the wonderful news that I am truly returned from the sea, that I have come back to you!"

She caught hold of his arm and tried to lead him toward the house. She was mistress of herself again, no longer driven by a strange force that harried and troubled her. She dismissed Luella with a single, scornful glance. Once she was inside Westhaven again, this girl, whose praises Simon Corbie had sung, would be sent on her way. It would all be accomplished quite easily, and then she would be free to search for the jewels, search every nook and cranny until she found them. . . . The very thought made her tremble with anticipation.

So she walked beside Quinn, her voice light and happy, and Luella walked behind, feeling as though all her world had dissolved into cold mists about her, while Quinn stared straight ahead, walking like a man in a dream.

Near the gates of Westhaven, Philip Janson came upon the odd trio as he stepped suddenly from a patch of shade into the moonlight. Luella recognized him at once as the fugitive she had met upon the moors. His face was gaunt with fatigue; his eyes were bright and clear as they stared contemptuously at the girl who drew back from him.

They all heard the sharp hiss of Marianne's breath, saw how still she was. She stared at him as though she could not believe her eyes, and Janson, who scarcely saw her two companions, nodded slowly.

"Yes, I have returned, Marianne. I am not dead, as you so ardently wished, even though you betrayed me—even though, after my escape, you tried to make it seem as though it was I who murdered an old woman from whom I stole food. Or was it the man from whom *you* had stolen the Flowers of Darkness, he who vowed vengeance upon you, who tried to make me appear a murderer?"

Marianne closed her eyes; she thought she was going to faint. The inexorable voice went on, pitiless, colder than death.

"You wanted my death, Marianne. It was your misfortune that when the man whom I called Mrs. Cazelet escaped from your trap and vowed to kill you, you came to me. You begged me to take you away. You said you had made it appear that you had been drowned, in order that Parnall would not pursue you, but he was not such a fool as to think you dead—of that I have no doubt! And *I* was blinded by my infatuation for you."

"No!" she whispered violently. "No! It is not true."

"Let him finish his tale!" said Quinn, with deadly calm.

"I had never spoken of my obsession with your beauty, your charm—but you read it in my eyes, and believed I would do exactly as you wished. I agreed to go away with you—I confess that fact, to my everlasting shame. I forgot that I was Eleanor La Vanne's nephew; I forgot that the aunt who had shown me such kindness in my youth had disappeared, and I feared she was dead, for I had received no word in many months, not since the note smuggled from France in which she told me she was being brought to England and would land in this part of Dorset."

He drew a long, shuddering breath. Marianne's face was like marble. When she opened her mouth, Quinn cried to her to be silent.

Janson continued: "It was not until you told me, Marianne, that you had a great treasure to share with me, a treasure you had stolen from Parnall, that I understood. You called that treasure the Flowers of Darkness. You did not know that I had seen them once, as a child, when the queen wore them at court. They were said to be unlucky. The tale was told that the devil himself had left the gift at the palace. I saw my aunt after the outbreak of the Revolution, and she told me she had them. I begged her to let *me* bring them to England, but she would not, for she had been entrusted with the task."

There was silence. Quinn stared at Janson.

"Let us hear the rest of your tale," he said wearily.

"There is little more. I had obtained employment as a tutor to fill the time of waiting for my aunt. When I knew that Marianne had the Flowers of Darkness in her possession, I was filled with horror and dismay, realizing that my aunt was dead. I vowed to hunt down Parnall. I demanded that Marianne give me the jewels, but she refused. Her last words, as she ran from the house, were that she would see me dead first. . . . Now I have returned—to demand that you give me the jewels in order that I may give them to those for whom they are intended!"

There was silence. Marianne opened her eyes and gave a great shuddering sob.

"Damn you!" she whispered, in sudden frenzy. "Damn you all! I have been cheated of my jewels, my beautiful jewels! I *will* have them, I swear I will! They have been taken from me! I went back to the sea tower and put them in one of the coffers in the old chapel, and they have been taken!" Her voice rose to a wail, like a child's. "I shall find them! I want them! I *will* have them!"

Her eyes glittered as she cried, "Parnall is dead! *You* cannot harm me, Philip Janson! The jewels are mine and I will tear Westhaven apart, stone by stone, to find them, for I swear before God that no one save Marianne Walton shall ever wear the Flowers of Darkness!"

"*You* shall never wear them!" Philip cried, outraged, and he stepped threateningly toward her.

He was unarmed, but he put out a hand, and as Quinn stepped forward, feeling violence in the very air, a strange thing happened to Marianne.

She stared at Philip Janson as though he was a ghost. She saw, not a weary figure in breeches and torn shirt, but a woman, dark, beautiful, decked in jewels, a woman with a look of terrible sadness in her eyes.

Marianne gave one small strangled cry of horror. The coldness was all about her, there was a fever of madness raging inside her head, and the stars seemed to spin giddily in the sky. The last brittle thread of reason snapped. With a strangely desolate cry, like that of a seabird, she turned and ran away inland, over the moonlit moors.

The three of them watched the flying, white-clad figure. She ran as though the devil himself was at her heels.

The sound of her cries floated back to them until she was out of sight. Quinn broke the silence.

"Come, Luella, and you, Janson. We are all in need of some attention," he said.

The three of them made their way to the gates of West-haven.

Luella was scarcely aware of the turbulence and confusion that came hard on the heels of their return. There were servants running to and fro, and a groom was dispatched for a physician. Vaguely, she heard Quinn's voice giving orders, calm and clear, as though nothing had happened, and she heard Mary's great cry when she set eyes on Philip Janson.

Luella submitted to being undressed, given a treacle posset, and put to bed by Betty Graddle, whose eyes were as round as saucers, and whose questions came thick and fast as snowflakes on a winter's day. Luella answered her sleepily—she had never felt so utterly weary, not even in the days when she had stumbled to her attic room throbbing all over from one of Henrietta's beatings.

Her last waking thought was of Marianne. Quinn would find her and bring her home, she decided; it wouldn't matter what she had done . . . he loved her. . . .

When she awoke for the first time, Mary was bending over her bed. She no longer wore the concealing veil, and her face looked gentle.

"Is there anything you need?" she asked.

Luella shook her head drowsily.

"Only to sleep," she murmured.

"Then do so, as long as you wish. Philip is sleeping. With my care and good nursing, he will soon be well again. . . ."

She sounded serene. Her eyes said: Perhaps, one day, there will be happiness for us.

"Did Philip tell you what has happened?" Luella asked.

"Yes. I never heard a stranger tale in my life, and the house has been in an uproar since last night."

"Where is Quinn?" asked Luella.

"In the sea tower. The chapel is being stripped and searched, so it is as well that Grandmother has been given a draught to make her sleep."

"Marianne?" asked Luella.

Mary hesitated.

"Such beauty as hers is a curse. Marianne is dead, Luella. Simon Corbie was riding back from Axminster, late last night, when she ran out in front of him and frightened his horse. The animal reared up and she was killed by its hooves. Simon is distraught. He says she looked like a woman pursued by the devil when she ran in front of the horse. How strange an ending to her life! Sleep now, Luella, and when you wake again, try to forget all that has happened."

How can I forget? Luella thought, anguished. Oh, Quinn, my poor Quinn! You loved her so. To have found her and lost her again is surely the most terrible thing that can happen. . . .

When she awoke the second time, it was almost dark. Alice had brought lighted candles and a tray of food. A fire snapped cheerfully in the grate. The maid looked at her with round, curious eyes, but she had been forbidden to ask questions.

Luella discovered that she was hungry. When she had eaten the food, she got out of bed, washed and dressed, and went to the sea tower.

It was quiet; the search was evidently over. In the big bedroom Grandmother lay propped against the pillows, wide awake. When she saw Luella, she stretched out her hands.

Luella took the thin, dry fingers in her own warm ones and smiled down at her.

"Such a fuss and pother," Jessica said irritably. "All day long there have been people coming and going to my room upstairs. They say they are looking for the jewelry that Marianne hid there. They will not find it. I told them so. I told them the truth: that Marianne has it. They think I am mad. They are wrong. I do not want them to disturb my peace again, so will you please tell my grandson that I wish to see him."

Luella nodded. She did not want to look for Quinn, but she knew that she must come face to face with him sooner or later.

She bent and kissed the lined forehead and went into the sitting room. She stared at the dark sea. It was quiet to-night, and there was no wind. She thought that the stars had never looked so bright, nor so near to earth.

"Luella," said a quiet voice from behind her.

She spun around from the window, her heart thundering in her breast. She was fearful that her face would betray all her love and yearning for the man who called her name.

Quinn no longer looked tired and bleak. There was a tenderness in his face that she had never seen before.

He came across to her and put his hands on her shoulders.

She held her breath. He towered above her, but he bent his head so that he could look into her eyes. She would not look up; she was trembling so much that he pulled her close against him, putting up a hand to hold her head against his breast, soothing her as though she was a frightened child.

She felt the strong beat of his heart; from her own heart a thousand singing birds were flying as though suddenly released through the open door of a cage. She felt the pain, the torment, the exquisite rapture of loving, and knew they were so blended together that one could never again be separated from the other.

To the ends of time she would love this man. Yea, and after death, she promised herself, as she put up her hands and clung to him.

"Dearest heart, I love you," he said softly.

"Say it again," she whispered, the tears running down her cheeks.

"I love you, Luella March. Will *you* not tell *me* that you love me?"

She had never heard that note of humility in his voice

before. Through her tears, she whispered, "I love you! Oh, how I love you, Quinn Mallory!"

"Do we know what love is?" he whispered. "To me, it used to mean the pleasure a woman gives; now I know that it is a meeting of mind and spirit as well as body. What is love to *you*, Luella?"

"It is being with you, for all the rest of my life," she answered simply.

He lifted her face and covered it with kisses: her forehead, her eyelids, her warm, wet cheeks, her sweet and willing mouth.

"Yesterday is done," he told her. "With all its lies, treachery, deceit, and violence. Last night, when I thought Parnall would kill me, I knew the strength of my love for you. A strange woman was taken from the sea. Poor Emmie has confessed that she would not look upon the dead woman, for she could not bear to do so. Her eyesight is better than Grandmother's and may have revealed the truth; however, it is all done with—Grandmother truly believed she saw all that remained of Marianne, and she shall not be told the truth now. Marianne died late last night, beneath the hooves of Simon Corbie's horse."

"I know," she whispered. "Oh, Quinn, I am so sorry!"

He said quietly, "The Marianne I knew died while I was in France, even though an unknown woman lies beneath her headstone. Perhaps it is true that the Flowers generate a terrible evil, and that those who look upon them are filled with a terrible greed and a longing to possess them. I do not know. I know only that yesterday is done, and tomorrow is ours."

He kissed her with great tenderness and passion, until her pulses raced at the thought of being possessed by this man. He would take her mind, her body, her heart, she thought—and give his own joyously in return. Their delight in one another would be fierce and sweet, and the years would not dim the splendor of their loving.

He kissed the hollow of her throat where the locket lay.

"I need you," he said simply. "I need you, Luella, for as long as I live. I will wait no longer than your seventeenth birthday for our wedding, and then we shall honeymoon in London, so that we may visit all the jewelers' shops and discover if you are a princess in disguise!"

"Oh, Quinn, it does not matter who I am! I want only to be your wife," she told him.

She lay against him, feeling his strength, knowing it would always be a shield and protection against the world; blissfully content, while he whispered words of love in her ear, until she turned her face to his again, and he kissed her with such ardor that she felt all the stars in the sky spin around her.

She sighed and said reluctantly, "We must go to your grandmother. She wishes to see you."

They went into the room where Jessica lay, still wide awake. Quinn bent over her and kissed her cheek.

"I am going to marry Luella," he told her.

"Shall I hold a great-grandchild in my arms before I die, Quinn?" she asked.

"Yes," he promised.

She smiled happily.

"The thought gives me such joy!" She looked at Luella and smiled.

"You shall have my jewels, child, as a wedding gift. Marianne has her own jewels, Quinn. It was this that I wished to tell you, in order that I may not be troubled by people searching the chapel. They are not there. Oh, yes, I know they *were* hidden in the coffer that contained Marianne's wedding gown. I found them when I brought out her wedding gown to put on for her funeral. They were so pretty—like flowers."

Quinn drew a long, steadying breath. Luella's hand found his, and he held it tightly.

"Like flowers," he said. "With leaves of emeralds, and rubies at the center?"

She nodded eagerly.

"Yes, yes! I did what she would most have wished me to do. I wrapped them in a piece of linen and put them beneath her head, in her coffin. She loved pretty things and baubles and said that, even when she was dead, she would

220

dance in the next world, wearing her jewels. Ah, but I should *not* have told her secret!"

She looked troubled. Quinn said gently, "Her secret is safe. Go to sleep now."

She closed her eyes. Together Quinn and Luella went from the room, through the sitting room, and into the long gallery, which was full of moonlight and candlelight.

"It is so simple, after all," Quinn marveled. "And so strange. An unknown woman, buried in Marianne's grave, with a dowry of jewels that belonged to a queen!"

"Can they not stay buried forever?" Luella pleaded.

"No, my love, but you need have no fear that *I* shall covet them! I shall get in touch with Sir Julius at once. Now that Eleanor La Vanne's mission is completed, may she rest in peace!"

Together they walked the length of the long gallery, their arms about one another, while the moon climbed high above the sea, spreading her silver skirts around her, and the stars sparkled like diamonds in the dark hair of night.

Luella could have sworn that a little wind touched her cheek, light as a mere brushing of fingertips. She thought she heard a sigh; the rustle of a skirt as someone passed by, and was gone out of their lives. . . .

It was all nonsense, of course, she told herself; there was only Quinn, walking with his arm around her shoulders, while the candleflames dipped in salute for two people going toward a tomorrow bright with the promise of happiness.

Dell Bestsellers

- [ ] **TO LOVE AGAIN** by Danielle Steel $2.50 (18631-5)
- [ ] **SECOND GENERATION** by Howard Fast $2.75 (17892-4)
- [ ] **EVERGREEN** by Belva Plain $2.75 (13294-0)
- [ ] **AMERICAN CAESAR** by William Manchester . . . $3.50 (10413-0)
- [ ] **THERE SHOULD HAVE BEEN CASTLES**
  by Herman Raucher $2.75 (18500-9)
- [ ] **THE FAR ARENA** by Richard Ben Sapir $2.75 (12671-1)
- [ ] **THE SAVIOR** by Marvin Werlin and Mark Werlin . $2.75 (17748-0)
- [ ] **SUMMER'S END** by Danielle Steel $2.50 (18418-5)
- [ ] **SHARKY'S MACHINE** by William Diehl $2.50 (18292-1)
- [ ] **DOWNRIVER** by Peter Collier $2.75 (11830-1)
- [ ] **CRY FOR THE STRANGERS** by John Saul $2.50 (11869-7)
- [ ] **BITTER EDEN** by Sharon Salvate $2.75 (10771-7)
- [ ] **WILD TIMES** by Brian Garfield $2.50 (19457-1)
- [ ] **1407 BROADWAY** by Joel Gross $2.50 (12819-6)
- [ ] **A SPARROW FALLS** by Wilbur Smith $2.75 (17707-3)
- [ ] **FOR LOVE AND HONOR** by Antonia Van-Loon . . $2.50 (12574-X)
- [ ] **COLD IS THE SEA** by Edward L. Beach $2.50 (11045-9)
- [ ] **TROCADERO** by Leslie Waller $2.50 (18613-7)
- [ ] **THE BURNING LAND** by Emma Drummond $2.50 (10274-X)
- [ ] **HOUSE OF GOD** by Samuel Shem, M.D. $2.50 (13371-8)
- [ ] **SMALL TOWN** by Sloan Wilson $2.50 (17474-0)

At your local bookstore or use this handy coupon for ordering:

DELL BOOKS
P.O. BOX 1000, PINEBROOK, N.J. 07058

Please send me the books I have checked above. I am enclosing $_____
(please add 75¢ per copy to cover postage and handling). Send check or money
order—no cash or C.O.D.'s. Please allow up to 8 weeks for shipment.

Mr/Mrs/Miss _____

Address _____

City _____ State/Zip _____

INTRODUCING...

The Romance Magazine For The 1980's

Each exciting issue contains a full-length romance novel — the kind of first-love story we all dream about...

PLUS

other wonderful features such as a travelogue to the world's most romantic spots, advice about your romantic problems, a quiz to find the ideal mate for you and much, much more.

ROMANTIQUE: A complete novel of romance, plus a whole world of romantic features.

ROMANTIQUE: Wherever magazines are sold. Or write Romantique Magazine, Dept. C-1, 41 East 42nd Street, New York, N.Y. 10017

INTERNATIONALLY DISTRIBUTED BY DELL DISTRIBUTING, INC.

Love—the way you want it!

Candlelight Romances